DERAILED

DOMINIQUE THOMAS

Author Note

Casting all your care upon Him, for He careth for you.

Peter 1:5

Ladies my heart is hurting because this world is getting worse and my kids are God willing only getting older and that's a pain that I want to leave. This book was not planned, but it comes from the heart. I pushed aside Bebe's story for this novel. *Oshun and Jaylah are so special to me.* This story will speak to your soul and you don't have to be black to relate to it. All you have to be is **human**.

I pray for you; I pray for this world and I especially pray for our babies.

Like the story then leave an Honest Review!

Disclaimer: This book will touch on police brutality, political views, racism and rape. If you are not comfortable reading on these topics as they could be a trigger for you then please DON'T proceed.

You can't separate peace from freedom because no one can be at peace unless he has his freedom.

-Malcolm X

PROLOGUE

location

Detroit

A nervous energy filled the kitchen as the family of four plus one stood inside of the vast cooking space. All eyes were on the youngest Lacoste man and for the first time in his life, he was scared. Pressure made diamonds and the pressure that was placed on his shoulders was enough for him to be the brightest diamond of them all. Only he didn't have the same aspirations in life as his family.

He wanted to choose his own path and was already making plans to do so. The baby inside of his girlfriend's stomach was proof of that but standing up to the family he had wasn't easy. Malik found himself sweating bullets under his oldest brother's questioning gaze. Oshun Lacoste was a force to be reckoned with and the strongest man Malik knew. He was frightened of his older brother and he respected him because while they shared the same father Oshun was the only dad he'd ever known.

"Young lady you looking beautiful today," Oshun said and their mom Angie blushed from the attention before waving him off. She went back to placing icing on the cupcakes she was making when Oshun peered over at Malik again. Malik maintained a cool front as he looked back at him. "What's good, young king? I got moves to make," he said taking a seat at the white island that was in the center of the kitchen.

Malik's limited-edition Jordan's shuffled from one foot to the other nervously. His wide-set brown eyes shifted down to his girlfriend and she gave him a reassuring smile that he couldn't return. He cleared his throat as his eyes drifted over to his mother.

"Tiff is pregnant. We found out two months ago and I decided to take a break from law school and focus on her and the baby."

Nervousness covered him like a cloak, and he knew that giving off any fear would set his brothers off. He was scared to let them down, but he also had to live for himself. Being a lawyer wasn't what he wanted anymore, and they would have to accept that.

His oldest brother Oshun pulled out his ringing cellphone and silenced the call. His hooded eyes a dark honey shade narrowed as he looked at Malik. "And you came up with this all by yourself?" he asked.

Malik nodded and Oshun raised his thick brow. That nodding shit was for kids. As a man, Malik knew that you had to use your words to get your point across.

"Yeah," Malik grunted with a shrug.

Oshun's jaw tensed and Malik wasn't strong enough to handle the intense gaze his brother was pushing his way, so he dropped his head. His girlfriend peered over at him and clear her throat.

"I think it's a girl! And we're already looking for baby names and buying things," his girlfriend of a year Tiffany stated wanting to alleviate the tension inside of the kitchen. "Malik and I have an apartment that we recently signed for in Southfield and once the baby comes, we will go back to school. Maybe even start a business together. It would also be something in the BOC. For the family."

Oshun smirked. He checked the time on his black Frank Muller and his eyes lifted to Malik. Disappointment swam in his lids and instantly Malik felt the shame, but he knew he had to stand strong on what he wanted.

"Is that right?" Oshun's deep voice asked. He smirked then

licked his full lips. In his grey designer logo joggers and his white crew neck Palms Angels t-shirt he looked relaxed but the anger rising from his being let Malik know that shit wasn't all good.

"For the family, huh," Oshun said lowly. He smiled and Malik knew his brother well enough to know that it wasn't a friendly one. "Having a baby at 21 while dropping out of college is for the family, Malik? Were you raised to make irrational decisions like this? Because only a dumb motherfucka wanders through life with no plan attached to the moves they're making. Right?"

Malik's eyes cut to his mom and Oshun's jaw tensed. He stood from the white marble island with his 6'4 and 230-pound physique commanding attention. He cocked his head to the side as he looked at Malik.

"You're a man and you made this decision, so I need you to stand on that shit. Look at me and not momma because despite being foolish at times you are not a coward. You weren't raised to be one either. Now is this how we do things as a family?" he asked sternly.

Malik shook his head as his shoulders dropped in despair. His hands went to his even fade and he clutched his head briefly while staring up at the ceiling. He looked around at his family as his anger rose inside of him.

"I did everything that was required of me. I graduated from high school with honors. I attended college, got another degree, and now I'm done with that. Law school is cool but that's not what I'm trying to do in my life, and I keep trying to tell y'all that," he explained with his tiredness from the situation showing on his handsome face.

Oshun's jaw tensed then he nodded and from doing something so minuscule it made Malik uneasy. From his presence alone Malik was frazzled. Their father died a year after Malik was born from a sudden heart attack and when he was old enough Oshun became the man of the family. Like their dad Phillip, he naturally took charge of things and because of Oshun, they were doing well in life.

Oshun and his mother created a plan for the Lacoste family to succeed while breaking generational curses in the process. It was because of their hard work that the Black Owned Community affectionately known as the BOC was born. They took care of one another and thrived without the help of the government. They didn't want shit from America if wasn't reparations and true freedom. Their family re-built the same hood that drugs tore apart for their people and while it hadn't been easy, they did it and was still going strong seven years later.

"Being a man means you do what you have to do. Not just what you want to do. Gio didn't want to go to school for accounting but he did. He did that for the betterment of all of us. Business school wasn't ideal for me either, but I did what I had to do for this family. We've worked hard to give you a good life. And all we asked was for you to become a lawyer," Oshun said to Malik.

Malik looked to his mom and shook his head.

"Momma, come on," he pleaded with his brows furrowed.

His mom Angie took a deep breath and exhaled as she looked at her handsome baby boy that was the spitting image of his late father with his mocha brown skin and chestnut-colored eyes.

"I don't know what to say," she admitted with hurt lacing her light voice.

Angie looked at her son's girlfriend and swallowed hard.

"And your family knows about this?" she wanted to know.

Tiffany smiled wide showing off her deep dimples and bright white teeth. "Yes, mam and they are excited about this baby," she replied quickly while leaning on Malik.

Malik cleared his throat.

"I know I'm young, but this is a gift from God. I can still help the family. I have to find what's right for me, but I will make sure that it is something that all of us will benefit from. I'm even doing some side gigs now that will be a good look for the BOC," he said displaying confidence that he didn't have minutes ago.

Angie nodded. She looked over her son's pricey threads then his expensive watch. He drove a car that carried a $500 car note and he spent money like it was going out of style. Malik was young and a baby didn't seem like a good choice for him. At 21 he should have been preparing for another round of college not becoming a father. Angie wanted her sons to be better than her. She wanted them to break generational curses so yes something as small as him having a kid out of wedlock was upsetting to her. Because it honestly made her feel like a failure. She brushed her hand over the jet-black short curls on her head and sighed.

"Sweetie can you give me and my son a minute?" she asked Tiffany nicely.

Malik frowned before shaking his head. His chin jutted out in defiance as he looked at his mom.

"Nah, whatever you have to say you can say it to me *and* her," he said in a deeper tone.

Oshun sat up and glared at Malik.

"Aye—"

"It's fine," Angie told Oshun cutting him off. She looked at Malik and admired his mocha skin and handsome face. He was no matter what age her baby and while she didn't like being the bad guy, she knew that sparing the rod did spoil the child and a baby was where she put her foot down.

"You have never had a job. You overspend like it's a sport that you have to be the best at. You don't even do your laundry sweetie. I only have a few rules and no babies before your career and marriage is one of them. I am not raising statistics. You boys will be better than this world ever thought you could be. A kid changes everything Malik. *Everything* and there is no way you and your girlfriend is ready for that. Then you want us to be happy for you but we're not. We didn't see this one coming and I'm worried because you're not ready you just don't see it yet," she said and although her words were honest and brutal, they'd been spoken from a place of love.

Malik's chiseled jaw tensed. He brushed his left hand over his fade as his eyes narrowed.

"And you get to tell me how to live my life? You're not God. I love and appreciate all that you do but I'm not Oshun or Gio. I have my own fucking mind and I can live my life the way I want to," he snapped so angry that his fist balled.

Oshun stood as Gio took a step towards Malik and Angie raised her hand in the air. Then like the queen she was everyone relaxed at her gesture. Malik's shoulders fell and his tough-guy act vanished before her eyes.

"I'm sorry," he quickly apologized.

Angie nodded knowing that he was.

"You have feelings and you're hurt by what I said. I won't take it personally. I also will never tell a woman what to do with her body. I would never suggest abortion. But I do hate that this happened so soon. You have so much life to live and this will hold you back for a while. That I'm certain of," she professed.

Malik's girlfriend blinked rapidly as her eyes watered.

"I have to go," she announced and sniffled before rushing out of the kitchen.

Malik looked at his brothers and mom before shaking his head. Anger once again vibrated off his 5'9 frame and Angie prayed that he kept it respectful so that she didn't have to slap his big behind.

"This whack as hell and I'm not believing what y'all saying right now. How are we going to promote black love and black unity when we really on some dictating shit?"

"I know you're mad brah, but show respect," Gio said in his deep voice making Malik peer over at him.

Malik threw his hands in the air exasperatedly as he looked back at his mom.

"You had it rough! Your family didn't accept you because you were the product of an affair. It was always tight for you and dad and we get it! We know you saw the struggle, but my kid won't! My kid will be good no matter who I have in my corner. All I need is God and my girl. I love you, but you can't tell me how to live. I control my life and if you want to stop paying for my shit then that's fine. I have a small savings. I'm not as dumb as you make me out to be. And when y'all ready to accept our baby give me a call but until then keep that negative energy over here," he said before walking away.

Malik exited his mom's house with a heavy heart. He got into his custom matte black Hellcat Charger and started it up. It purred softly like a kitten before rumbling like a lion. Malik's nerves started to ease up once he was out of his mom's home. His chestnut eyes slid over to his girlfriend as she cried softly in her seat.

"My mom's just mad. She'll come around," he said knowing his mom wouldn't shun her grandchild.

Tiffany shook her head as she wiped her face. She was a pretty young woman with caramel hued skin, thick curly black hair that hung down her back along with doe-shaped brown eyes, a straight nose, and full lips. She was a runner and it showed with her toned legs and fit body. Her beauty was uncanny and had been one of the things to get Malik's attention.

"Cheer up baby. It's like I told you today. It's me and you forever, and I'll never let you down. Whether we work out or not and we better fucking work out, we will always be a family," he assured her.

Malik winked at her once he was done talking and she nodded. Tiffany smiled at him as she turned her body his way.

"You promise?" she questioned quietly.

Malik looked over at her deeply while biting his bottom lip. He nodded not having to think about it and peace washed over Tiffany.

"On my pop's life, I promise. I would never dog you out. Hell, my dad would come from the grave to kick my black ass then my brothers would finish me off."

Tiffany laughed lightly.

"Then my brother would get the final licks in. But seriously I want this to work."

Malik nodded. He backed out of his mom's driveway and sped off down her residential street. He pulled up to the stop sign and partially stopped before hitting a right and speeding towards the main street. Tiffany shook her head while grinning at him.

"I told you about doing that. I hate you even got this damn car. It's too fast," she complained while smiling.

Malik smirked and she swooned at how sexy he was to her.

"You like it though. Whenever we fuck in the car your pussy be on water wet. On gushy, gushy, and shit," he remarked and licked his lips.

Tiffany's body temperature rose as he turned onto another street. His hand slid up her thigh and right before it made it to her center where her body was the most heated a local cop switched lanes and flicked his lights on.

Malik's brows tensed as he placed his car in park. Because of the Lacoste name in Detroit, the police made it a habit to harass any of the Lacoste brothers that they could, but they loved to antagonize Malik the most. Because of his young age and temper, he was always angry and hot mannered with them. Any negative light that they could put on the Lacoste family was a plus in their book.

"Please relax and place your hands on the steering wheel. Think of the baby," Tiffany whispered.

She attempted to rub Malik's leg and he jerked away from her. Malik angrily swung his car door open and emerged from his car with a deep scowl on his face. He looked at the pale-faced tall officer approach him with disdain.

"What the fuck your bitch ass stop me for today? I drove a car while being black motherfucka!" he based.

The tall, stocky officer with the pale ivory skin and dark

green eyes smiled with mischief. He peered over at his black partner another tall man as well with an athletic frame and they smirked at one another.

"We received a call that your vehicle just took place in a drug transaction. We will need to search your car. Calm down, boy," officer Polk spoke evenly.

Malik's head snapped back at the disrespect and his fist balled.

"Boy? Do I look like your fucking son? I'm not no fucking boy my nigga! Y'all on some bullshit like always and you not checking shit I know my rights!

"Malik calm down, baby. Just do as they say," Tiffany said getting out of the car.

"Miss please put your hands in the air!" the black officer Milton yelled and raised his gun.

Malik's heart expanded and pounded ferociously at the sight of the cop drawing his weapon on his unarmed girl-friend that was carrying his child.

"Look she has nothing in her fucking hands! This that bullshit, wait until I call my brother!" he yelled.

Officer Polk touched the top of his gun that was still in the holster while eyeing Malik. He looked over his nice car then his expensive clothing and shook his head.

"Drug money got you looking real good. I see your dad dying didn't slow the cash flow up," he snarled saying anything he felt he could to set Malik off.

Malik took a step towards him as his chest started to hurt.

It heaved up and down rapidly as his body struggled to breathe.

"Fuck you just say? Huh, nigga," he rasped and touched his chest.

Tiffany's eyes widened at the sight of Malik touching his chest.

"Malik, baby you okay?" Tiffany asked as the black officer cuffed her.

Malik fought for air as he looked at officer Polk.

"Hands in the air! Please put your hands in the air!" officer Polk yelled drawing his gun.

Malik's eyes closed briefly, and he remembered his inhaler was in his car door. He turned from the cop and leaned down. He reached for his inhaler and Tiffany's piercing scream grabbed his attention.

Malik attempted to look up and the feeling of an intense burning sensation caused him not to. He fell into his car door as the officer shot him three more times.

Pop!

Pop!

Pop!

"You motherfucka's, he was reaching for his inhaler! Malik! Malik get up!" Tiffany yelled in the loudest voice she could muster up.

Officer Polk slowly walked up on Malik and stared down at him as his ivory skin turned red in worry. His eyes landed on the inhaler that was sticking out of the inside of the door slot and he swallowed hard. He put his gun away and leaned down to check Malik's pulse.

He felt no beat as he looked at his young face.

"Malik, baby get up! You killed him! You killed my boyfriend!" Tiffany yelled with tears streaming down her face.

Officer Polk discreetly grabbed the inhaler and placed it in his pocket. He put the weed he had on him on the inside of the car door and slowly stood.

"He was trying to hide the weed. It's right in the door. Take her to the car while I call Bishop," he replied speaking of their chief.

His partner officer Milton looked at him with a slight frown before clearing his throat.

"Is he okay, though?" officer Milton asked.

Officer Polk shook his head but didn't respond. Tiffany's knees went weak as she thought of Malik. The life they were supposed to live. The baby they would eventually have and the love he gave her. Her heart tore into pieces as she fell back. Her eyes closed and consciousness left her being as her world came to an end.

CHAPTER 1

A WEEK LATER

baymoor falls

His eyes were lifeless. The beautiful hazel color that was mixed with specs of green usually shined bright but for the day they were dull. Despair clung to his stocky physique and from his upset disposition, Jaylah grew nervous sensing something was wrong.

She'd never seen her father look so desolate.

Ever.

"Baby what's wrong?" her mom asked rubbing his hand gently.

Jaylah's father didn't respond right away. Instead, he looked from Jaylah to her mom then sister wearily before sighing and even while under stress his handsomeness showed. Her parents were only seventeen when they had she and her twin. So, Jaylah often got that "girl where your daddy at" Question from her friends that she detested.

Jaylah shifted on their oversized sectional and pulled the blanket up over her frame that was maturing already at the age of sixteen.

"Daddy what's wrong?" she found the voice to ask not able to take his silence any longer.

"Yeah daddy, you okay?" her twin Jael added always cosigning her words.

Jaylah hated and loved that about her twin.

Her father shook his head. He adjusted his expensive watch a gold and diamond timepiece that he'd recently purchased before licking his thick lips. His eyes went to their mother and watered before he spoke.

"I'm sorry, sweetheart. So sorry," he apologized calling her mom by his favorite term of endearment.

Jaylah thought it was cute and to watch her parents openly show affection made her teenage mind yearn for a marriage like that.

"Sorry about what? You scaring me Clay," her mom said softly.

Jaylah's father was nicknamed Clay because of his café 'Au Lait hued skin and dark gingered colored hair. Her father shifted on the suede sectional and Jaylah briefly admired his custom grey suit and shiny black loafers.

"Sometimes what we do in life isn't always right, but the sad thing is we don't see that until it's too late," he replied speaking in codes.

Jaylah cleared her throat.

"What happened?"

"Yeah, what happened?" Jael asked.

"Life happened," he replied, and before he could elaborate the front doors were burst open.

"FBI! FBI! FBI!" the plain-clothed officer yelled as a group of men wearing black jackets rushed into their large home with guns drawn.

"Jaylah snap out of it! The set is falling asleep waiting on you to finish your interview," the producer Ricky hissed into her earpiece in his normal demanding tone.

His words were enough to jar Jaylah from her intense flashback. She crossed her legs, licked her heart-shaped lips, and gave the woman before her a generic smile ignoring the pain that the memory left her within its wake.

"Can you explain to me what exactly your show is about?" she asked looking at the woman she was interviewing.

Simply looking over the biracial woman with the lavender tinted hair and colorful tattoos Jaylah felt nothing. The woman looked so damn white trashy to her that she didn't know what to do.

"My name is Swan and my radio show started as a podcast. I was coming off a breakup and wanted a way to positively release that hurt I was feeling you know? I also knew that I wasn't the only woman in pain. I wanted to help my sisters overcome their pain as well and I felt we could do it together. From there, my radio show was formed and six years later it's still standing," the woman Swan said proudly.

Jaylah nodded not impressed. She detested Swan's show that spoke about feminism, crystals, and heartbreak. It was a joke and she wasn't sure what anyone saw in that bullshit. If anything, she felt Swan should have been telling women how to erase debt and create the life they want to live. Speaking on not needing a man while placing yoni eggs up your pussy wasn't Jaylah's thing.

Jaylah sighed wishing she'd called into work. She wasn't feeling it and was struggling with keeping her fake mask on for the day. She yawned and was able to quickly cover her face to mask it. She shifted on the small sofa and gave Swan a tight-lipped smile.

"Well, you've certainly made an impression. You got our attention at the station. A few of the women here love the jargon," she commented.

Swan stopped smiling and sat up. Her bangles of brass and gold clanked together, and Jaylah cringed at how many she wore on her left arm. It looked messy, childish, and dirty. She was into clean, classy dressing. Jaylah was big on looking well put together. She knew that how you presented yourself to the world mattered. And what she got from Swan's look was that she was the kind of woman that went panty less. The woman that got fucked but never the woman to be proposed to.

"But how do you feel about the show?" Swan asked raising her tattooed brow that was an ombre color to match her lavender-hued hair. Her colored eyes peered at Jaylah in a way that told Jaylah she was fucking with her.

Jaylah sat up straight and gave her another fake smile.

"I feel nothing about it. I'm sorry sweetie but I haven't listened to it. However, at the station we are proud to support a woman like you today on, this Woman is Winning Wednesday segment. Keep up the good work and tell everyone what channel your station can be found on," she replied.

The camera shot to Swan and Swan's eyes peered at Jaylah questioningly before her pretty face relaxed and a smiled covered it. She rattled off her station's channel and the camera's cut. Jaylah stood and cleared her throat as Swan rose to her feet as well.

"Thank you for coming on the station. Enjoy the rest of—"

"Save it bitch and before you judge me make sure your own house is clean. I can't believe this was your endgame. You have nothing but negative energy surrounding you and destruction is following you like a black cloud. I'll be cleansing myself of it the rest of the week to ward your bad spirits away," Swan shook her head as she looked at Jaylah. "Five is your number and now I can see why. Find yourself and you will find the peace your soul longs for because you need it hoe," she told her and walked off the set.

Jaylah's jaw fell slack before her face formed a smile. Swan carried sass to her and while she still wasn't shit in

Jaylah's eyes, Jaylah loved that she spoke her mind. Jaylah was perplexed as to half of the shit that Swan said to her and didn't care enough to ask her about it. Instead, she pulled off her mic and walked to the back of the studio. As she entered into the office area her mind started to drift to that dark place that sometimes kept her up at night. She shook her head and took a deep calming breath as she headed for her desk.

"Hey chick, that was an interesting interview you just did. Her show is bomb as fuck. You would know that if you listened to it," Charise her co-worker said walking up.

Jaylah peered around for her assistant while shaking her head.

"Charise I have no interest in listening to that Erykah Badu shit she talks about and if you keep sticking those things up your coochie they're going to get— what the hell happened to you?" Jaylah asked finally looking at her co-worker.

Charise stood before her with a bruised lip and slightly darkened left eye. While Jaylah only worked on set doing her Wednesday segment and 6 AM to 9 AM morning schedule Charise worked the street news out of the studio for the station three times out the week. Jaylah felt blessed to never have to do that bullshit but didn't knock Charise's position.

"Let's talk," Charise said quietly and pulled Jaylah into her cubicle. They sat down and Jaylah's arched brows drew together as she stared at Charise. "I was marching with a few of my people the other day on Broad Street. Things are getting worse Jaylah and I'm tired of it. Aren't you?" she asked.

Jaylah cleared her throat then shook her head. She was stumped on what to say because her views on the world weren't the same as most black people she knew.

"Bad as in what, Charise? You're out on the street a college-educated woman with a child putting your life on the line for low life's. These men and women would be alive if they did what the police asked of them. I mean how hard is it to follow directions?" she countered with a shrug.

Charise's eyes widened and she blew out hot breath.

"Wow," she muttered. She laughed lightly before speaking. "I know that life for you has probably been easy. I see the way people cater to you because of your looks. You've got that whole black Barbie thing going for you with the slim thick body, light chinky eyes, and long hair. Even your light damn near white skin has got you to the morning segment but make no mistakes about it, you're still black. You are nothing more than a *nigga* to these people that own this station Jaylah," Charise told her.

Jaylah's heart raced as she stared at Charise. They were both the same age. Had been hired in at the same time only the boss Jerry saw something in Jaylah that he didn't see in Charise. Charise and she were friends in college. Had studied together, cried together, and graduated together. But somewhere along the way they disconnected and now they felt more like strangers than friends. Jaylah never taken Charise as the jealous type but as she sat across from the pretty caramel shaded beauty with the round face, pretty smile, and shoulder-length locs she saw the green monster sitting on her shoulder.

Jaylah sat up and licked her lips. She pushed her left hand through her long luminous inky black curls and flashed Charise a startling white smile. She'd always known she was gorgeous. Her beauty however brought along her greatest pain, so she didn't rely on her looks and never had. She was educated and the hustle in her was so strong that she made it out of her circumstances. What she would never let anyone do was try to make her feel bad about being successful.

Her nose crinkled as she looked at Charise.

"See that's the problem with you people. You always try to place every black person in the same box. You don't know my story Charise. Yes, I am beautiful and yes that comes with perks, but it came with pain too. I have been at the top of my class since high school. I even graduated Baymoor University as the valedictorian, and you know that. I am more than just a pretty face," Jaylah stopped talking and she stood. She adjusted her watch, the female version of her father's favorite timepiece before giving Charise a cocky smirk. "I'm the complete package. Instead of fighting for grown-ass people that are so stuck on the past that they can't fix their future and adjust their present you need to be wondering why you're still on the road doing segments while I sit at the desk sipping my coffee in a cozy studio."

Jaylah smiled and walked away.

"Enjoy the rest of your day Charise," she called over her shoulder.

Jaylah headed for her boss's office remembering he wanted to speak with her after her segment and when she looked to her left, she spotted her assistant Anthony asleep inside of the break room. Her eyes narrowed and she frowned as she headed into the small room that housed a round white table with a black fridge and microwave.

"Anthony, I told you before my segment to grab my dry cleaning. What the fuck!" she hissed sneaking up on him.

Anthony her twenty-two-year-old struggling college student assistant jumped in his seat at the sound of her voice. Slob dribbled down the side of his face as he looked up at her with blurry blue eyes.

"Sorry, I've been studying for school and my mom is sick," he replied wiping the sleep from his eyes.

Jaylah took a deep breath and exhaled. To her excuses were for the weak.

"And somehow you felt that made it okay for you to come in here and be mediocre today? Nothing will come to a lazy man not even a fuck for me to give. You don't have to return here, and I will not be writing any letters of recommendation. Now you have time for school and your mom."

Jaylah walked away before Anthony could reply and headed for her boss's office. Lightly she tapped on his door as her nerves began to peek through. She battled with anxiety but would never tell a soul. For Jaylah strong, beautiful, and successful was the only way she wanted people to perceive her. Her trust issues with people made it hard for her to show her flaws because she knew that once someone saw your flaws, they could use them against you.

"Come in Jaylah!" her boss based in his raspy tone.

"You wanted to see me. Is everything okay?" she asked stepping in.

Jerry Hegler was the executive producer for the news station that Jaylah was employed at. Jaylah did her research while in college and learned that Jerry was someone of importance because the news station that he worked at was also co-owned by his family. He had connections in the media industry and was in the kind of crowd Jaylah wanted to be in. The who's, who of Baymoor Falls you could call it. Jerry was respected, stern, right-wing as hell, and very successful. Jaylah took to him immediately. He was someone she respected. He'd taken her under his wing and shown her the ropes. From the start, he believed in her and because he did, the other people in the television industry did as well.

She took a seat in front of his desk and crossed her legs. Her eyes briefly cast down to the saucy ass Fendi heels that she wore before looking back up to her boss that was a badly aging Caucasian man that carried a husky build to him. Jerry's brown hair was thinning, his facial hair was nonexistent, and his eyes were the color of dirty river water. He was nothing spectacular to look at, but he was successful, so many women treated him like he was handsome.

"I did. Do you remember the story that Earnest covered last week on that drug dealer that was shot down in Detroit?" he asked with his murky brown eyes on her.

Jaylah nodded although she didn't. Black men died on the regular and the station she worked at quickly told the story then moved on to the next topic for the day. They weren't for black lives and Jaylah didn't blame them. Black men didn't know how to stay out of trouble. Instead of living the right way they chose chaos, illegal dealings, and blame-shifting. She was over the narrative that black men deserved a break because of slavery. If she made it despite all the bullshit, she'd been through then they could as well.

Jerry sat back and rubbed his protruding belly.

"All hell has broken loose because of that shooting. I mean for heaven's sake he was a drug dealer and the media is making him out to be a college boy saint," he grumbled, frowning.

Jaylah nodded not sure what any of the things he said had to do with her. It was another hustler dead and she knew it wouldn't be the last. For black men to survive and be taken seriously they needed to get their shit together. She was tired of them resorting to the street life because it made the whole race look bad.

"I saw that and I'm already over it," she co-signed feeling the need to say something.

Jerry gazed at her with tensed brows. He sat up and placed his elbows onto his cluttered desk.

"The thing is. I just heard from my son in Detroit and the officer that did the shooting is a part of my fraternity. He's received death threats and is afraid for his life. His home was recently set on fire and he was forced to go into hiding. He's put out a call for us to help and as a fellow brother of mine, I have to. I need a favor from you and if you do this whatever salary increase that you want within reason will be granted to you, my girl. You can also have your morning slot locked in. No one will get it," he explained, and Jaylah's ears perked up at the sound of what he was proposing.

"Do tell," she crooned making him chuckle.

Jerry pulled out two blue label Maduro cigars and passed her one. He then lit the cigars while grinning at her.

"I love you, Jaylah. You are the daughter that I wish I had because those little sluts Heather gave me aren't good for shit. I need you to take a trip to Detroit. Stay as long as you need. Get close with this thug's family and get me some dirt. Anything that can help prove the innocence of officer Polk. As of now he's still working but if they make enough noise about this, he could be suspended or worse arrested," he replied.

Jaylah shook her head in disbelief. None of this was making sense to her. The boy he shot was a thug. He was dealing drugs and that was the life he'd signed up for. A cop should never have to hide because they did the right thing.

"All for doing his job? Wow. They're animals and they expect the world to treat them with respect when they don't even respect themselves. It's sad really and it makes my life harder. Sometimes I hate to be even tied to this lazy ass black race," she huffed in irritation. "Whatever you need I will do it. I'm tired of the black lives matter walks. All lives matter, Jerry," she replied.

Jerry beamed at her with pride. He blew smoke from his mouth and passed her a manila folder that was sealed.

"You're different from them. Always have been and always will be. That's why I chose you and put you where you are in this company. You are what they should be. In this folder is what we have on this family. You will have a new name and identity for this. If at any moment you feel afraid leave and come home but I'm hopeful that you can get what we need. Can I count on you to do this for me?" he asked peering at her deeply.

Jaylah nodded eagerly looking to please Jerry. Out of all of the men in her life he'd been the only one to consistently stay by her side.

"Of course. Why not take them all down since they want to complain about some shit," she smiled.

Jerry chuckled loudly and smiled at her.

"My girl. I knew you would be on board."

Jaylah nodded and winked at Jerry before leaving his office.

After leaving work Jaylah picked up her dry cleaning

then grabbed dinner from Tabito Grill her favorite sushi spot in Baymoor Falls. Her car had a mind of its own and when she pulled up to the gated home inside of the pricey Woodland Hills subdivision she lingered near the bottom of the long driveway.

The estate was grand with its wrought-iron fence that protected the eight-bedroom mini-mansion. Jaylah could feel her heart racing and her palms grow sweaty from just the sight of it. She wasn't supposed to be there. Shit, really not even care. The home carried her past and she was now in the present. She wasn't Jaylah from the Southside projects. She was now Jaylah Cole, anchorwoman for one of Baymoor Falls leading news stations HLN2o. Her life turned out well and was only getting better however a sinking feeling that she couldn't shake was starting to keep her up at night again. It was trudging up memories that she'd locked away in her mind years ago. It kept creeping into her daily life and now starting to affect her work. She didn't want to open her chest of horrors from her teenage years.

No fuck that she wasn't going to be like so many black people. Crying over spilled milk. The shit happened and now she was over it.

Right?

Honk!

The loud horn blaring at her made Jaylah nearly jump out of her skin. Her eyes widened in alarm and shot towards the gate. The white Wrath held a glossy shine to it as it attempted to pull out of the driveway. The gate securing the mini mansion was open and the window tint was so dark on the car that Jaylah couldn't see inside.

She sped off in her two-door black E450 coupe with her eyes watering.

"It was for the best, it was for the best," she whispered repeatedly refusing to cry.

As the sunset, Jaylah pulled up to her home. It wasn't the extravagant Woodland Hills area she'd just left, but it was still in a middle-class neighborhood that housed good eateries, clean parks, and nice boutiques. It was the Northside of Baymoor Falls and Jaylah adored her loft. It reminded her of the home she once had when she was younger back before her father had been sent to prison. It wasn't far from that street and while that place wasn't available her loft was and the second, she'd seen it she was sold on the property.

Jaylah pulled behind her boyfriend Garris, slate grey Lexus and parked. She grabbed her food, purse, and cellphone before exiting her car.

"Babe I'm home! Come grab this hot ass food!" she called out stepping into her place.

She shut the door with her foot and seconds later Garris rushed down the stairs. His grey joggers hung loose on his narrowed waist as he grabbed the takeout containers. His full pink lips that were outlined with a bushy brown mustache brushed against hers and he smiled.

"I missed you. How was work?" he asked with his dark brown eyes on her.

Jaylah admired her sexy ass man that looked like a clone of the actor Orlando Bloom. Garris walked into her life one rainy morning a year ago while she was grabbing coffee at Rojo's and he never walked out of it. He was an accountant that was smart, funny, and attentive. It was nice to come home to someone because she'd been alone for so long, so she welcomed him into her private space and didn't mind Garris staying at her place most of the time she preferred it that way.

Being the control freak that she was.

"It was long sweetie. How was yours?" she asked stepping out of her heels.

Jaylah found Garris in her upscale kitchen making their plates. She inhaled the alluring aroma of sushi and her stomach growled with excitement. She was good at many things, but cooking was not a favorite of hers. She knew how to thanks to her mom, but she did not have time to slave over a fucking stove. That was basic bitch shit and she was too busy for that.

"It was work, baby. I thought you said you would make my favorite dish since my birthday is coming up," he commented grabbing a bottle of red wine from the marble island.

Jaylah rolled her eyes while washing her hands.

"I have a lot on my plate and cooking homemade lasagna is not one of them at the moment. Maybe next week, Garris," she exhaled dramatically. "Like I'm fucking tired. I helped my assistant with his homework today and I drove Charise to the dealership to get her car back," she fibbed with a frown on her face.

Garris looked at her with an empathetic gaze.

"I understand you do a lot and I'm sorry. I can have my mom make it," he replied, and it made her smile.

Garris didn't bring her drama over anything and she loved that about him.

"That's good. She should do that anyway seeing as how you're her son and when will I get to meet her? Am I invited to the birthday celebration she's having for you?" she asked turning to him.

Garris looked up from pouring the wine and his brows knitted together.

"Not this time, she's old school and wants me to settle down with a wholesome Italian girl, but she'll come around soon bellissima," he replied in a hopeful tone. "Let's eat," he said, and Jaylah nodded hating his reply.

She liked Garris and felt herself slowly warming up to the idea of them being together. He was Italian and his family didn't believe in mixing races, so she hadn't met any of them yet.

Garris watched her closely while frowning.

"Are you mad?"

Jaylah joined him at her round glass dining table and shook her head. Even if she was, she wouldn't let him know it.

The last thing she would ever do was allow for her emotions to peak through. Being vulnerable for Jaylah wasn't an option. So instead of complaining and crying about it, she smiled.

"It's fine. I wouldn't be able to fly down with you anyway. I have to cover an exclusive story in Detroit. I might be gone for a month or two depending on how it goes. Jerry wants me to do this and I can't say no."

Garris ate some of his sushi before shaking his head. His eyes narrowed as he looked at Jaylah.

"He's always demanding all of your time and that shit isn't cool. It's like he's obsessed with you or something. Has he ever come on to you sexually?"

Jaylah nearly dropped her fork. The mere thought of Jerry coming on to her in a sexual manner was enough for her stomach to churn in disgust.

"Garris, never. He's the father I wish I had," she told him.

Garris nodded with his thoughtful eyes looking her way.

"I guess that's cool but here's an option. You could also reach out to the man that brought you into this world. I see how he calls here for you all day every day. I couldn't imagine not having my father in my life. You know he's done prison time as well baby."

Jaylah checked out of the conversation at the mention of her sperm donor. His bad decisions changed her family's life forever. She hated him with every fiber in her being and she didn't give a damn if he called until the world was over. She would never forgive him for what he did to her and her family.

I have to get a wax.

Go shopping.

Get something ghetto as hell done to my hair.

Shit, I might have to look at some videos online for street terms. I might be too smart for them.

Jaylah smiled at her thoughts and Garris frowned.

"Did you hear any of what I said? I asked what day are you leaving?"

Jaylah shrugged because she wasn't sure.

"Um, in a few days babe. Why?"

Garris licked his lips as he sat back in the seat.

"I'm trying to see how much time I have with you. Come here and show me how much you are going to miss me," he said stroking his lengthy member through his grey Champion joggers.

Jaylah's body woke up at the lustful words he spoke to her.

"I'd love to do that," she said in a sultry tone and rose from her seat.

Thoughts of her upcoming trip went to the recess of her mind along with the manila folder she'd forgotten in her car as she slipped off her dress and walked up on her man ready to give them both a pleasurable ride.

CHAPTER 2

Mom: Call me baby please and cut on your GPS we're worried about you.

Gio: Aye mom looking for you, you good?

Latoya: Call me king. Please.

Brando: You been on my mind heavy, call me back.

Mom: please call me!

H is teeth sunk into his bottom lip so hard that they punctured the skin. On his lap was something he never thought he would ever have to use. An AK47 Pistol. In his late teens, he wanted to be a hood celebrity. Shit like that was intriguing to him. The dope boys had the money and the women. While he never needed help in the lady's department, he did want money. His family needed the extra ends so he told himself he would sell dope. He did odd *jobs until he had enough money to buy some drugs and a gun. The crazy thing was Ray from his old hood that sold weapons only had a choppa left. Oshun had never seen anything so dangerous in his young life. The steel felt heavy and was life changing. Even while being blissfully ignorant to a lot of shit he knew what the gun was capable of, so he stowed it away. His dreams of being the next kingpin never came into fruition thanks to his boy and he was glad.*

However now as he sat outside of the home of the person responsible for his pain, he was certain he would put that bitch to use. His anger was overtaking his will to make the right decisions. The two-story home inside of the city of Rochester was nice. Oshun figured it was at least $350,000 and any regular cop would be glad to have such a residence. All day Oshun had been perched outside of the place waiting for movement.

Blinding hot rage seared his core and the only thing on his mind was revenge. He wanted the people responsible dead for taking away his brother.

Thick tattooed fingers tapped against the pistol grip impatiently. He released his lip and tugged on the collar of his black Amiri distressed hoodie. He then pulled his black Gucci beanie low and swallowed hard more anxious than tired and before he could blink the door to the garage slowly ascended.

Oshun's teeth gritted as he raised the choppa. He lowered his window not giving a damn if they saw his face and tossed the front of the gun out of it. His fingers brushed against the trigger *and before he sprayed the black Lincoln SUV a calmness washed over him. The shit was crazy because he was in the midst of a fucking storm. Standing in hell with the devil by his side but temporarily he felt peace.*

He tried to fight it, but the stillness was too loud. He lowered the choppa, and when the Lincoln drove past, he was able to see that it was a woman and child in the car.

No man, just them.

"Damn," he grumbled from what could have been.

Oshun tossed the choppa into his passengers' seat and his chest tightened. Had he almost killed a woman and a child?

What the fuck.

He was shook. His mind couldn't stop traveling to the what if's. Yes, he wanted officer Polk because despite the footage being lost, he felt in his soul that Polk was responsible for his brother's death. He even had a reliable source, one of the members of the BOC and he saw everything go down as he was walking his dog. He trusted Mr. Franklin however the cops weren't trying to hear Mr. Franklin's statement but for Oshun that was all the proof he needed.

He closed his eyes as he fought for control over his anger because if he didn't stop, he was bound to take a lot of lives while making his own worse than it already was. His eyes opened as he still carried the rage with him that came from losing his brother. If he couldn't get Polk, he would ensure that the scary motherfucka had no home to return to.

"Talk to me," his friend spoke in a raspy tenor.

Oshun leaned his tall muscular frame against the wall in the hallway with his hooded eyes on the ground. He couldn't stop thinking about the fire and what he'd almost committed. He wasn't a violent man. Hadn't been in many fights because from one look you could see he wasn't the person you wanted to fuck with. However, he was in pain and hurt people tended to, *hurt people.*

His heart was shattered and keeping up the facade that everything was good was gutting him from the inside out. He wanted to make the streets of Detroit bleed red. He wanted the families of the officers involved to mourn. He wanted them to cry, feel his pain ten times over, and have to sit on that shit and do nothing.

He was at a battle. Facing the fucking Devil head-on. He could cross the street and let the devil direct his steps some more or he could do the right thing and allow for his lawyer and the law to lock the officers up. The shitty thing was the law had never been on his side, so it made it that much harder for him to want to do the right thing.

"I'm conflicted," he admitted, and only with his nigga could he drop his guard and keep shit real.

Pain and anger clung to him like a needy bitch and whenever he told himself that he could make it through the day without thinking of murder, he always failed.

"That's natural to feel that way. I ain't got much time fam because Sterling is sick so this will be quick. My mentor told me the story about when he'd been shot. He said the bullets and hate came from someone that was his friend but only by business. He knew the nigga hated him, but he still kept him around. Always looking to have his enemies close and in the process, he made money with the dude. Anyway, he said it all came to a head and one day the nigga pulled on him out of the blue. Popped two bullets into his chest and left him leaking while walking away with their cash. My mentor said he took months to recover and when he went to re-pay the favor his enemy said some shit that made him think," Brando spoke.

Oshun cleared his throat. His worried dark honey eyes brushed against his black Balenciaga sneakers before lifting. His thick brows pulled together as he listened to his close friend speak. Brando was wiser beyond his years and that was one of the reasons why Oshun was so close to him.

"I'm listening."

"He said the nigga looked him in the eye and said. *I always showed my hand still you kept me around. I only did what was expected of me, so why you mad at me?* You and I both know how this shit goes for us in America. The law was never on our side. We always knew what they were capable of. You have to be smarter, quicker, and better. One slip up and the BOC could fall. Your mom could be burying two sons then it would really be a fucking war out here. A man with great patience, that can think past the moment and look into the future is a wise man. Making un-rational decisions based on feelings will get you killed. Come see me when you free. One love king," Brando said and ended the call.

Oshun went to put his cellphone away feeling stronger because of Brando's talk when a text message flashed across his large screen.

Letoya: I love you and while I know you have to be strong for the family, you need someone to be there for you too. Please don't shut me out. The family will get through this. I'm here for whatever you need, and I do mean whatever king.

Oshun felt no way about reading over his friends' message. Latoya knew texting wasn't his thing. He preferred face to face interaction. He needed to see the person he was connecting with. Feel their energy and engage with them on a more personal level. Texting never gave him that feeling. That was one thing from technology he could do without.

Without responding he placed his cellphone into his jean pocket. He stepped off the wall and went back into the room that was filled with his family and friends. He fell into his seat with his heart racing. This moment wasn't about how he felt. It was for Malik. It was to protect his legacy and as long as he remembered that he would be able to get through it.

"Everything smooth?" Gio asked peering over at him with pain in his almond-shaped eyes.

"I'm good, you?"

Gio shrugged. He was always the calmest of the Lacoste men. Malik had been hot-tempered, Oshun was known to be grouchy despite his giving nature and Gio was chill. It had been that way since they were kids.

"I'm Gucci," Gio mumbled avoiding eye contact with him.

Oshun nodded certain that Gio was lying like he was about his feelings. His angry eyes ascended to the high ceiling inside of the room and like clockwork, his thoughts drifted to his youngest brother. He wanted desperately to pull at the black short curls adorning his burst fade but refrained. Oshun was rarely the kind of man that lost his cool but to lose your little brother to the same people that were sworn in to protect him was about enough to push him to his limit. His eyes zeroed in on the large wooden fans on the ceiling as he thought of Malik.

"Tell me why you mad?" he asked Malik as he got into his car.

Malik's fist was balled as his chest rose up and down rapidly. He looked over at Oshun with his brows furrowed and he shrugged.

"I didn't make the team," he said angrily. "That's some bullshit," he mumbled and because he was so down trout Oshun allowed for his curse word to slide.

Oshun placed his white 745 Beamer in park and looked out of his car window.

"Is any of those boys taller than you?" he inquired.

Malik shook his head and he continued.

"Stronger?"

Malik sighed.

"Nah," he mumbled.

Oshun nodded.

"Then why do you think they made the team and you didn't?"

Malik sat up straight and his eyes went over to the group of boys that made the varsity basketball team. He swallowed hard as he watched them laugh and joke around outside of the school near the gym doors.

"They did practice more when I felt like I would automatically get it. I know Jacob did and even Reese," he spoke up.

Oshun nodded.

"Then do you have a right to be mad? They put in the work and you didn't. Nobody on this earth is getting something that's not available to you. As a black man in this world, life will be harder for you, but you can still go out and get it. I'm *not letting that stop me and you better not let it stop you either. Suck that shit up, put in the work, and try again. You have to fight for the things you want in life,"* he told him.

Malik nodded with determination covering his face.

"I got you. I'ma put that work in, Oshun. I'll make you proud."

Oshun started up his car and smirked over at his brother.

"Just saying that makes me proud of you. And don't do it for me. Do it for you," he told him as he pulled away from the high school.

"I let this happen," Oshun mumbled pulling himself away from his thoughts.

Every memory of Malik hurt. His insides were ruined, and his heart was broken. A real-life fucking heartbreak and he didn't know what to do.

After witnessing the cops speak on Malik and his family as if they were the next Black Mafia Family, he knew he had to say something. Not speaking on the incident would only lead people to believe that Malik was a drug dealer when that was far from the case.

"You good?" Ameer asked grabbing his attention.

Ameer Matin was Oshun's unofficial big brother. Oshun could still remember the day he walked up on Ameer looking to hustle. His family needed the money and Ameer turned him away. However, Ameer gave him a job at one of his businesses and from there a bond was formed. Oshun valued Ameer's opinion and when he formed the BOC with his mom and brother, Ameer was the first person to invest in the community with them. He was a real nigga and Oshun loved him like he was blood.

"I'm straight," he lied because he knew his friend well enough to know that he was itching to take matters into his own hands.

Ameer peered at him questioningly before he went back to talking to one of Oshun's cousins. Oshun sat up in his seat and shook off thoughts of his younger brother. His hooded eyes a shade similar to dark honey peered around at his family and friends with gratefulness. He adjusted his black AP and his eyes drifted down to the tattoo's covering his fingers. It was a prayer, and damn did he need one.

Psalm was on his right hand spelled out in a neat calligraphy font while 59:1 was on his left fingers. Oshun had gotten the tattoos a year ago, after having an intense run in with the law.

"*Deliver me from my enemies. Be my fortress against those who are attacking me,*" he said lowly more to himself than anyone in the room before he cleared his throat. His eyes lifted to his people as he spoke. "I appreciate everybody coming down for this. The family isn't perfect but if we don't move as a unit, we won't make it. Our foundation has to be strong. Losing Malik has shown me that petty family beef and being in your feelings about things that happened years ago isn't worth it. All that matters is spending your time on earth with the ones you love," he said standing.

"The family is far from perfect but we're family and we got you," Deen Lacoste his estranged older cousin said looking at him.

Oshun nodded. He had seldom memories with Deen and his brother Sayeed because of their mother's petty drama but he knew him and despite it all, he did have love for him.

"I appreciate it."

"I don't want them out there acting a fool for Malik. He wouldn't want that either. Make sure you let them know to not go about getting justice that way," Angie said peering over at Oshun with red-rimmed eyes from the black sofa she sat on with her three sisters beside her for support.

Oshun sighed at his mother's words.

"I got you momma. Just try to keep your blood pressure down young lady," he replied thinking of the fainting spells she'd been having since losing Malik.

Oshun exited the backroom and went into the sanctuary of his family's church. He found his pastor the esteemed Domani Miles sitting on stage in the front of the large room. Oshun's sneakers hit the carpet with determination as he walked towards the man that showed him a real way to build a relationship with God. He'd known pastor Miles since he was a teenager and he respected and loved him like he was family.

"—Hey Oshun," Tegan the first lady of the church spoke softly.

Oshun stopped walking and turned to the light voice that

held great grief in it. Tegan Miles was a stunning woman. She possessed glowing dark skin and thick inky black hair that hung down her back. She was a gentle soul that wore her first lady title well. She was a mother, a minister, a lawyer, and an author. From stories retold to him by pastor Domani, he knew that Tegan had a spunky side to her, but she never let it show. She carried herself well and Oshun saw himself settling down with someone as poised and educated as her in the future.

He smiled at the beautiful Tegan and gave her a quick hug. She sniffled holding in her tears as he respectfully rubbed her arm.

"It's all good Mrs. Tee. Malik is with God. He's doing a lot better than us," he said wanting to alleviate her pain as well and the only way to do that was remind himself that Malik was with the Lord.

Tegan's eyes stared up at Oshun for a moment before she nodded. His words made her stand taller and he could see her mood lighten a bit.

"You're right he is. Thank you for that," she said appreciatively still in pain but looking better with his words of encouragement and he nodded glad to see that she wasn't about to fall apart.

That was what he was used to doing. Being there for everyone. If there was a problem. Oshun fixed it. That was part of his DNA. A doer, a fixer, a thinker, a—*king*. Naturally, he took charge, and nobody fought him on it.

Ever.

"I just love him so much and I'm so mad this happened. My dear sweet, stubborn Malik. God comfort us," Tegan said before walking off in a haste.

Oshun swallowed hard. He closed his eyes briefly and when they opened, he was at a hundred. He met his pastor on the stage and they gave one another a quick embrace. The pastor's camera crew was already in place and as Oshun sat in the chair across from pastor Domani he loosened the buttons on his plaid Canali sport coat. He'd woken up that day not wanting to do shit but handle the cops involved with killing Malik. But the man in him pushed him to get out of bed. Check on his mom, handle shit in the BOC, and interview with his pastor. He looked like he was ready to be featured on a magazine in his Palm Angels blue jeans that he'd paired with a white designer button-up shirt and black sport coat. Effortlessly Oshun dressed the part because he did that fashion shit in his sleep. His AP watch, white gold Cuban link chain, and diamond left earring showed off his wealth, and still even while wearing such nice things he felt like shit.

For all of the money he had, he'd eagerly give it up easily if it meant he could have his brother back.

"Oshun thank you for doing this. We love Malik and we know the real him. However, the media is trying to portray him as something he wasn't. What do you want the world to know about Malik? What did they take from you and your family when they killed him for grabbing his inhaler?" Pastor Domani asked.

Oshun could hear someone sniffling behind him in the sanctuary and his jaw tensed. Never had he felt a pain so raw. His hatred for the cops, shit the world he lived in was embedded in his soul. He knew that there was plenty of good police out there but the same way the world labeled all black people one way he was starting to do the same with law enforcement. The lines were blurred, and his hatred was strong.

Oshun sat up straight in his seat damn near filling it up. His eyes shifted from his pastor to the monitor and he prayed that the people responsible for taking away his brother was watching. He wanted them to feel his pain and know that soon judgment day would be upon them.

"Malik was smart, funny, and gifted. He could have gone to school for ball, but he wanted to be a lawyer." Oshun stopped speaking and his last words with Malik drifted into his mind. His hooded eyes fell to his lap in despair and he took a deep breath. After a few seconds, he looked up at his pastor and shook his head. "He was about to be a father. He wanted to make his own way in life and I'm sure that what-ever path he chose it was going to be great. Nothing, Malik did was average. I mean look at his grades. Look at the degrees he had already then look at his age. He was far from ordinary. Nothing like what the media is saying about him. My brother didn't have to sell drugs and even if poverty would have made him feel like that was his only choice, he would have still done something else with his life. The problem with America is that they don't understand the strength that's in black people. Malik would have made a way out of no way. Losing wasn't in his DNA. Just because a black man in America has money does not mean they are doing something illegal. Officer Polk played God when he killed my brother. He showed the hate this world has for a colored man and I want people to remember that if they did it to Malik they can, and might one day do that to them," Oshun replied.

Pastor Domani nodded with his brows furrowing. It sometimes caught Oshun off guard how young he still looked but he also knew that black didn't crack. It also helped that his pastor was active, ate a good diet, and worked out regularly.

"Do you think the cops have the footage of Malik grabbing for his inhaler? And how do you feel about the man that came out against the police? He said that he was there when it happened," the pastor said to him.

Oshun's teeth sunk into his bottom lip. He waited for his heart rate to slow to an even level before responding. He looked at the monitor and a sly smirk fell onto his handsome mug.

"We all know that it's out there. Several videos have popped up with Malik being shot on the internet. I just hate that the view we need wasn't captured. However, I have spoken to the man that witnessed it all. He's a good man and he has no reason to lie on officer Polk."

"The police officers involved with this case have gone into

hiding after officer Polk's home was set on fire. How do you feel about that?" he asked Oshun.

Oshun struggled to hold in his smile then he thought of his brother and his body grew tight with anger. Even officer Polk looking for a new home didn't ease the pain in his heart.

"I'm too busy comforting my family to think of that *boy* replacing his house," he said smugly, and his pastor cleared his throat.

Pastor Domani looked at him with a concerning gaze.

"Beloved, never avenge yourselves, but leave it to the wrath of God, for it is written, Vengeance is mine. I will repay, says the Lord. You are a God-fearing man and I know you know the word. I also know that you would never try to play God, would you Oshun?" Pastor Domani inquired with curious eyes.

Oshun shared an intense stare down with his pastor until the good side of him won.

He shook his head.

"Nah, never that," he said quickly.

Pastor Domani nodded with relief.

"Good. The officers involved are still working and a petition is going around for them to be fired and charged. How do you feel about that?"

Oshun sat up and placed his elbows onto his knees. He was a big man. He stood at 6'4 and he weighed 230 pounds of muscle. He wasn't bulky in the kind of way that eluded to him being on steroids. Instead, he was solid, and it showed that he cared what he put into his body. Strength vibrated off his frame and as he looked at the monitor the rage building in his core started to show. To display weakness or even anger wasn't a good play for him however sometimes you just couldn't control how the fuck you felt.

His umber hued skin turned a shade darker as his dark honey-colored eyes peered at the pastor.

"No petition, no judge, no jury can save the cops involved from getting—"

"And what does the BOC stand for? The media has not said one word about all of the good things your family including Malik has done for the community," the pastor said cutting him off.

Oshun's fang showed as he glared at his pastor. He wasn't used to anyone cutting him off. Yes, this was the church, a holy place but he couldn't fight the urge to let the cops know that wasn't shit sweet. His fist balled and when his pastor younger than most pastors cocked his head to the side questioningly Oshun was brought back to reality. He remembered that Domani only wanted the best for him and with that, he was able to relax. Pastor Domani was everything but his enemy.

Oshun sat back and tugged at his thick beard adorning his handsome face.

"Black Owned Community was started by my family over five years ago. We went back to my mom's neighborhood that she grew up in and we bought it," Oshun's handsome face shifted into a smile at the thought. "We started with the homes in the area then we did the stores and before we knew it, we owned eight blocks of houses and businesses. They are for us and owned by us. Two gas stations. A market with fresh food that's not overpriced. Even a charter school. We're looking to expand in the near future," he explained.

Pastor Domani looked at Oshun with pride in his slanted eyes.

"Are you telling me that instead of being a black mafia family you all are a corporation?" he asked.

Oshun chuckled. He'd never saw it that way, but he liked the sound of that shit.

"I guess you could say that. What we're doing is for our people and that's why the cops are so mad. They've been targeting us for years. They chose to antagonize Malik daily because of his age. They finally got what they wanted though," Oshun replied with his mood shifting that quick.

Pastor Domani looked at him with curious eyes.

"And what's that?"

Oshun looked at him then at the camera. He stared at the monitor for several seconds allowing for his chiseled jaw to flex before responding.

"Our attention," he said evenly with a face void of emotion.

Pastor Domani cleared his throat.

"Thank you for that. I don't know your pain and I never will pretend to, but I know you and your family, and my heart is hurting right now. I watched Malik grow into the man that he was and I'm angry. His service will be private, and the family asks that you all respect their wishes. Thank you," he said, and his cameraman stopped filming.

The cameraman placed his camera towards the ground and began to walk away as pastor Domani sat up in his seat. He looked at Oshun with empathetic eyes as he clasped his hands together.

"I also called you up here to speak on the anger you have Oshun," he spoke lowly.

Oshun shifted in his seat and he peered over to his mom and brother that stood in the back of the sanctuary with Domani's wife Tegan. He looked back to the pastor and frowned.

"I'm not following you," he admitted.

Pastor Domani nodded.

"Your youngest brother was murdered by a cop Oshun. I know there is a fire inside of you that you have never felt before. I also know that the media and police are watching your family's every move. I don't want your mother to have to prepare to bury another son or two," the pastor explained.

Oshun looked at the pastor with nothing but respect. He understood where the pastor was coming from, but it wasn't needed. The cops would never catch him or Gio slipping. They weren't smart enough and for that reason alone was why they'd targeted Malik. He was young and irrational whereas they were older and wise. He was too much of a real nigga to let the bitch ass police knock him off his square.

"Everything's good pastor. It won't be any DPD bloodshed anytime soon if that's what you are referring to."

The pastor stared at him skeptically as he nodded.

"I want to believe you Oshun. I also have never felt what your feeling so I guess only time will tell. I just want you to remember all of the good you've done for this city. You and your family made it safe to be in the hood again. Nothing but black-owned businesses and homes reside in your part of town and that's something to be proud of. Don't allow for pain or anger to take away all that you've done. Those young boys that you mentor every day at your youth center still need you. You should see your brothers face in all of them," the pastor added.

Oshun felt his blood pressure rise at the pastor's words. He thought of his brother and how he'd been lying when he'd pulled onto the scene of his shooting and pain shot through his chest as if someone was piercing him with a sharp-edged knife.

"Slow down brah, he good. It's not him," Gio said glancing over at Oshun.

Oshun's car whipped in and out of traffic as he headed towards the location of Malik. They all possessed an app on their phones that alerted the family of their whereabouts. It was their mom being overprotective, but the brothers honestly didn't mind. They also got a kick out of pulling up on one another just for the hell of it and pissing the person off that had their day interrupted.

Oshun was kicking shit with Gio at their mom's house when they got a call that Malik's car was pulled over and surrounded by cops. After calling Malik for ten minutes straight the brothers decided to locate him and was currently en-route to his destination.

"Oh, shit there his whip go!" Gio yelled.

Oshun pulled onto the street Malik's Challenger was sitting on and his stomach knotted up in worry. He quickly parked his white Alfieri, Maserati, and got out of his car. He felt as if he was stepping outside of his body as he bypassed the crowd of people and rushed over to Malik's car.

"Sir you can't—"

"That's our fucking brother. Touch his shoulder and I'll lay your bitch ass out right here," Gio gritted out drawing his pistol on the young Chinese cop.

The man nodded with empathetic eyes.

"Let me get my captain to help you. I'm sorry for your loss," he said, and his words made Gio lose it.

Gio brushed passed the cop and ran over to Malik's driver's side door that was opened. His yell was gut-wrenching and painful enough to make the crowd quiet down to study his breakdown.

"Aye, that's his brother! Those the Lacoste boys that re-did the Northside! Damn, that's fucked up!" one onlooker yelled pulling out her cellphone.

Gio dropped down to his knees and his tears fell from his eyes quickly like a flood down his face. Oshun moved slowly not wanting to see what he knew was waiting for him.

Don't let it be.

Please don't.

Come on, God don't do us like this.

He silently prayed.

"You can't move his body!" another cop yelled angrily and Oshun stopped walking to glare at the man.

Oshun's nostrils were flared as his fist was balled. He didn't need to pull his gun. Off anger alone he could handle the man with his bare hands.

"What the fuck did you just say to me?" he asked through gritted teeth.

The cop took a step back with worried eyes.

"Let him be," the head officer in charge said low enough for the man to hear.

Oshun nodded relieved they weren't trying him, and he advanced on Malik's car door with his heart pounding ferociously in his chest. It beat at a tempo he wasn't familiar with. And with the rate it was thumping he was sure to fall out at any minute from the drum of it.

"That's the Lacoste boys!" he could hear someone yell out.

However, the crowd around Oshun was nonexistent. All that mattered was what was before him. Gio sat on the ground holding Malik's lifeless body as his cream-colored designer shirt was stained with blood.

Oshun's knees buckled and his heart tore into two.

"Nah, man. Nah! Nah, man. Malik. Malik come on man. Malik," Oshun said feeling utter despair wash over him. He shook Malik's arm until two women officers walked over with wet lenses. They peered down at Oshun and Gio as they tried to revive Malik.

"The CSI needs to see him. You all must move, or we will be forced to arrest you," she spoke softly.

"Ah hell nah! They are making them move!" another man yelled as the crowd of onlookers grew bigger.

Gio reached for his gun and their mother's piercing scream made him stop.

"No! No! No! Not my Malik! No baby, I'm so sorry about earlier. I didn't mean it!" Angie yelled running up.

"Ma, you don't need to see him like this," Oshun said grabbing her before she could see Malik's bloody body.

Angie hugged Oshun tightly as her body shook.

"Is he dead?" she asked with her face buried in his shirt.

Oshun hugged his mother tighter not wanting to respond. Wishing he didn't have to deliver such horrible news. Was this the American dream? Living the right way then being gunned down by the law? It sure as hell felt like a bunch of bullshit to Oshun.

"Is my son dead Oshun David Lacoste? Is he?" she asked again in a stern tone.

Oshun sighed and when he blinked his tears fell from his

hooded dark honey eyes. He nodded and his mother's legs gave
out as more officers approached them.

"We're good pastor. Something is telling me that I need to
show the cops the same love that they've been showing me
and my family. I gotta be up though. I appreciate you calling
and doing this for us," Oshun said after snapping out of his
thoughts.

Pastor Domani stared at him intently.

"God is with you. He never left your side and although this
happened that doesn't mean He wasn't watching over your
family. As people, He gives us the free will to do as we please.
The same way those cops made a bad decision you have the free
will to make the right one," the pastor said standing with him.

Oshun smirked. If only Domani knew what he was
thinking he would be praying for him instead of trying to
lecture him.

"And what decision would that be?" Oshun asked.

Pastor Domani cleared his throat.

"The right decision is for you to let God be the judge and
juror. Vengeance isn't yours to take, Oshun," he told him.

Oshun nodded done with the conversation.

"Thanks again for having us," he said and walked off.

Oshun caught up with his family outside of the church.
They stood in the front near the parking lot embracing one
another while talking quietly.

"We will get through this as a family," his oldest aunt

Mrs. Lacoste said to him as he walked up. She was the mother of his cousins Deen and Sayeed. Oshun didn't care for her too much because she wasn't the nicest woman but out of respect, he gave her a quick embrace. Still in the recess of his mind, he remembered all of the hateful things she'd done to his mom because his mother was the daughter of their fathers' mistress.

"I know," he mumbled.

"Baby come here," his third aunt who was his cousin Chevez's mom spoke and a genuine smile covered his handsome mug. To Oshun, she was the sweetest of his mother's sisters. She always showed real love and even when his mom's family shunned her his aunt still made a habit of being in their life. He walked into her outstretched arms and hugged her tightly. "Auntie is so sorry," she whispered choking up.

Oshun's shoulders fell as he hugged her tighter.

"I am too, auntie. It's all good," he whispered.

"We gone get those motherfucka's. You just wait and see baby," she whispered, and he smiled.

That was why she was his favorite. She was the realest one in his opinion.

"Enough said auntie," he agreed making her smile through her tears.

"We need to be up," Gio said walking up with their cousins and his friend Ameer.

Angie looked from Oshun to Gio and she shook her head.

"What's going on? I wanted us to all go home and watch

some movies. Maybe spend some time with Tiffany. She's sick right now and I don't like that," she said sadly.

Oshun walked over to his mom and placed a quick kiss on her forehead. He then grabbed her hand and pulled her to his side protectively.

"Mom we're good. You need to rest, and we need to make sure that business in the BOC is good. Don't worry about us. I swear on my life we'll be fine. Call me if you need me and stay out of the streets. You don't need to be bombarded with talks about Malik or get harassed by the cops. Because then I won't be at peace. Feel me, young lady with your beautiful self?" he asked and winked at her.

Angie slowly nodded before smiling.

"There goes that smile I was looking for. I'm taking care of everything. Let your sisters be there for you as they should be. Okay?"

Angie sighed. She ran her hands through her short cut while looking at Oshun.

"Okay, but keep your location on. Please be safe."

Oshun smiled down at his mom.

"I will. Go get some rest. Love you," he replied and walked off before she tried to convince him to leave with her again.

Oshun called up Malik's girlfriend Tiffany as he got into his brother Gio's car. He reached over looking for Gio's fob and Gio chuckled.

"Brah, this my shit. How you gone try to whip me in my

ride like I'm the bitch? You should have drove your own fucking car," he commented only half-joking.

Oshun's brows tugged together as he stared at him and Gio tossed him the fob while shaking his head.

"On God, you irritate the fuck out of me sometimes," Gio mumbled looking like Malik and their father with his dark skin and chestnut-colored eyes.

Oshun smirked as Tiffany picked up the phone.

"*Hi*, Oshun," Tiffany said in a somber tone.

Oshun started up Gio's Lexus and pulled away from the church. As he followed his cousins, he made sure to check out his surroundings for the cops.

"Hey, Tiff. I won't even ask how you feeling? That's stupid people questions. I do need to know if you ate and got some rest today, however?" he asked.

Tiffany breathed heavily into the phone instead of responding and Oshun shook his head.

"I won't lecture you but your baby needs food and rest. Malik wouldn't want you out here starving yourself either. I set up a spa day for you and your best friend. She will be at your house in the morning at nine and a car will be there shortly after to pick you up. Tiff, don't go anywhere besides the spa, and if anybody pops up asking questions call me."

"Or my dad?" she asked quietly.

Oshun cleared his throat.

"Yeah, him too but me first. The driver that's picking you up is someone we trust, and he will guard you with his life.

You need this break and I need you to promise me you will do better to take care of yourself. Okay?" he asked.

Tiffany cleared her throat.

"I will. Thank you so much for being there for me. I see why Malik looked up to you the way that he did. He always said that if it was a boy he would be named after you. You were his hero," she replied.

Oshun's chest tightened at her revelation. He shook off his emotions as he pulled onto the freeway.

"—Alright Tiff. Enjoy your spa day and call me if you need me. Also, Gio sent you some money on that app. Make sure you put it in your savings," he told her before ending the call.

"How she sound today?" Gio asked sparking up his blunt.

Oshun peered over at his younger brother briefly before placing his eyes back onto the road.

"Better than she did yesterday."

"And you still don't know where the cops hiding at? I'm ready to handle these niggas and be done with it. Especially since you didn't take me with you to set that niggas house on fire," Gio remarked and took a hit off his blunt.

Oshun frowned at the way his brother spoke to him. He wanted everything for his brother *but* that type of activity.

"Nah, I don't. Like I said before. Just be easy and make sure the BOC is good. I don't need you trying to chase after them and I didn't do shit to that man's house. I already told you that so don't say that shit again," he let him know.

Gio's brows drew together and he frowned.

"Malik was my brother too and I want to help get at the people responsible for killing him. You can't decide what's right for me! I'm not your fucking child my nigga," he said angrily.

Oshun took Gio's anger to the chin because hell what Gio said didn't matter. As long as Oshun was alive his brother would never have to get his hands dirty. Gio wasn't a killer and he would never allow for his heart to be stained with the blood from another man's life. If anybody's soul was to be ruined it would be his. It was the price he would pay to keep his brothers' soul good.

"Like I said make sure the BOC is good and look after momma while I handle everything. And you can take that fucking base out your voice. Fuck you thought this was? This shit wasn't up for debate, your hands will stay clean," Oshun replied and turned up the music as Gio began to talk shit.

After driving for thirty minutes Oshun pulled up to his cousins' business The Boys Club. He parked in an available spot near the door and pulled out his ringing phone.

"You can head in, I need to take this," he said not bothering to look over at his brother.

Gio chuckled. He rubbed on his bald head while cutting his eyes at Oshun. Like Oshun, he was tall with a muscular build, but he wasn't quite as big as his brother. It was clear who the older brother was.

"Nigga, again this is my shit. How the fuck you gone take over my car?"

Oshun lifted his head to peer over at his brother. Irritation covered his mug and he flexed his jaw. Gio was trying to make power moves when none needed to be made. Oshun cocked his head to the side challenging Gio and his brother sighed.

"Fuck it," he grumbled pushing his door open.

Oshun waited for Gio to close the car door before he spoke into his cellphone.

"What's good, Tori?" he asked relaxing in his seat.

Tori breathed heavily into the phone and Oshun could almost anticipate his next words. Tori was doing a bid for a crime he hadn't even committed all in the name of love. Tori was one of his best friends and even though he was locked up he was still very much attached to the streets.

"King, what's good? Been calling your ass for a week and shit. I would say tell me it isn't real, but I saw the news and all I can say is, *damn*. I'm all fucked up behind this. You remember those bad lil jawns we used to fuck with on Rosa Parks?" Tori asked.

Oshun's ears perked up at the mention of the street. They hadn't fucked with anybody on Rosa Parks in years, but Tori possessed a very lucrative bando in that area that Oshun was certain still made him good money.

"I do my guy. What's good with them?" he asked

watching attractive women prance into the club wearing close to nothing.

Tori coughed into the phone.

"They wanted to come see me but I told them to wait. Prison not the place for all that shit. However, you could fall through and check them out for me. They still stay at that same house and they always looking for a nigga to fuck with. They thirsty as shit," Tori expressed.

Oshun nodded reading between the lines. He made a mental note to check out Tori's spot to see what he was talking about.

"I'm already on it. You good in there? Need anything?"

Tori chuckled.

"Same old Oshun. I'm as good as I'ma be my nigga. I didn't just lose a brother, you did. You need to find somebody to hold you down. Nobody can carry the weight of the world on their shoulders, not even you," he told him.

Oshun grunted at the thought of being with a woman that was special enough to satisfy all of his needs.

"Everybody don't have a Miesha in their life and I'm not the kind of man to just fuck with anybody. You know I'm picky as fuck. If she doesn't spark my interest in the first few minutes from talking to her then I'm good," he jested but he was very serious.

"Yeah well, even I don't have a Miesha. Not like that anyway. Fall through to Rosa Parks and holla at them bitches. You know it's all love," Tori said and ended the call.

Oshun sat his phone in his lap and he briefly wondered what his friend was speaking on before exiting Gio's car. He wanted a break. Some type of escape from his reality even for a night before he lost it. Shit, he needed one but didn't see it coming anytime soon.

He lit his weed he'd rolled earlier as he stepped into the club and took deep powerful hits of his cigarillo. He wanted the gorilla glue strain to take him away from his pain.

"What I know is that Polk is part of a fraternity of some rich white motherfucka's. I'm sure they're the ones that's helping him hide. I'm not sure about that house nigga though. We need to get both of their asses," Omelly who was close friends with his cousin Sayeed said as he walked up.

Oshun took a seat on the black sofa facing the stage of beautiful exotic dancers. His tired dark honey-hued eyes traveled over to the voluptuous women that easily swirled around the pole like it wasn't hard work. Oshun appreciated his cousins trying to get involved. The love was real because despite their bond not being as strong as it could be, they were family. However, what he wasn't feeling was talking about his brothers' case in a club filled with people he didn't fucking know. And what he definitely didn't like was discussing things like murder in front of Gio. That wasn't for him and he would never make him into something he wasn't. Gio was a good guy and Oshun wanted him to know that it was okay to be that.

"But what happened to the house for them to be hiding in the first place?" Gio asked looking at Omelly.

Omelly shrugged.

"Shit I don't know. That wasn't us," he replied. He went to say something else and Oshun shook his head.

"This isn't the time or place for this conversation. The family business will never be discussed in a fucking strip club. It's not that kind of party so dead that shit. I'll be back," his deep voice said sternly before he stood up and went over to the stage.

"We on the same side," Deen his older cousin said as Oshun pulled a few blue faces from his wallet.

Oshun walked up on the stage and tossed money at the dancer that was putting in the most work while pulling him into a trance with her exotic looks and curvy body. She sauntered his way and turned around to give him a full view of her ample chocolate bottom. Oshun smacked her flawless ass and tossed more money on it before hitting his blunt that he made sure to take deep pulls from wanting all of the weed into his system that he could get.

The dancer was attractive, and her body was inviting but fucking her wasn't the play so after hitting her with more cash than she'd made all night he stepped away.

"You want a private dance!" she called out in haste rushing off the stage.

"He's not interested Sienna. You, not his type," Deen responded for Oshun.

Oshun peered over at his cousin with a frown marring his face.

"I appreciate you and your people coming through to the church. Since shit went down you have been there, but all this isn't needed. I came by for a drink and to chill. I'm not looking to run down plays with y'all about this shit."

Deen grabbed his arm and he peered back at him angrily.

"We haven't been close, but you know the funny thing about a phone my nigga is that the bitch works both ways. You could have called us too. We've been dealing with a lot of shit as well. I lost my dad and could have lost my mom to her house fire. Your mom came through and even attended the funeral, but I didn't hear a peep from you or Gio. I'm not holding that shit against you two so cut us some fucking slack. Take the help we trying to give, receive the love we showing, and lets finally mend this broken family. I'm hurt behind Malik dying too. He might not have told you, but I talked to him regularly. He was about to intern at one of my companies. I don't show fake love. I don't give a fuck who it is, and my time is valuable. Cause a nigga like me don't have time to spare on some real shit but your family and I make time for what's important. I want to help. Those niggas can't walk away from this and I won't let your anger push me away. And I hope you ready to make that ride in a few hours up north with me. I still want you in on this hospital shit and I need you by my side for it, nigga so get your shit together," Deen told him and walked off before he could respond.

Oshun smirked as he realized that for the first time someone had gotten the last word in on him.

"Shit won't happen again," he mumbled holding in his smirk as he headed back to the section where his people were at.

CHAPTER 3

1:30 AM

baymoor falls

J aylah's car slowed and she sat outside of the gates inside of the pricey neighborhood once more. Garris being away for work always made for a restless night for Jaylah. She'd tossed and turned on her plush mattress until she couldn't take it anymore.

Her tired eyes lingered on the gate that blocked her entry to the home and with every breath that Jaylah took her heart ached. She sat back in her seat and held on tightly to the steering wheel not sure what to do. For years she'd been good with every decision she made but for some reason, things were changing. Nightmares were coming back. Memories were resurfacing like she'd subscribed to a fucked up episode of her life and she was stumped on what to do. For someone that thrived off being in control of her life, she felt helpless and that was a frightening emotion for Jaylah to have.

"Oh fuck, why do I keep ending up here?" she asked out loud wishing she could let the pain go once and for all.

Jaylah's thoughts drifted to her past and the anger she still held onto crept onto her as she thought of the moments that shifted her into the woman that she now was.

"Jaylah stop pouting. He owes your dad a lot of money, so we need to go see him," her mom Lisa said trying to pull her arm out of Jaylah's grasp.

Jaylah was being a brat and she didn't care. Everything in her life was turning sour. The last thing she wanted to do was sit outside of the projects. It was she and twin's special day. They were supposed to have a good time on the day they had been born but once again life was being cruel to her.

"No! I want to go to Crust Lust and to the mall," she whined gripping her mom's arm tighter.

Her mom glared at her and snatched her arm away. She popped Jaylah's arm three times while looking at her. The quick but hard gesture made her immediately get some act right. Her eyes grew wide and her twin looked on in shock by what their mom had done.

"Ma?" she asked nervously with questioning eyes.

"Yes, ma?" her twin co-signed with sad eyes like she'd been reprimanded as well.

Their mother a beautiful biracial woman with fair freckled skin and dark doe-shaped eyes cleared her throat. She smoothed out the wrinkles in her blouse and gave Jaylah half a smile with defeat hovering over her thick frame.

"I'm sorry but I told you to let me go. Mommy is stressed and I've exhausted all of my funds on your fathers' case. I know it's your birthday and I know you are angry with everything that's happening. I'm sorry I am but I need to go visit daddy's friend. Then afterward we can go meet up with your friends at Crust Lust," their mom replied.

Jaylah held in her cries as she nodded. She gave her mother a forced smile that her mom sighed with relief at.

"Okay now, no matter what happens I want you all to stay in the car. These people are dangerous and some of them still feel a certain way about your father. So, let's not take any chances by hanging around them. Okay?" she asked Jaylah and her twin.

Jaylah's sister nodded and she simply stared at her mom.

"Okay," her mom muttered and pulled away from their home that was in Merrisville Heights, on the Northside which was considered the middle-class area of Baymoor Falls.

Jaylah's twin grabbed her hand and gave her a reassuring squeeze as their mom took them to a more urban part of Baymoor Falls.

The Southside.

After forty minutes of driving, she pulled up to a row of buildings inside of the projects and parked her shiny red four-door, Lexus, it was one of the last nice luxury items they owned.

"Okay, I'll be right back. Don't forget to lock the doors," their mom said and smiled at them nervously.

Jaylah and her twin watched their mom exit the vehicle and rush towards the middle building. Jaylah hit the locks on the door as the group of boys that were standing outside of the row homes looked their way.

"Oh, that's Greedo! He raps and stuff. He has that one mixtape we were listening to last night," her twin said excitedly and pushed the door open.

"Twin! No!" Jaylah harshly whispered.

Jaylah jumped out of the car and caught up with her sister as she advanced on the older group of guys.

"Aye, I heard about your smart-ass twin that be curving all the niggas on the Northside. She sexy as hell too. What's up?" one young guy asked smiling Jaylah's way.

Jaylah immediately turned up her small button-shaped nose at the sight of the pimple-faced, badly dressed boy.

"Not you," she retorted, and the group of men laughed except for the man she capped on.

The man pulled up his dirty sagging Ecko Unltd. jeans while snarling at her.

"Hoe don't think you better than us. Your pops in jail now and that nigga not coming home unless he snitching. Pretty soon your bitch ass gone be in the jects with us then we'll see how high and mighty you are," he said angrily.

"Greedo get your boy. He can't be disrespecting my sister like that. I'll slap some pretty on his bumpy face ass," her twin said pulling Jaylah to her side protectively.

Greedo the most attractive older teen in the circle looked at his boy and shook his head.

"My apologies that nigga has no manners. He didn't mean that," Greedo quickly spoke up but Jaylah wasn't convinced.

She stared into the man that disrespected her, beady eyes and the cold hard glare he pushed her way was enough to send a chill of fear up her spine. There was a rage in his glare that was so startling it made her hug her twins' side harder.

Jaylah swallowed hard as the fear she felt all those years ago covered her body from the memory. Anger and sadness encased her heart as she realized that she was still afraid of him.

That stung then angered her.

"You weren't there, daddy. You weren't fucking there," she whispered with anger hanging onto her words.

She pulled away from the grand estate not wanting to have the cops called on her and she drove back to the Northside. Her car pulled over at the first bar she came across that was still open.

Club Luxure was owned by the Roi family and had always carried a mystic to it that Jaylah was intrigued by. It was exclusive and chic as fuck from the seldom photos she'd seen online. Jaylah joined the club a year ago to get intel on the business for a story but had come up short. Shortly after gaining her membership, the owner fell ill, and the club was shut down for six months.

She had no clue that the club had opened back up for business.

"One drink wouldn't hurt. Maybe I can drink enough to fall right into sleep when I get home," she said grabbing her blue Bruce Glen egg bag.

Jaylah raked her hands through her long strands and coated her lips with the Queen lip gloss by Glamhercosmetics before exiting her car. She pulled out her membership card as she headed for the large black double doors that let you into the establishment.

"The club's just opening up. You're right on time beautiful. What floor and I'm going to need to see your license as well, along with your car keys?"

Jaylah's arched brows drew together as she peered up at the man.

"All of that? It must be something life-changing inside of there," she joked.

The tall, stocky man that could have been a linebacker in his heyday smirked down at her.

"Club rules. Upon leaving you will be checked for liquor

consumption and as long as you're under the limit your keys will be given back to you. If not, our car will take you home. You're a black card member. Our highest level. This comes with your membership," he explained.

Black card member?

Jaylah was stumped. She was also sad and was in desperate need of a drink. The liquor stores in Baymoor Falls closed at nine PM on Sunday. She was desperate so she conceded. She passed her car keys and license to the man while huffing.

The bouncer meticulously checked her information, taking the time to swipe her card through a reader before looking back at her.

"What floor, Miss?" he asked again.

Jaylah sighed. This was supposed to be a drink and nothing more. The club was elusive, and she got that but damn they were doing too much. She checked the time again on her phone wondering if a more relaxed club was still open.

"Maybe I should go? This seems like a lot," she said taking a step back.

The bouncer looked Jaylah over and when he peered behind her his eyes widened in delight.

"Hey Mr. Roi!" he said excitedly and pushed Jaylah to the side to dap up the owner of the club.

Jaylah frowned as she watched the bouncer, a grown-ass man fawn over another man as if he were God himself.

Mr. Roi looked as handsome as he did in the photos,

she'd seen of him online with his chocolaty brown skin, intense dark eyes, and sexy face. His black suit was surely custom made the way it fit onto his tall, lean body and his presence was somewhat intimidating. Jaylah cleared her throat as her hand shot out for her belongings and the owner of the club stopped looking at the bouncer to peer over at her. The way his eyes bored into Jaylah made her swallow hard.

"Floor five for her," the owner said and shot Jaylah a sexy smirk before walking into the club.

He was in his early forties that Jaylah was certain of, but damn he looked no older than thirty without a grey hair in sight on his head or in his full beard. She was impressed and saw firsthand why the women went wild over him making him the most sought out bachelor in Baymoor Falls.

"Fifth floor it is. Cherry show her the way," the bouncer called out and smirked at Jaylah.

Jaylah took her license and membership card from the bouncer and stepped into the club after the owner. She sniffed the air discreetly loving the owner's masculine scent as an attractive woman wearing a black pantsuit advanced on her sporting a big smile.

"Jaylah?" she asked.

Jaylah nodded while looking around. The entrance into the club was dark and no music could be heard. The hallway was short, and it led to a set of smoked glass elevators.

"Right this way and welcome to Lust," the woman said

sweetly with a hint of sultriness to her tone that wasn't lost on Jaylah.

Jaylah gave her a tight-lipped smile and stepped onto the elevator. The woman walked in beside her and silently they rode the cart up to the fifth floor. When the elevator doors slid open Jaylah was greeted with a pleasant floral scent. She nervously stepped off the cart and the woman cleared her throat.

"It's the first door to the right, enjoy," she said and the doors to the elevator closed.

Jaylah took a deep breath and sighed. She'd come in for a drink, but things were feeling heavy. The club carried a mysterious dark vibe to it that she wasn't sure she liked. She walked down to the first door to the right and stepped in.

"Oh wow," she murmured taken in by the large space.

However, what Jaylah expected to be a club was everything but that. She was inside of a bedroom that housed a king-sized four-poster bed along with a black loveseat and fully stocked bar. Jaylah looked around the room slowly taking it all in as her heart thundered in her chest.

"Is this a sex club?"

"I'm figuring anything that has the word lust in the title is just that. What's your name?" a masculine voice asked with a tenor so deep it made her eyes widen.

Jaylah jumped at the sound of it and the man chuckled.

"Turn around, love. Is this your first time coming to a place like this?" he asked.

Jaylah turned and when she peered at the wall facing her, she gasped at the monitor that sat on it. A man draped in a designer suit sat at the front of a king-sized bed in a room similar to the one she was in. His head was down as he rolled up a blunt on the small coffee table before him but still, she could see his handsome visage. He was tall, muscular, and attractive. Even with only half of his face visible that much she could tell. Jaylah's eyes looked nervously over at the bedroom door and she swallowed hard.

"I only wanted a drink. I did a story on this club a year ago wanting to answer the burning question on if it was a sex club and before I could investigate the club closed. I had no idea this was that kind of place. Well I thought it was, but I didn't know for sure that it was," she said worriedly fumbling over her words.

"Relax and make yourself a drink. This isn't meant to be anything bad. Shit, I came here for an escape. Well for business but with all the bullshit happening in my life I figured I could steal a few hours to get myself some pleasure before my pain gets worse," he told her.

Jaylah watched the man take his time rolling up the large blunt. She shifted from one foot to the other not sure what to do.

"I shouldn't be here," she said wanting to leave but not doing so.

This was a black man and she hadn't been attracted to

one of them in years. So long ago she'd honestly forgotten that she could be.

"And I'm with someone," she said quickly.

The man chuckled. He sealed the blunt with his long tongue and Jaylah looked away as her fair cheeks reddened.

"And I'm only here for one night. Your overthinking something that isn't meant to be complicated. Leave if that's what you need to do and stay if that's what you want, sweetheart. The number five symbolizes balance, independence, versatility, and adaptation. What's crazy is I was never into that numerology shit until I came here for the first time. They sent me to a floor that I needed without even knowing the shit. It was crazy and when I walked in tonight the woman Cherry said floor 5 like the shit was clear," he said and chuckled.

Jaylah focused on the doorknob for a moment in deep contemplation. She could leave and be alone for the night or she could stay and have a conversation with a man that she didn't have to see again. The situation was weird. Crazy as hell considering she wasn't the daring type, but it was also — intriguing. She sighed as she decided to have at least one drink.

"The owner saw me and immediately said five as well. I'm not sure what I need balance for though. My life is good," she finally said making her way to the bar.

Jaylah grabbed the tall bottle of Clase Azul Reposado tequila loving how fancy it looked and took two shots to the head after opening it. The tequila burned as it went down and she welcomed it. She wanted to forget about the pain inside of her and push it back to the place it had been hiding in.

"I'm sure I need balance with some shit. I'm dealing with a lot of pain, sweetheart," he explained, and Jaylah took another shot before stepping out of her heels.

The man's deep voice was soothing, inviting, warm hell like hot chocolate and she found herself growing comfortable with talking to him. It also helped that she was drinking in a private room away from the stranger, so she felt she had nothing to lose by staying.

She went over to the bed and perched herself in the middle with the bottle of tequila. She watched the stranger smoke on his blunt while gazing up at the ceiling. Somewhere along the way, he'd shed his sport coat along with his button-up shirt and her eyes had a mind of their own when they ogled his umber toned body.

His chest was muscular, and he possessed a six-pack that was cut so deep she could run her finger across the dents in it. On both of his pecks were what she presumed to be bible scriptures in neat sans script. On the side of his neck was a crown tattoo then there was more ink on his hand—numbers she realized but she couldn't make out what it was without squinting and being obvious.

Jaylah inhaled sharply when he finally looked at the

monitor. His hooded dark honey-hued eyes bored into her deeply and finally, she was able to see his face.

He was fucking handsome.

She hated that fact.

From his wide nose to his full lips and hooded eyes he was a looker. The kind of man you would see out and wonder what woman was lucky enough to lay in his bed and be in his life. He rocked a short curly fade style that she actually liked, and it was lined to perfection. A manicured beard covered the bottom of his face and when he cocked his head to the side to assess her as well, she knew, that he knew, that he was the shit.

"Your beautiful, love," he expressed before puffing on his blunt.

Jaylah get your shit together. This is a black man that you don't even know. He's probably a drug dealer or worst. A killer. Look at him! Fucking tattoo's everywhere and he does drugs. Pull it together!

Jaylah's inner thoughts battled with her emotional side. She gave the sexy stranger a coy smile as she gripped the bottle tightly.

This scene wasn't for her but damn she didn't know how to get up off the fucking bed and leave. It was insane and if it hadn't been happening to her, she wouldn't have believed a soul that would have said her night would end up that way.

"Thank you, so are you," she replied shyly.

Really? You like him, Jaylah? What the fuck, he's a thug. Don't be stupid.

Jaylah shook her head and took a large sip of the tequila to rid herself of her thoughts. The internal battle she was fighting was sure to drive her crazy.

The man chuckled lightly at her words and just from doing so Jaylah was blessed with a glimpse of his perfect white teeth. His hooded eyes held amusement in them as they peered at her.

"I've been called a lot of things and beautiful has never been one of them, ma. And just being honest you seem like the type to call a nigga like me a thug or some shit," he jested and cracked a crooked grin Jaylah's way.

Jaylah laughed lightly as her body temperature rose.

"I would never," she lied quickly.

The man's brows rose, and he nodded before licking his lips.

"Probably never even been with a black man before. Have you?" he questioned.

Jaylah's tongue grew heavy and she pictured the villains in her story. Stripping away the last part of her that wasn't tainted and her eyes watered. She nodded slowly and took another sip of the tequila while avoiding eye contact with the inquisitive stranger that possessed the dirty mouth.

"I see that affected you and I apologize, ma. What do you do? Talk to me, sweetheart," he said with his dark honey gaze searing into her.

Jaylah shook her head and sat up straight on the bed. Her mouth opened to tell a perfect uniformed version of her life, but the fibs wouldn't come out. Her mind was as tired as she was of the lies. The tequila snuck up on her like a thief in the night and that quickly she found herself becoming emotional.

Jaylah dropped her head and brushed her left hand through her long black tresses while sighing. Drinking was an escape, but she detested how raw it made her feel.

"I don't live a life that's worth discussing," she painfully admitted.

The handsome stranger coughed then grabbed a bottle of water from a nearby table.

"I'm sorry to hear that, beautiful. What's holding your happiness back? Family shit?" he asked.

Jaylah nodded without overthinking it. She fell back onto the bed and placed the bottle of tequila onto the nightstand beside it. Her hands had a mind of their own as they started to brush up and down her stomach that was covered by her black silk blouse.

"Isn't it always family shit?" she quipped.

The alluring stranger cleared his throat.

"If I told you my problems you would see how blessed you are, ma. When faced with real pain you realize that lil shit you were upset over for whatever reason isn't that important. Trust me it isn't," he said to her.

Jaylah frowned at his words.

"I don't know your pain and you don't know mine so let's

not compare trauma to see who's had it the worst in life," she said thinking of the home inside of Woodland Hills that possessed her greatest pain.

Jaylah hadn't pegged the stranger as a woe is me type of black man and the second, he started on what the world had done to him she was getting the fuck up out of the room.

"Sweetheart the last thing I'm trying to do is compare pain and you're right I don't know what you've been through. How was your childhood?" he asked catching her off guard.

Jaylah's eyes drifted to the ceiling and she was surprised to see that a mirror was on top of it. She stared at herself cautiously while biting down onto her bottom lip. The stranger was assertive with knowing her business and she was at a loss on why that wasn't an issue for her.

Must be the liquor. She thought.

"I grew up with my family, here in Baymoor Falls. On the Northside," she said revealing something that she hadn't in so long.

It felt strange but to speak on her family wasn't as bad as she thought it would be. Jaylah closed her eyes and slowly unbuttoned her blouse as the room grew warm. Her body was antsy, and her hands felt bored. It was as if she needed to constantly put them to work or else, she would lose her mind.

"I have a twin sister that I'm two minutes older than and when we were younger, we would hang out at the movies and sneak over to Crust Lust," she giggled at the memory. "Life was good back then. My mom was a stay at home mother and my dad owned auto body shops," she revealed.

The handsome stranger whistled.

"Sounds legit as fuck. Sounds like a nice upbringing," he told her pouring himself a drink of 1942.

Jaylah removed her blouse and stared at herself in the mirror. Her perky C-cup breast sat up high in the nude lace bra that she wore. She stared down at the tiny date that was inked over her left breast and her smile faded. That date, those numbers would forever follow her. They had the power to alter her mood instantly.

"It was until it wasn't, you know? Curse of the black family," she said suddenly irritated.

The stranger shook his head while looking at her.

"And what is the curse of the black family to you? What does that mean, sweetheart?" he asked.

Jaylah sat up on her elbows ignoring how her upper body was exposed and glared at the handsome man.

"My father was a freaking drug dealer! All those years of him telling me and my twin who to love, how to love when he wasn't anything but a common criminal. He got sent away and we eventually lost everything. Our home was taken, his businesses were closed, and our accounts were frozen. We were left with nothing when it was all said and done. Some amazing father he was."

Jaylah's eyes watered in anger at the thought of her father Clay.

"I'm sorry to hear that."

The stranger's words were sincere in his deep tone but instead of comforting Jaylah, they made her angrier.

"You didn't abandon your family because you wanted to live out some dream of being the neighborhood dope man so don't apologize for his bad behavior. He made his bed and now he's lying in it. He has ten more years to go and I won't be waiting for him," she said coldly.

"*Damn*," The stranger said shaking his head.

Jaylah's eyes narrowed as she looked at the man.

"What?" she asked with a bite to her light voice while cocking her head to the side.

The man smirked before his brows pulled together.

"Relax, sweetheart. I can see you pissed about your pops. I can also assume you haven't spoken to him in a long time. The thing is clarity comes from engagement not thought. Talking to your pops and learning why he chose to make the moves he did will give you the peace you need to accept what happened. Assuming which only dumb motherfucka's do has built this rage inside of you that even you can't put out. And I'ma need for you to stop looking at me like you want to square up unless you really about that life, ma," he told her.

Jaylah rolled her eyes hating how his statement made some sense. She fell back onto the bed and rolled her eyes.

"Whatever," she mumbled not looking to argue with a stranger over her past.

Silence greeted Jaylah and when she looked up the

stranger was gone. Her brows tugged together and when the mirror that was on the wall to the right of the bed opened, she jumped in alarm. The man stepped into the room holding his liquor while frowning at her.

Jaylah's heart raced as she felt fear instantly wash over her.

"I—I—"

The man shook his head. His face relaxed as he shut the mirror door that led to his room.

"I'm not here to hurt you. Do you want me to leave?" he asked.

Jaylah looked him up and down intently and his smell, a salacious scent that was mixed with notes of bergamot, ginger, and vetiver wafted her way as he walked over to the loveseat.

"—No," she whispered with her heart racing. It was the most confusing thing because a part of her was scared of the man entering into her personal space while the other part was still intrigued by him. Jaylah didn't want to fawn over his impeccable looks, sexy voice, and alluring body but he was just too fucking fine to ignore.

The man sat in the center of the loveseat and took his bottle of liquor to the face. His alluring eyes never left Jaylah's as he finished his drink. He sat the long brown bottle down once it was empty and licked his full lips. A drop of the dark liquor was clinging to his beard and Jaylah wanted to desperately lick it off.

She studied his sexy visage in angst. He was a few feet

away from her gazing at her like a lion would its prey only she wasn't sure if running was her only option.

She could stay and enjoy what was to come. She could then leave and never tell a soul. Jaylah had morals and had never cheated on Garris, but this was different. She'd gone to the club looking for a break. She wanted a drink to ease her unsettled mind but had gotten so much more. It was as if it was meant for her to meet the stranger.

Serendipity perhaps.

Sort of in the cards for their paths to cross and Jaylah was intrigued by that. He was a black man, covered in tattoos, smoking weed while using the word *nigga* still she wasn't turned off. Usually, men such as him made her stomach coil in disgust but he was different.

Something about this man told Jaylah that he wasn't your average black man.

"Can I be real with you, beautiful?" he asked breaking the silence.

Jaylah nodded with her heart racing. She admired his hooded shaped eyes. She lusted over his thick lips and she liked his curly fade that showed off his dark hair. The chiseled jaw he possessed and wide nose was appealing as well and when his flushed skin an umber toned hue shined under the lamp's lighting her sex creamed.

She discreetly rubbed her thighs together while staring his way.

"Yes," she said breathily.

The handsome stranger smirked and it was so fucking cocky because she could tell he knew she was frazzled. Jaylah wanted to look away and not feed into his ego, but she couldn't. This man was a force that even she wasn't strong enough to move through at the moment.

"I need a release. Something very bad happened to me and my family, love. My life like yours is fucked up right now. Only mine won't ever go back to being how it was. I came here for a break. This is my third time in two years being here and for the first time, I've met someone that I can see myself letting go with. I need to release this pain. Do you understand what I'm saying?" he asked sitting up.

Jaylah nodded although she somewhat didn't.

"I don't want to die in here," she whispered and clamped her lips shut at her confession.

The stranger stood from the loveseat and unbuckled his pants. His eyes stayed glued to Jaylah as his slacks fell down his narrow waist. Her eyes landed on his massive imprint in his grey boxers and she swallowed hard. Garris was a good five inches but he was thick, and he worked his penis well enough to gain her one climax. However, the man before her was hung.

Like a fucking horse, his dick swelled in the fabric holding it back and it was long and begging to be freed. Jaylah closed her eyes as the man gently grabbed her foot.

"I don't want to even dignify that shit you said with a response, but you have to know I would never do anything like that to you. I like giving the kind of pain that makes you cry because you're tired of cumming. The kind of pain that makes your pussy fart with relief when I pull out of it. I mean I want to give you the kind of pain that makes you pull at that long as hair on your head while I stretch your pussy out so tough that you squirt all over my dick. That's the kind of shit that I'm into," he said huskily as his thick hands roamed up her legs.

"—If you can take that," he said lowly but loud enough for her to hear.

Jaylah closed her eyes as her sex thumped with anticipation. Never before had she been so anxious for dick.

Ever.

It was alarming, because this wasn't her. She didn't do irrational, spontaneous things but as the man unbuttoned her ripped jeans, she found herself looking forward to the fucking he was offering.

"Say yes, sexy," he whispered and kissed her belly button.

His lips were soft and warm. They sent a volt of pleasure up her abdomen and into her veins. Jaylah's chest heaved up and down as she nodded.

"Okay," she conceded not strong enough to say no. "One and done, right?" she said lightly.

The man smirked. He stood and grabbed a condom from the pocket of his slacks. He then grabbed the Balenciaga belt from his pants and licked his lips.

"Just for tonight, let's be each other's escape. Can I use this on you?" he asked holding up the belt.

Jaylah looked at the thick belt he held in his left hand while he massaged her center through her jeans with his right one.

"For what?" she asked loving the pleasure that came from him rubbing on her clothed vagina.

"Because I only like fucking women that know how to submit. Can you do that?" he asked peering down at her.

Jaylah's head nodded before she registered what was happening.

Slap.

It was light.

More of a love tap but damn when the stranger slapped the bottom of her face her eyes widened. He then leaned down and sucked on her bottom lip while caressing her breast.

"*Sir*. Say yes sir. Don't fucking nod at me," he said against her lips.

"Yes—sir," she whispered nervous as fuck but wet as hell.

The stranger with a demanding tone, aggressive attitude, and big dick smiled at her response. Jaylah couldn't fight the swarm of butterflies from forming in her stomach as she peered up at him.

"Is this really happening? I don't even know your name," she said praying the situation wouldn't end with her dead in a nearby ditch down the road.

The man cupped her chin and sucked on her bottom lip while peering deeply into her eyes. He was so fucking fine, he smelled so fucking good and Jaylah was in awe of it all. She knew her best friend would keel over and die if she could see her in the room with a man like him.

"It's happening sweetheart and my name is Oshun. Now turn around so I can see how wet you are," he demanded.

Within minutes she was naked and on her stomach as the man named Oshun laced the belt around her wrist. He did it tight enough for her to wince but not hard enough for her to cry out in pain. Her thighs were then pushed open from the back and fear of the unknown made her body tremble.

"Relax. You are so fucking beautiful. Damn," he said appreciatively and rubbed her ass slowly.

Slap!

It was hard this time and his palm hit her ass in a way that told Jaylah he wasn't new to the dominant game. He knew just how much pressure to apply before shit went from sex to a police investigation.

Jaylah bit down hard onto her bottom lip and his hands opened her bottom.

"I said you're beautiful. What do you say after that?" he asked and yanked on her strands enough for her to gasp.

A long thick finger then entered Jaylah from the back causing her to moan. Her eyes rolled as her head lolled from one side to the other.

"Thank you, sir," she whispered in rapture.

Oshun slid another finger into Jaylah's opening and slowly he moved them around as she writhed on the bed.

"Your welcome, love. Arch your back some more and don't ever hold back how you feel. If it hurts tell me, if it feels good, say that shit, and when you get ready to cum, ask for permission. Okay?"

"Yes, sir. Yes!" she yelled out as Oshun worked his fingers faster quickly finding her spot that took Garris a good fifteen minutes to locate.

Jaylah's legs began to shake, and he removed his fingers.

"Not yet, that pussy feels so good. I want to taste it," he said and dropped down to his knees.

Oshun pulled Jaylah to the edge of the bed and opened her legs as wide as they would go. From the back, he feasted on her sex. His long soft tongue slurped up and down her kitty making Jaylah's body quiver in pleasure. Her eyes watered and when Oshun sucked on her clit from the back her stomach knotted up.

"Permission to cum," she begged with quivering lips.

Oshun sucked harder on her clit while thumbing her butt. His left hand smacked her ass hard as he pulled back just enough to torpedo his tongue onto her love button. Jaylah took his insistence to suck the soul from her pussy as a yes and her body spasmed on the bed. Her mouth fell open, her tears leaked, and her knees grew weak. She fell forward as her body orgasmed in a way like it never had before while Oshun's phone started to ring.

Oshun waited for her arousal to move through her being before standing. He loosened the belt and kissed her back as she cried softly on the bed.

"I gotta be up, sexy. I wish I had more time with you, but this is where our story ends." He hovered over her body as he allowed for the sheathed head of his thick dick to slowly push at her tight hole. He reframed from pushing in as his lips brushed against the side of her neck. "If I see you again, I'm a write my name in that shit. Own that pussy and give you a reason to trust a black man again. Get some rest, you can stay here until nine in the morning," he whispered and kissed her neck one last time.

Jaylah moaned softly as her body vibrated on the bed. She allowed for Oshun to place the cover over her and kiss her lips one last time then like a dream, he was gone.

Two days later Jaylah sat inside of the hair salon with her head lost in her thoughts. Her eyes couldn't stop peering down at her wrists that were darkened by the tightness of the leather belt Oshun used on her. Her sex tingled from the mere thought of him and she wasn't sure if she should be proud or disgusted with herself. She'd allowed for a stranger to have oral sex with her at a sex club. A black man at that. Just thinking on the ridiculous, immature, reckless thing she'd done made her shake her head.

Oshun wasn't real. Jaylah swore he wasn't but when she woke up that next morning to a swollen clit and sore wrists, she knew it hadn't been a dream. She'd done the unthinkable and was plagued with an array of emotions. As she prepared to make her trip to Detroit her spirit was down. The happiness she'd once felt for having such an amazing opportunity was gone. She'd also misplaced the file Jerry gave her not sure where it was at and was too ashamed to ask for another one. She wasn't on her A-game and that angered her.

Jaylah couldn't stop thinking of her past and now her mystery guy and it was all too much. She knew she needed to get back on track and fast because her future depended on it.

She refused to allow for anything to derail her from the good things that were awaiting her.

"I never thought I would see the day your anti-weave behind would be up in here getting a lace unit," her hairdresser Miesha said spinning Jaylah in her seat.

Jaylah's tired eyes looked at herself in the mirror and she soaked in her new look. Instead of getting a traditional sew-in, her stylist convinced her to get one of her custom lace front units. It was a Brazilian body wave texture and instead of going for the rainbow-colored hair she requested, her stylist instead gave her a coppery red shade that complemented her dewy fair skin.

"I know, things change," Jaylah said softly as she pulled out her ringing cellphone. "Hello," she answered with her heartbeat increasing.

"Jaylah, the results for Chlamydia and Gonorrhea came back negative. You will have to wait a few more days for the rest of the results to be in. Is everything okay?" her gynecologist asked in concern.

Jaylah sighed with relief. She smiled as she realized she was still disease-free.

"Yes, and thank you for the speedy results," she replied before ending the call.

"Jaylah *Miss Prissy*, looking like a bad bitch now. I would fuck you!" A young stylist said animatedly grinning Jaylah's way.

"Girl," Jaylah's stylist mumbled while shaking her head.

Jaylah's hairstylist was a talented up and coming hairdresser in Baymoor Falls and Jaylah was pleased to be able to sit in her chair. The problem was she didn't care too much for where her stylist worked. She was stationed at a salon on the Southside and it wasn't particularly the safest area. Jaylah also hated that part of town because it reminded her of the worst times of her life. However, her stylist that she'd known for six months didn't mind being around people with mediocre lifestyles and ghetto personalities. She seemed comfortable in the hood and even spoke of opening her own salon up down the street from the one she worked at.

Jaylah didn't know how she did the shit.

She'd been at the shop for only two hours and was already irritated as fuck. The women in the salon spoke louder then normal and used rachet lingo instead of proper English but Jaylah used their ignorance for a greater cause. She stored certain words in her memory bank for later use so chilling in the hood hadn't been a total fail.

"You just might catch you a real one, though Jaylah. I heard Pharaoh was back in town. I know y'all seen princess of the church Bebe on the news for shooting her husband and shit," another stylist in the salon said smiling.

Jaylah's hairstylist Miesha cut her eyes at the young lady to the right of her that had too much damn mouth.

"Bebe is good people. What we won't do is discuss her business like our backyards is clean. As women, we have to love each other better. Talking about Bebe's problems will not better you in any kind of way Keanna," she scolded her.

The stylist Keanna smiled before curling her client's hair with a thin black ceramic flat iron.

"Well if I don't spread the gossip somebody else will," she smiled, and a few women nodded agreeing with her.

Typical crab in the barrel mess. Jaylah thought rolling her eyes.

"But do you honestly feel like white women sit up and discuss things like this in the salon? They're too busy talking about the trips they've taken and the houses they've built. As black women, we have to do better. We need to be discussing new business ventures. I like talks of things concerning my IRA and my FICO score. Life is about much more than what happened to the one chick we don't like," Jaylah butted in, refusing to let the gossipy hairstylist slide with her comment because although she didn't personally know Bebe she did know of the beauty that was tied to the megachurch in Baymoor Falls and had even covered the story of the shooting.

The stylist Keanna smacked her lips before laughing.

"I forgot you think your hot shit because you on the news. Girl, bye. The Northside may be a better fit for you because of your light skin and proper tone but trust they still see you as one of us. And white women are just as messy as black women if not more. They're the real definition of mean girls. They bully a bitch until she is committing suicide and shit. All we do is mildly discuss people's problems on the low. You need to look in the mirror and don't forget where you came from. I remember when you and your people were moving back to the Southside and staying in the projects cause your daddy got knocked by the FEDS with his fine ass. So, keep all that bullshit that way because you're no better than us. Matter fact, Alexa! play Jay-Z "OJ"!" the stylist said and a few of the women inside of the salon laughed as the speaker started to play the rap song that was requested.

"Messy ass. Don't pay her no mind," Jaylah's stylist

mumbled taking off Jaylah's cape. "Your all set for your trip. Have fun in the Bahamas," she told her.

Jaylah nodded while boiling hot on the inside. The problem she had with black people was that they hated for a motherfucka to surpass them. So, what she had to move back to the Southside? She wasn't there now and would never be there again. However, the bitch with the mini-van shaped body, in-expensive weave and ghetto lingo was still in the hood and she was looking down on her? She was pissed at the notion.

"Yes, I can't wait," Jaylah replied playing into the lie she'd told her stylist on why she needed such a drastic look. Jaylah stood assessing her new hairstyle and while she wanted it to be over the top and eye-catching the style was the opposite of that. The lace front appeared to be melting onto her scalp as if it were her hair and the color did compliment her bright skin. By choice, she would never go for such an eye-catching look but for her current predicament, it was perfect.

"Aye, she looks like Nicki Minaj with that red hair! Remember them pics she put on the gram bae, of when she was in Miami wearing that brown dress?" a deep voice said as Jaylah passed her stylist six hundred dollars for the hairdo.

"Nigga I do, but the real question is why do *you* remember that shit? You better calm your thirsty ass down," the stylist Keanna said frowning at the man.

Jaylah grabbed her bag and thanked her stylist once more before looking at the man that said she looked like the popular female rapper. He was standing beside the stylist that just tried to read her, and while the stylist was peering over at him with daggers in her dark brown eyes the man was staring at Jaylah with stars in his eyes. Jaylah laughed on the inside never missing an opportunity to clap back. Petty was most certainly her middle fucking name.

"I think I've heard that a time or two. I don't see it, however. Could you get the door for me though, baby?" she asked sweetly while looking at the man.

"Joc, you better not—"

Before the stylist Keanna could finish her sentence, her man was holding the door for Jaylah while sporting a big smile. Jaylah giggled and shook her head as she headed for the door. She made sure to walk past Keanna slowly while grinning her way.

"And just maybe if you elevated your mindset, he would open the door for you too. Instead of making fun of how I am, you should be taking notes," she told the stylist and took her time walking away.

Although Jaylah was past the hood life, she wasn't a stranger to protecting herself. She and her twin had been fighting each other since they were younger, and she had no problem laying a bitch out if she had to.

"Well see if that bitch is gone cook and fuck you tonight with your friendly ass! Since you want to open up doors and shit! Nigga open up a legal job! Shit, open up a fucking bank account. Hell open up some fucking soap, with yo dirty ass!" Keanna snapped as Jaylah walked through the salon doors.

Jaylah exited the salon and slid into her car. As she pulled off, she received a phone call from someone she hadn't spoken to in months. Brooke Morris was not only connected in Baymoor Falls she was also working at one of the highest-ranking news stations in the country MLN. Jaylah met her through Jerry and looked up to her for many reasons because Brooke was at a place in her career that Jaylah badly wanted to be.

"Hey Brooke!" she said excitedly.

"Hey, Jaylah! I spoke with Jerry and he told me about your secret mission and I'm all here for it. However, last night I talked with Alex about it and he said something that surprised me. He believes that if you can bring down this family which would be a huge news story, he could get you in at our station. You would have your own thirty-minute segment talking on the latest topics. This is everything you've ever wanted, and I know you love Jerry. Hell, I do too but this is business not personal. Mixing the two will only hold you back. What do you say?" she asked talking fast like usual.

Surprised by the nature of the call, Jaylah pulled her car over at the gas station and placed it into park. Her thoughts shifted from Jerry and how he helped her over the years to having a possible new job at MLN. This was what she was grinding so hard for, but she hated to step on Jerry to get there.

"I don't know. Jerry brought this opportunity to me and he's offering me a position basically for as long as I want along with a pay increase Brooke."

Brooke snorted.

"Honey, Jerry needs you it's not the other way around. You're the talent so you're the asset. You are the reason why people watch that shitty ass news show of his that Heather is trying to take from him. She's screaming divorce again," Brooke replied.

Jaylah shook her head. For reasons unknown to her Jerry and his wife Heather filed for divorce every few years, they would fight like cats and dogs then out of the blue drop the case.

"Wow, I'm sure one of them will not go through with it," Jaylah replied.

"I'm sure as well but what if this time they do? Nobody wants to be working for someone that has no clue what the hell they are doing. And this is no shade to Jerry but without you, the station would be trash. He knows that and for that reason alone he's trying to keep you around. You're going places but if settling for your position at HLN20 is where you want to be then I won't stop you. I just thought you were a woman that was about her career. The next Oprah is what you said when I first met you and look at all of the years you've given Jerry. Yes, he helped you in the beginning but that doesn't mean you have to forever work with him. I never knew that loyalty meant ownership. This would be you on a prime-time show and a black woman at that Jaylah!" Brooke said laying it on thick. "I mean if you were bad Jaylah you wouldn't be on his show anyway. You don't owe him anything. Trust you've more than made up for the chance he took on you a long time ago," she said laying it on thick.

Jaylah nodded agreeing with Brooke. Part of the reason why she stayed at Jerry's station was because of the way he looked out. He had her back and she had his, but they weren't a duo. She was her own person and she wanted to keep elevating. Jerry was not at the top so she knew eventually she would leave him behind. The opportunity had just come quicker than she imagined it would.

"I'm in," she sighed. "What do I have to do?"

Brooke clapped excitedly on the other end of the phone.

"I knew you would be all for it! I mean come on; you're a shark like me. We eat our fucking way to the top," Brooke laughed while Jaylah merely smiled at her response feeling guilt fall over her for what she was doing. "But yes, all I need is proof that this family is corrupt. This story has gained national headlines and if we could do an exclusive story on them that would place us at the top. This whole thing is a mess and I don't know what to believe. The cops say the boy was a dealer and he sure does look the part. I mean his brothers do as well with their tattoo's, nice cars and flashy clothes. They look nothing like the black men in my family," Brooke said with a laugh, and Jaylah nodded although she hadn't made the time to check out the family's background because she'd misplaced the folder and was now rushing to get last-minute things done.

Between having nightmares about her past and meeting the mystery man Oshun her mind was frazzled however she was ready to get herself back on track. She planned on reading up on the family as soon as she got home on the internet.

"No, that's fine. I'm ready," she told Brooke while nodding.

"Great! Like I said all I will need is enough to cover a story on the facts about this family. I look forward to working with you Jaylah because we sista's have to stick together," Brooke said and ended the call.

Jaylah put her phone away and sighed. She wanted more out of life. Prayed about it and even wrote about it. Things were changing rapidly for her and she was happy at the start of it, but now she wasn't so sure.

Her spirit was uneasy, and she hadn't felt so unsettled since before college, around the time of her assault. Back then she was damn near suicidal and the only way for her to tune out the pain and push forward was to turn her emotions off. She pretended nothing happened and when everything was said and done, she left her home and her family behind for good. It was the only way she could make it without going insane. She became a new Jaylah with a better outlook on life. She became the kind of black woman she felt every woman of her race should be and life for her got better. Looking back into the past would only cause her pain and strife. She refused to go down the rabbit's hole because nothing good would come from it.

"And I might not recover this time," she whispered pulling off.

Jaylah went home, sent her best friend Kylie photos of her new hairdo before she started to pack. Before Jaylah could finish pulling out her jeans for her trip her cellphone rung.

She smiled to herself as she quickly answered the call on speaker.

"Babe! You look like you stepped off the set of Greedo's fucking video!" Kylie laughed so hysterically that she snorted.

Jaylah stilled at the mention of Greedo. She closed her eyes and was transported to a time when Greedo had been the nice guy in her eyes.

The streets were littered with trash. Filth was all she saw. And it looked vastly different then the Northside area she'd grown accustomed to living in. Homeless people decorated the sidewalks begging for monetary help while drug dealers were cemented to the corners selling drugs. Jaylah had never seen anything like it before. It was scary, downright frightening but her twin seemed to love the change. She adapted well to the hood.

Almost too well.

"Hey Greedo!" her twin yelled excitedly as they walked down the street headed to the bus stop for school.

Thankfully they were able to finish up school in the

suburbs for the rest of the year and Jaylah was grateful for that. It would give her time to adjusting to the gritty neighborhood and the people that lived in it.

Greedo's slanted brown eyes a chestnut hued inviting shade peered over at Jaylah and her twin with intrigue. He looked Jaylah and her twin over staring at Jaylah longer before smirking.

"What's good, bad twin?" he chuckled while leaning against a black 1980 Regal that was decked out with 22-inch spoke rims and a shiny black paint job.

Jaylah's twin blushed as Jaylah discreetly rolled her eyes. She continued walking not looking to entertain anyone as her sister flirted with the local hood star that was also a drug dealer.

"Jaylah, watch out!"

Her twin's light voice screaming her name made her abruptly stop. Strong arms pulled her back onto the curb as her heart pounded in her chest. Jaylah gasped and looked up at the man that had saved her from being hit by the car that ran the stop sign.

"You good?" Greedo asked peering down at her.

Jaylah's mouth was dry as her chest heaved up and down rapidly. She nodded, still in shock and he rubbed her arms up and down slowly. Her pretty eyes assessed Greedo in a new light as he stood close to her with a slight frown on his face.

"You sure? I can go find that nigga that almost hit you," he insisted and his determination to protect her reminded Jaylah *of her father. It gave her comfort that she hadn't realized she was missing.*

It made her feel safe.

That was something her father once did but now he was gone.

"I'm fine," she said breathily flashing Greedo a genuine smile.

He was attractive with his mocha brown skin and slanted eyes. Greedo was tall with a stocky build and while his boys were on the immature side he wasn't. He wore a confidence on him that his friends didn't possess. He walked and talked like he was that nigga and Jaylah was now seeing why. He was cute and it helped that he housed deep dimples with an even fade that was always lined up.

Her eyes landed on his thick lips and she swallowed hard. Greedo caught her staring and he winked at her.

"Yeah, you definitely the good twin. Fine as shit for no reason. If you ever need anything and I mean anything. Let me know," Greedo insisted and Jaylah smiled.

"Thank you," she whispered for the first time wanting a boy to give her a kiss.

The kind of kisses her dad would rain down onto her mom just because.

"I will," she responded peering up into eyes dreamily.

"Jaylah! You okay?" Kylie asked raising her voice.

Jaylah snapped out of her thoughts and cleared her throat. More frequently the flashbacks were coming and each time they were longer, more vivid than the last scaring the shit out of her.

She grabbed some of her belongings while trying to slow her racing heart down.

"Yeah—yeah, I'm here," she stuttered stumbling over her words.

"Oh, okay. I saw the picture and you were looking very Nicki Minaj-ish with her smutty ass. Like a straight up section eight bitch," Kylie added in her snooty voice before laughing.

Unlike Jaylah, Kylie was born into wealth. Her family owned a chain of jewelry stores and she'd been given one as a wedding gift to set her and her family up. She never worked a day in her life and while she wasn't the most attractive woman, Jaylah had never seen a bitch dress nicer than Kylie or live a more lavish life. Kylie had the kind of money that made designers personally make you items and while Jaylah would never admit it. She was attracted to Kylie because of the luxurious lifestyle she lived. She was a black woman with a fine ass white husband, beautiful biracial kids, and money. Kylie was articulate, worldly, and not ghetto. She was indeed everything Jaylah felt black women should be.

Jaylah snorted at Kylie's assessment of her new look. Thinking of the red lace unit she wore made her gradually forget the scary flashback she had.

"I told you that was what I was going for! I need to look the part," she replied stuffing her toiletries into her suitcase.

"Hmm, well look the part you do. Make sure you don't post any photos on your IG while wearing that ridiculous looking wig. You look like your name should be Diamond or some shit," Kylie laughed.

Jaylah's packing paused as a frown fell onto her pretty face. She wasn't sure how to feel about Kylie's joke.

"That's my niece's name, Kylie," she reminded her in a clipped tone.

Kylie stopped laughing and cleared her throat.

"*Oh*, well you barely speak of those people. I forgot you had a twin sister let alone a niece. I mean isn't she a stripper? I wouldn't claim a woman like that, and you shouldn't either. Ugh, the foolery. I mean you don't have the education for a proper career, I get it but at least lay down with a man that has money. Shit don't be a complete fool," Kylie scolded her twin making Jaylah's frown deepen.

"So yeah, I have to finish packing, I will call you once I'm settled," she said quickly ready to end the call.

"No, wait! I didn't mean to offend you. You and I are like sisters and I would never do that babe. It's just I know where you are trying to get to in life, and I want you to get there. I want you to buy the house in my neighborhood and have the man like I do. You deserve all of the things you want, and you've worked so hard to put the Southside behind you. Don't forget that. What you are about to do will set you up for life. Who knows it could even bring you an athlete as well. I mean Garris is cool, but you need an NFL player or something like

I have on your team. That's where the real money is at but no need to worry. Your BF is on the job babe. Love you lots, call me later," Kylie said and blew kisses into the speakerphone before hanging up.

"And even after belittling your family, and me you still don't correct her about it. Are you that ignorant that you feel like all of the bullshit that she just said is okay?" Garris asked.

The sound of his deep voice made Jaylah jump. She turned and looked at him with wide eyes. Garris stood in her doorway donning a black two-piece suit with a white dress shirt and black shoes. His handsome face held a scowl to it as he glared her way. She shifted from one foot to the other caught off guard by his presence.

"I thought you were out of town," she said nervously.

Garris dropped his bags while frowning. He moved around the spacious bedroom with ease as he allowed for the silence to linger for a moment.

"I came back early to catch you before you left for Detroit. I need to talk with you about something very important," he replied.

Jaylah watched Garris sit at the black-winged chair that was in the corner of the room and stare at her. His gaze was intent and the pain swimming in his eyes made her uncomfortable.

"About?" she asked wondering if he'd heard about her being at Club Luxure the other night from someone that could have spotted her there.

Garris took a deep breath and exhaled.

"It's like this Jaylah, I met someone else and while I didn't intend to it happened. She works for another company, but we share the same building."

Jaylah snorted. Her anger with Garris rose in her body as she glared at him.

"And let me guess she's the kind of woman you can take home to your mom, huh?" she asked while shaking her head.

Garris dropped his head solemnly. He looked back up at her and his beautiful eyes were red-rimmed.

"I don't give a damn about that and for that reason alone I wasn't sure if I should tell you the truth, but she is my race. However, that has nothing to do with it and you know that. She's sweet, honest and doesn't mind being herself. She likes to cook for me and she's open to change. She's not holding on to pain the way that you do," he replied.

Jaylah took a step towards Garris as her face tightened in anger.

"Open to change? What the fuck are you talking about? I let you come to my house and practically live here even though we're not married. I have a life with you. I gave you my body and this is how you do me?"

Garris sat up while looking at her.

"Jaylah I'm just here to pass the fucking time and you know it! You hold on to so much hate that it's ridiculous. The sad thing is I think you hate your own race and that's scary for me. I can't have a life with someone that hates who they are.

You don't talk to your family and the people you do hang around, Kylie for example are horrible individuals. Including Jerry! I don't know what you like to do or eat. I know nothing about the real you because you're so busy trying to be better than every black woman in this world. When I just need you to be the best Jaylah you can be, but I don't think you even know who you are, baby."

Jaylah's eyes widened at his outburst. Her eyes watered and she found herself crying at Garris's assessment of her. While she didn't love Garris, she did care for him. She'd been genuine with her affection and to see how he felt about her hurt.

And it was a low blow because for Jaylah she was certain that one day he would come around to proposing. He was her safe, easy-going guy. This wasn't supposed to happen to them.

"I hate I did this to you, but I don't regret meeting Rosalie. I'm falling in love with her and that's who I want to be with. You're looking for perfection when you are so fucking far from perfect that it's not even funny. I hope you find what you are looking for, however. I really do," he spoke sincerely as he stood up.

Garris moved past Jaylah and headed towards the closet as she stewed on his words. Jaylah took a seat at the edge of her bed and sat with her hands in her lap. Yes, she had Kylie, but she'd needed Garris too. He'd been there since the day they'd met, and it felt good to come home to someone. Now she was back to having no one and she couldn't ignore the pain that it came with.

"Call your family and reconnect with them. Stop trying to be perfect and just be you. Love yourself Jaylah then maybe you can love someone else," he said and pulled his clothes that were already packed out of the closet.

Jaylah realized that he'd been preparing to leave, and she felt stupid because she hadn't even noticed it. She laid back on the bed with her eyes drifting to the ceiling and before she could mourn the loss of her relationship her cellphone rung.

She snatched the large black device up from her bed and glared at the screen. The all too familiar federal prison number slid across it like it did three times a week. Her father's handsome smile popped into her head and she found herself missing him.

Jaylah was emotional and decided to take the call while holding her breath.

"This is the federal penitentiary calling on a recorded line with a collect call for *"Jaylah Cole"* would you like to accept this collect call? If yes press 1."

Jaylah quickly ended the call and pressed the phone to her chest. She hadn't heard her father's voice since she was eighteen years old and as a thirty-year-old woman, he sounded the same.

He actually sounded the fucking same.

She whimpered at that and before a tear could fall the ice

in her veins froze over her heart. Jaylah sat her phone down and sat up straight.

"You are a winner. You will succeed. You are not a victim. You are not a statistic. You are everything you want to be in life," she spoke robotically.

Her eyes closed and when she opened them, she felt renewed. Garris, her father, and her family could all go to hell. She would be fine without them. She didn't need anybody but herself.

CHAPTER 4

What's free?
Free is when nobody else could tell us what to be
Free is when the TV ain't controlling what we see

Oshun lowered the volume inside of his car and his tired eyes peered over at his brother. Rage hovered over Gio as he sulked in the seat beside him. On Gio's lap was a bottle of Remy and Oshun couldn't stop peering down at the liquor. He felt like every time he saw his brother; he was clutching a fresh bottle of alcohol. He was all for a drink, but he didn't want Gio to become an alcoholic. He needed a more positive way to handle his pain.

As they sat outside of the men boutique in Oak Park

Oshun felt stressed. Between handling arrangements for the funeral, flying in family, doing shit in the BOC he was way past tired.

"What's good, brah? That's your new best friend or some shit?" he asked relaxing in his seat.

Gio smirked but didn't reply. Instead, he took another swig of his liquor. He lowered the window allowing for the cool April weather to breeze into the car.

"I'm doing me. Malik gone, my fucking girl crying pregnant and you won't let me do shit about the cops. I'm all fucked up right now," he replied.

Oshun frowned until he registered what his brother said to him. He looked over at him and smirked.

"Is that right? Your ass finally slipped up and got Tamara pregnant. You tell mom?"

Gio shook his head.

"Nah, not yet. She's all fucked up about Malik."

Oshun nodded, his eyes searched the streets for the cops always on the lookout for them as he sat in the car.

"And you're her son too. Tiff's pregnant and now Tamara. The family needs this."

Gio shrugged and despite understanding his pain Oshun found himself getting upset. The problem with being the strong person for everybody was that no one took the time to see about you. Oshun wanted comfort too. Malik was more like his son than his brother and he wasn't anywhere close to dealing with his death. He was too fucking busy checking on everyone else. At times he hated that he went so hard for the people he loved but that was him.

He was just a man with a good heart.

"I know your hurting, but a baby is a blessing. Losing Malik is proof that time is of the essence. Yes, we fucked up about this shit, but you can't drink your pain away. Your about to be a fucking father, like nigga that shit is big. Do you understand the gift that God is giving you? You get the chance to shape someone's life. Be there for them and love them. That should make you feel blessed," he told him.

Gio finished his drink and tossed his bottle onto the floor. Oshun's brows lifted as he watched the empty liquor bottle roll on his black custom Mercedes floor mat.

"Pain or not don't be littering in my fucking car, pick that shit up," he based and Gio chuckled.

Gio grabbed the empty bottle and looked at him.

"Brah, I'm in mourning. Fuck this car," he smiled with red-rimmed eyes.

Oshun chuckled. He scratched at the back of his head and checked the time before grinning at his brother.

"Nah, fuck that ugly ass car you got. Respect my shit now like I was saying, your about to have a baby. Be thankful and before you grab another bottle of Remy to drink hit me up. We can kick shit until that yearning to drink goes away. Even with the funeral approaching you on daddy time now. You need to be tightening your shit up. No hoes or bullshit will come before this kid. Be a man that your child can look up to," he schooled him. "And ask Tamara to marry you before you tell mom," he cracked just to fuck with him.

Gio's eyes widened before he started to laugh.

"Man fuck all that! I swear when she told me that shit all I could do was think of mom and what she said to Malik. She gone throw us the fuck away and start with some new sons," he jested pulling another bottle of Remy from his back pocket.

"What the fuck?" Oshun grabbed the unopened liquor bottle and shook his head. He placed it in the middle console as he stared at his brother.

"We just talked about that shit. There is no amount of drinking or fucking we can do that is going to heal this pain we're feeling," he told him.

Gio sucked his teeth.

"Maybe some get back would," he said lowly looking out of his window.

Oshun's dark honey shaded eyes peered out of his window thoughtfully. He bit down hard onto his bottom lip as he thought of the news, he'd received thanks to his friend Tori that was locked up. He now had a location on the black officer involved in Malik's shooting and it was on his call what happened to that man and his family.

Oshun wasn't a saint but killing had never been for him either. He was still shaken at how he'd almost sprayed a car that was occupied with a woman and a child. That one incident showed him that he didn't want a death on his soul, but this was Malik.

His brother, his shadow, his blood.

He didn't know if he could walk away from the opportunity to handle the people responsible for killing Malik. Because the thing was no matter what he did he would never have Gio execute the plan with him. He looked over at his brother and cleared his throat.

"You think taking a life would make the pain go away?" he asked Gio. Before Gio could respond Oshun continued. "Nothing we do would make our pain go away. Nothing," he told him shaking his head. Oshun's eyes peered out at the street that was darkening thanks to the sun going down and his chest tightened. "True strength is making the right decision when you have the ability to make the wrong one. Do you understand what I mean by that?"

Gio moved around in the seat while frowning. He pulled his black Detroit Mitchell and Ness fitted cap lower on his head and sighed.

"Look I'm not a kid. I don't need you to be always trying to school me on some shit," he said aggressively.

Oshun nodded.

"The funny thing is it's plenty of niggas out here that wish they had a big brother to show them the way. You never too old to learn something new Gio. Even with all the shit I know, I still take advice because only a fool thinks he knows it all. Now what I was about to say is that it's nothing for us to find who did it and run down on them. That wouldn't be a problem Gio, but to know where them clowns at and still not make that move shows our strength. It's never wise to make decisions based on emotions. Despite how I look I'm mentally unstable right now brah, and that's real shit. I've never felt a pain like this before and the last thing I need to do is make an irrational decision that could change our lives forever," he explained.

Gio's jaw tensed as he glared at Oshun.

"So, we let them get away with this shit then? They lying on Malik and they killed him for no damn reason!" he barked so angry that he bounced in the seat with aggression.

Oshun shook his head. He pulled his fob from his ignition while looking at his brother.

"Men can't afford to be careless. Ever. One fucked up decision from us and it would change everything. So yeah, we could act on our anger. Go run down on the cops and flip they shit back. Then we could get our black asses locked the fuck up. Tamara would be out here preparing to have a baby without you while momma runs the BOC by herself leaving the community at risk for thieves and gangs to overrun it. Would it be worth it then?" he asked looking at Gio.

Gio sat back and his eyes lowered to his lap before looking back to Oshun.

"Nah, guess not but I mean who's to say we would get caught? We're smart as hell and that's why the cops don't fuck with us like they did Malik. We could handle them niggas and be on our way," Gio replied showing Oshun that he still was immature about a lot of things, but it was cool because as long as he was breathing, he would push as much knowledge into his brother that he could.

Oshun pushed open his door with his eyes on Gio.

"The difference between a man and a boy is that a man does what he needs to do while a boy does what he wants," he told him and exited the car.

Gio begrudgingly exited the car with him and picked up his suit for the funeral service with Oshun. Once they were done Oshun took Gio to his home that was off the water in downtown Detroit. He pulled into the circular driveway and stopped near the front door. He unlocked the car and looked at Gio with narrowed eyes.

"I know I give you a lot of shit, but it's only to make you the best person you can be. I'm not trying to be pops. I'm only trying to be your big brother because if you fail in life then I failed in life. We're a family and the entire tree needs to be strong not just the trunk. I love kicking back with you and talking shit, but I really enjoy telling you things that will make your life better. I want you to be better than me Gio so pray tonight and thank God for this baby your about to have. And ask him to help you with your anger," Oshun said as sincere as he could not wanting his brother to feel anything but the love, he had for him.

Gio's shoulders relaxed and he nodded solemnly. He dapped up Oshun as his girlfriend stepped outside in a long black fluffy robe with pink slippers on her feet. She waved at Oshun and he hit the horn twice.

"And if you don't want her then don't string her along. I don't give a fuck about y'all not having the title. She's about to have your child so you will put her on a pedestal fuck the dumb shit, right?" he asked.

Gio nodded pushing his door open.

"You already know, I appreciate you, brah. I really do," he said and grabbed his suit from the backseat before exiting Oshun's car.

Oshun made sure Gio was good before driving away. He drove to his apartment instead of his home and the second he entered the penthouse suite his eyes drifted over to the black sofa.

The dark chocolate beauty with the short red hair and brown doe shaped eyes smiled at him. She was sitting on the leather loveseat donning a black trench that stopped mid-thigh. She stood as Oshun shut his front door and dropped her coat.

"Welcome home, sir," she murmured sexily.

Oshun leaned against the door and folded his hands in front of himself. This was one of his favorite girls. Her body was stacked in all of the right places with her juicy thighs, perky breast and fat waxed pussy. She knew how to take directions and dick. Both pluses in his book but the release he needed wasn't trying to come to him. Usually on sight he was ready to bust her walls and throat down. He wanted to fuck his hurt away. Release his pent up anger onto the beauty but his member was refusing to thicken up for him.

Something was off.

Oshun closed his eyes and took a deep breath. He exhaled a few minutes later as sadness clung to his frame.

Damn, he was hurt. Malik's burial was two days away and the pain he'd been ignoring was getting closer with each second that passed. He lifted his head and placed his dark honey hued gaze onto his special friend Alicia.

"You have to excuse me, sweetheart. Tonight, just isn't the night for me," he said stepping off the door. Oshun pulled open the door for the tall stallion as she stared at him in confusion.

"I can't begin to understand your pain. I want to be here for you in any kind of way. Fuck me as hard as you need to," she begged and licked her lips with her long tongue that had brought him great pleasure in the past.

Oshun shook his head regretting having the beauty over to his place. He turned to the door as his tongue grew heavy. His body tensed and his eyes watered.

He was close to losing it.

"I'll hit you up another time, ma," he spoke lowly still his words were heard.

The beauty quickly grabbed her trench and covered her voluptuous body. She walked towards the door and before she could pass Oshun her small hand rubbed at his strong back.

"I'm sorry," she whispered before leaving his penthouse.

Oshun shut the door not bothering to respond. He grabbed the statue he'd gotten from Egypt and threw it as hard as he could against the wall facing him.

Bam!

It hit the grey wall hard and cracked before falling to his marbled floor. Oshun leaned against his front door and his tall frame slowly slid down it as his face became wet with tears.

Fucking tears.

He couldn't believe it.

They were upon him and he couldn't stop it. They came fast and his chest quaked with great sorrow. Oshun held his face as the pain from losing his loved one finally poured out of him.

CHAPTER 5

Oshun David Lacoste- AGE 31 no kids, no police record,
bachelor's degree in business administration, master's degree
in business administration.
Giovanni Jacob Lacoste- AGE 28 no kids, no police record,
bachelor's degree in accounting, master's degree in
accounting.

H oly fuck.
Her hand couldn't stop shaking as she held the paper. Her skin shivered and as she clicked on the link to the latest video that was uploaded onto the BOC community social media page, she held her breath.

"Malik was smart, funny, and gifted. He could have gone to school for ball, but he wanted to be a lawyer." Oshun stopped talking and his last words with Malik drifted into his

mind. His hooded eyes fell to his lap and he took a deep breath. After a few seconds, he looked up at his pastor and shook his head. "He was about to be a father. He wanted to make his own way in life and I'm sure that whatever path he chose it was going to be great. Nothing, Malik did was average. I mean look at his grades. Look at the degrees he had already then look at his age. He was far from ordinary. Nothing like what the media is saying about him. My brother didn't have to sell drugs and even if poverty would have made him feel like that was a choice, he would have still done something else with his life. The problem with America is that they don't understand the strength that's in a black person. Malik would have made a way out of no way. Losing wasn't in his DNA. Just because a black man in America has money does not mean they are doing something illegal. The cops played God when they killed my brother. They showed the hate this world has for a colored man and I want people to remember that if they did it to Malik they can and will might one day do it to them," Oshun replied.

Jaylah's shaky fingers shut her rose gold MacBook Pro, and her eyes closed.

His brother.

Malik was his brother. The same man she'd received her greatest orgasm from was none other than the man she had to grow close with to find out his family's deep dark secrets. Jaylah dropped her head and took deep meaningful breaths. She regretted losing the file and waiting until the last minute to do her research. That was amateur shit. She was better than that. Had never been a slacker but her life lately had been unraveling at the seams.

Her current predicament was proof of that.

"I can't do this. I can't," she muttered opening her light eyes.

Jaylah grabbed her phone from the hotel bed and called up Jerry. She opened her laptop and stared at the paused video of the handsome Oshun as she waited for him to take the call.

"Hey babe, what's going on? You know that son of a bitches funeral is tomorrow," he said answering the phone.

Jaylah stared intently at the video of Oshun before looking away. She thought of the pain in his deep voice and on his face when he spoke of his brother and guilt hovered over her head like a dark cloud.

"About that. I um—I um don't feel too good Jerry. I know how important this is for you and—"

"And you have to do it. Jaylah now isn't the time to drop the ball. My brothers are depending on me to pull through for them. I told them you would do this. I work under the weather all of the time and you can too. The funeral is tomor-row. Don't back out now, damn," Jerry replied with an atti-tude and ended the call.

Jaylah held the phone while frowning. What Jerry was requesting her to do wasn't her job and she was highly pissed that he wasn't giving her a chance to change her mind. His uncaring attitude towards her reluctance to push through with the plan made her feel less guilty about leaving the news station. She nibbled on her bottom lip as she called up a number that she rarely used.

"—Jaylah? Hey," Charise said with a surprised voice.

Jaylah groaned.

This wasn't her.

At all.

She cleared her throat before speaking. "Hey. Uh, you busy?" she asked nervously.

"No just prepping my letter of resignation. What about you? I heard you had some big story you were working on for Jerry. What's going on with that?" Charise replied.

Jaylah relaxed on the bed as her brows knitted together.

"Why are you quitting?"

Charise laughed.

"After you tried to read me back at the office I thought about my career at the station and I decided that even though you are full of shit you were right. I haven't elevated and they don't appreciate me. I won't keep taking peanuts when I know I'm worth more than that. Jerry is racist as hell and I would rather work odd jobs than be his house nigga," she replied.

Jaylah rolled her eyes.

"Why is it always about color with you?" she asked over the race talk.

Charise snorted.

"Because Jerry makes it that way. I asked him if I could

cover your Wednesday segment while your away and that fat greasy motherfucka said I wasn't what the station needed to see so early in the morning. He then laughed it off and walked away like I was going to let that shit ride. I have a lawyer and everything. I'm over being a slave to that station," Charise vented.

Jaylah's pretty face fell into a frown at Charise's words. She regretted calling up the bitch because she always had to make herself a victim.

Typical angry black woman behavior.

"Maybe if you weren't so aggressive and wore your hair in more appealing styles instead of locs, he wouldn't have said that. My hair is naturally curly, and you don't see me flossing my curls. I wear work related styles. I smile, I'm polite and I'm happy. Being an angry black woman will always hold you back. You walking around with a chip on your shoulder for no damn reason. Jerry doesn't care about the color of your skin. He cares about ratings, that's it. I'm black and he likes me," she defended him.

Charise began to breathe heavily into the phone.

"I don't know why I even bother with your simple-minded ass. I keep thinking of the Jaylah that I met when we were in college and I give you chance after chance to show me that person again. You were sad back then, but you were real. You had a heart and you cared. You're so lost now that you can't tell that your face is all up in masta's ass. Get out of the house boo please, because I would rather die in the field fighting for my rights than sell my soul to fit in. I love my dreadlocks even when they're nappy. I love my brown skin and I love my attitude. I'm a bitch when I don't have coffee or dick in the morning. I'm a bitch when somebody parks in my spot or cuts me off on the freeway. And I'm a *downright* angry bitch when I can't find anything good to eat and I'm forced to eat some bullshit. I will never change my mood or alter my appearance to make people like me. What you see is what you get. I'm going to pray for you Jaylah," Charise told her.

Jaylah sat on the bed with her face turned up at Charise's words.

"Pray for me? You're the one about to be without a job, why do I need the prayer?" she quipped.

Charise sighed.

"Because in the words of the late great Dr. Martin Luther King, *nothing in the world is more dangerous than sincere ignorance and conscience stupidity.* Please don't call me again until you've gotten your shit together. Goodbye Jaylah," she replied and ended the call.

Jaylah sat the phone down onto the bed and opened her laptop. As she prepared to search for police shootings on black men, wanting to see just why Charise and so many other black people felt compelled to protest while calling out the law enforcement, a message from her MLN connect Brooke popped up onto her computer screen.

Tomorrow we need a small video of the service with pictures of

the family members. Make sure to zoom in on their jewelry
and cars. Good luck! Primetime here you come!

Jaylah closed her laptop and laid back on the bed. She could pack up, go back home and find something to tell Jerry or she could push through. Oshun had been remarkable at Club Luxure but that didn't mean a thing to her. It couldn't because she only had herself to look out for. She had big things awaiting her and feeling sorry for people that brought strife onto themselves wasn't something she was comfortable doing.

"I have to shake this off. I'm too close to my dream to give up now. I mean what the fuck has a black man ever done for me? My own father let me down," she said bitterly and from thinking of her dad and his fuckups she became angry.

Jaylah rolled onto her side with a snarl on her face ready to get intel on the Lacoste family so she could head back home.

A day later she sat in the back of the semi-packed church. She was surprised to see that the family didn't want outsiders at the funeral and the only way she'd gotten in was by sneaking in through the kitchen area and finding a seat towards the back.

Jaylah knew it was wrong to scheme in the Lord's house, but she also knew that He would understand. This was what she needed to do to get to the next level in her career. Jaylah knew in her soul that she was the next Oprah. She was too

fucking determined not to be somebody of extreme importance. Her hustle was too strong and her will to make it was
too great. The devil couldn't stop her even if he tried.

"This is so sad. Malik was just about to have a baby. He
was on his way to becoming a lawyer," an elderly woman
whispered leaning towards Jaylah.

With drug money I'm sure.

She thought but when she glanced over at the older
woman, she smiled.

"I know he was a good man," Jaylah," said in such a
sincere voice that she even surprised herself.

"He was," the older woman agreed, and Jaylah nodded
while discreetly rolling her eyes.

Pastor Domani Miles that Jaylah heard of being an
amazing figure in the church world stood. She watched him
take the podium before sitting back and hoping the service
didn't take too long. Patiently she sat through two hours of the
church service forcing herself not to look at Oshun who she
could tell was sitting in the front pew next to his beautiful
mother that Jaylah felt resembled the actress Jada Pinkett in
many ways. The service had been emotional for Oshun's
family yet surprisingly peaceful.

No loud exaggerated crying.

No women falling out over the casket and no RIP t-shirts.

Jaylah was impressed thinking that for the family to be
connected to the drug world she expected a different kind of
sendoff for Malik. One more buoyant and louder.

Men in all black entered the church grabbing everyone's attention as the service was being wrapped up and everyone peered back at them. They wore stern looks on their faces as they lined the walkway leading to the casket.

"That's the security for the event. They work for the minister," the older lady whispered, and Jaylah's eyes widened in surprise.

Now, why on earth would the nation of Islam be supporting this family? She wondered.

She watched Malik's mother Angie take the podium as the men in the front row stood in respect for her. Everyone in the family wore white which she thought was strange. They weren't as flashy as drug dealers were known for being, but wealth was visible on the family even with them trying to downplay it. The suits and dresses the family wore was nothing off the rack while their jewels were real sparkling pieces that would be seen in Kylie's jewelry store. Jaylah wasn't sold on every man in the funeral being rich, but she was certain that Oshun and the men sitting on the front pew with him had healthy funds available to them. She'd been around people with money long enough to know what rich looked like.

Oshun's mom smoothed out her short hair and licked her thin lips. She wore a white shift dress with a purple and gold wrap around her waist. Her makeup was natural and despite losing a son she was poised with a regal look to her that made Jaylah sit up straight to stare at her.

His mother dropped her head and took a deep calming breath. Her eyes lifted to the crowd and she offered a sad smile.

"I would like to thank each and every one for coming to my son's home going. As you all know we wanted the service to be intimate. Malik's death will not be in vain and his funeral will not be a circus. The only way to drive out hate is love. Malik was a light that could never be dimmed. Those officers that did this to my son who has never been arrested or even expelled from school will pay. Either here on earth or in the afterlife. Please keep us lifted in your prayers as well as his unborn child. As a family we will not let his memory fade away. Thank you," the mother said and kissed Malik's handsome face before placing a worn-in teddy bear into the casket.

"And the spirit shall return unto God who gave it," the mother said before returning to the young lady's side that Jaylah assumed was the pregnant girlfriend.

The young woman was gorgeous as well and Jaylah was again caught off guard with how calm she was. The funeral was serene like with minimal breakdowns. Many people stood and spoke highly of Malik in an intelligent way making sure to not go over their time to speak. Even a professor from a HBCU university talked about Malik and how special he was. Jaylah had never seen a hustler's funeral be held in such away.

It was if she were at the home going service of a public official or something.

Ring. Ring. Ring.

The loud annoying ring of her cellphone made Jaylah jump in her seat. She quickly retrieved her phone from her black caviar bag and silenced the call. Her eyes flew up in alarm as she realized that her presence was known and when they connected with Oshun, Jaylah nearly shitted herself.

Oh my God!

Oh my God!

Oh my God!

She panicked. Her body grew cold and her leg started to shake as Oshun's brows tugged together. He stared at her inquisitively before looking back to his mom.

"You can stop shaking, baby. These boys are good men. They helped me and my Otis get a home in their community with no money down and you don't even want to know what my mortgage is. Pennies. They are heaven-sent," the older woman whispered.

Jaylah nodded. She was so spooked by Oshun's stare that she couldn't think straight. Her heart was racing as she watched him walk towards Malik's casket.

"I shouldn't have come," Jaylah mumbled only it was loud enough for the older woman beside her to hear.

The older woman looked at Oshun and she smiled wide.

"They won't mind that phone call, dear. That's Oshun the oldest brother. That's my baby right there with his handsome self. That boy is always a phone call away. He keeps the streets of the BOC clean. No drug dealing and no gang violence. It's really a shame how the police here hate him," she replied.

Jaylah closed her eyes at the woman's response and sunk into her seat. Oshun was smooth. She'd give him that. From the club, she'd off top felt he wasn't living right. Hell, most black men weren't but upon talking to him she thought he might have been different. But now she knew it was her fragile mental state mixed in with tequila that had her open to being around a black man again.

She'd been weak and had fallen for the con. He was clearly into something illegal. Degrees, no police record, and all he was still a hoodlum. Because how else could he explain the money? He started up a community from what she knew and something like that wasn't cheap. No black person she knew had done anything of that magnitude because it wasn't easy. Things like that took capital and having degrees in business administration wasn't enough for all of that. Jaylah saw through the smoke and mirrors.

When the service was over Jaylah rushed out of the church and called back Brook from the MLN station as she headed briskly towards her car. Although Oshun was surely a wolf in sheep's clothing she wasn't ready to be back in his presence. Just seeing the sinfully handsome man made her nerves go haywire. Jaylah also found herself upset with him.

"Jaylah, I got those photos you sent of the inside of the service. They definitely look like the black mafia 2020 style. If you could snap more pictures of the family along with their cars, I would really appreciate that. The big leagues are where you belong. Keep up the good work," Brooke said excitedly.

Jaylah moved past the funeral goers in a rush as she walked towards her car.

"Glad you liked them," she said with no enthusiasm, thinking of the photo's she'd snapped the second she snuck into the funeral service.

"It is you! You came! Where is Diamond?" a jovial voice asked approaching Jaylah.

Jaylah's body froze in fear at the mention of her twin sisters' newborn daughter being brought up. Through social media, she knew that her twin was in Detroit and working as one of the higher-earning dancers, but she never thought that anyone would see her out and get them mixed up. Detroit was much larger than Baymoor Falls making the chance of someone seeing her out and getting her confused with her sister slim to none.

"Let me call you back, Brooke," she whispered in a haste and ended the call.

Jaylah turned and her eyes landed on a tall woman with cocoa brown skin and a round pretty face. She was dressed in the family's color of white and wearing her hair in long large knotless braids that touched her waist. She was beautiful and as she pulled Jaylah into a hug, she rubbed her back endearingly.

"You are not Jael, girl. You must be her twin," the woman said pulling back.

Jaylah smiled nervously while staring at the cocoa hued beauty that possessed pouty lips with almond-shaped brown eyes.

"I am. How exactly do you know—twin?"

Simply saying the word made Jaylah's stomach knot up. This was unfamiliar grounds and making her even more nervous because her real-life was on display.

The woman before her smiled showing all her pretty white teeth.

"We attended beauty school together last year. She graduated and I had to do another year," she revealed surprising the hell out of Jaylah.

Twin went back to school?

Jaylah shook off the thought of her twin bettering herself and she nodded feeling overwhelmed with everything that was happening.

"Oh, that's nice," she quipped.

The woman looked her over and held out her hand.

"My name is Stasia, but I go by Pinky. It's a childhood nickname," she explained.

Of course, it is. Like lil momma or baby girl.

Jaylah thought looking Pinky's way.

"Um, well it was nice meeting you," Jaylah said and when she went to walk away Pinky grabbed her arm. "Yes?" she asked looking at her with narrowed eyes.

Pinky shifted from one foot to the other.

"Last I heard your sister has a beauty bar in Southfield. I believe it's on nine mile and Southfield road or in that area. It's very popular and she's already in the works of opening another one. Word around town is that she's the next big thing in the beauty world. Twin is getting to that bag, okay. You should go by and see her. I remember from beauty school how she would reminisce about y'all younger years. She misses you a lot. That I know for a fact," Pinky said and let her arm go. "It's weird seeing you here but I am a firm believer in everything happening for a reason. You needed to hear that. Bye, good twin."

Pinky let Jaylah's arm go and gave her a gentle smile before walking off. Jaylah stood on the pavement lost in her thoughts.

"You did this, and I'll never forgive you for it. You know that right twin?" she asked hoarsely as she rested in bed.

Even after being given meds she was still sore. Her body was in an extreme amount of pain, but nothing trumped her shattered heart. She felt violated. Her sad eyes peered up at her sister that was hovering over her with tears in her eyes.

"Why are you sad?" Jaylah asked frowning.

Her twin shook her head. She looked runway ready in her Iceberg outfit with her side ponytail and pretty face. Life for her hadn't changed however for Jaylah she knew she would never be the same.

"I'm sad because your sad! I didn't mean for any of that to happen!" Jael cried.

Jaylah closed her eyes refusing to feel sad for her twin. It was because of her that she even went to the party. She was done with her.

For good.

"You're stupid. Your so fucking dumb, this is all your fault and I will never forgive you for this," she whispered coldly wanting her sister to feel the hate she now carried for her.

"Aye, just follow me!" someone yelled in a distance to a man and Jaylah realized that the family was piling into their cars, headed for the cemetery.

She went to her vehicle and slipped inside with her heart racing. She'd left Baymoor Falls praying the flashbacks would stop yet they were following her into a new city. Jaylah couldn't deal. Shit was heavy and having a drink was the only thing she felt would alleviate the pain. She sat back in the seat and her eyes ventured out of the window and over to Oshun.

His dark honey eyes were red-rimmed and as he looked at the men in front of him, she could almost feel his pain. The love he had for his brother was palpable and when he spoke of Malik at the service his words had been filled with a love that fell over the sanctuary. Jaylah couldn't believe the situation she was in. She rolled her eyes in irritation wishing she was back home.

Oshun was undoubtedly one of the most attractive men she'd ever encountered. Jaylah saw that even outside of Club

Luxure he was a looker. It wasn't her imagination. He was fine as sin with his tall, athletic frame and flawless umber tone skin, he'd decorated with tattoos. Her eyes zeroed in on his thick lips, the same ones to grace her sex and she shuddered.

She knew she needed to leave but her body was immobilized to her seat. Jaylah studied Oshun in his white two-piece tailored suit and she swallowed hard. Tattoos crept his neck and covered his hands. Those same strong hands that handled her body in a way like never before and she felt shame at what she was thinking. This wasn't the man for her.

No, Oshun was Malik's brother. A hustler, like she thought. In the end, he was exactly who she assumed he was, and a part of her felt bamboozled because in her mind she'd made him out to be a good black man. Shit maybe the last good black man she would know, and he'd failed her. Like all of the other black men that entered her life he ended up being a letdown.

Tap.

Tap.

Soft knocking at her window jarred Jaylah from her thoughts. She looked out of her window and there he was. Tall, muscular, and handsome as hell. Sorrow clung to his hooded eyes but not a tear fell. Instead, he looked well and in charge of everything much like he was back at the club. Jaylah swallowed hard and with shaky fingers lowered her window. She flashed Oshun a nervous smile as his eyes peered into her deeply.

His stare was brazen as he studied her inside of the car. He rubbed the soft curls on his burst fade and Jaylah swallowed hard. Oshun was serious and his presence like before was intense. He surely wasn't for the faint of heart. She couldn't see a shy woman being able to peer his way let alone look him in the eyes.

"Is hitting up funerals your thing or some shit, love?" he wanted to know and while the words were spoken in a charming way, they held a bite to them that she didn't miss.

He was serious.

Maybe even angry that she was there.

"Um. I—," she muttered and Oshun touched her shoulder. Jaylah's body went still as she watched his tattooed hand slide up and down her arm soothingly.

"Relax and speak from your heart. Now one more time and I need for you, Jaylah from Baymoor Falls that works at a news station with pussy sweeter than fruit to tell me just why you're here. How do you know my baby brother?" he asked looking her in the eyes.

Jaylah swallowed the huge lump that formed in her throat. She looked at Oshun and sighed.

Fuck it.

She would tell the truth.

Somewhat.

"I've seen everything that's going on with your brother, his story, and my heart went out to your mom. I had no clue that you was his brother until a day ago. I just wanted to come and pay my respects," she said nervously.

Her leg slowly shook as she waited for Oshun to respond.

His gaze was intent and had Jaylah damn near sweating bullets. He chewed on his bottom lip. His thick, soft, brown lips that Jaylah had admired from afar before he responded.

"You snuck into my brother's funeral to pay your respects. Is this for a story?"

Jaylah shook her head quickly.

"Of course not!"

Oshun didn't respond only stared at her and when Jaylah blinked tears filled her eyes. He already knew so much about her. She hated that he knew what her sex tasted like. She hated that he knew her background. This wasn't part of the plan and now she would be forced to go above and beyond to get what she needed for her job.

"Something's calling me to your brother and the injustice that was done to him," she said softly.

Oshun stood, placed his hands into his pants pocket and like the stalker she was, Jaylah checked out his dick print that was very noticeable.

She swallowed hard at the sight of the long, thick, muscle filling up his pants. Jaylah sat back in her seat with her pussy throbbing and was shocked when Oshun opened her car door. He leaned down and was eye level with her. His eyes closed briefly and when they opened, she saw love in his orbs for his brother that was so real it made her body shiver. He was in mourning and no matter how fine he was that didn't take away how much pain he was in. She could see and feel the grief pouring out of his large frame.

Her hand had a mind of its own when she touched his arm and offered a consoling smile.

"I'm so sorry. I really am," she whispered.

Oshun nodded. He looked her in the eyes and his gaze was unearthing her as she felt him peer at her in a way like no one had before. She felt vulnerable and fake.

Very fucking fake.

Something she'd never felt before.

Jaylah quickly removed her hand and placed it on her lap.

"You came down here to see the service and leave?" his deep voice asked.

His question was low, but she'd heard it, and when Jaylah nodded his nostrils flared.

Did I say something wrong? She wondered.

"Nah, you'll stick around for a few days. Didn't I tell you what would happen if I saw you again?"

Damn, there he was trying to place his spell back onto her. Jaylah knew that could work to her advantage, but she wasn't trying to give up pussy for a story. That had never been her style.

"Love, you being here is kind of fucking me up right now. I almost didn't recognize you with this wig on and shit, but it fits you. I support the switch up," he said as his right hand brushed the top of her left one. The shock made both of their eyes widen in surprise. Oshun smirked as she snatched her hand back. "What's there to think about? You're here and you're staying," he told her smoothly like it wasn't a demand, but Jaylah knew from his bedroom skills that coming from him it was.

"I need to go be with my people but before I do that. What's your number? I wanna see you tonight."

Jaylah wet her lips and when Oshun pulled out his phone she rattled off her number while staring at him. The draw to Oshun was strong and she hated that the first spark of real interest she had in a man came from a black one.

"I know that the club connected us but one and done is what we agreed to. You don't call the shots for me Oshun. I don't mind staying. I could see about the BOC and get a first-hand look at what your brother was about. However, it will be on my terms," she felt the need to tell him while praying her boldness didn't make him shut her out.

Oshun smirked and leaned into her car. The heat from his body made Jaylah's nipples harden against her black lace bra. She closed her eyes and inhaled a deep breath as he whispered in her ear.

"You'll see sooner than later that when in the presence of a king, you willingly submit. See you in a couple of hours, sweetheart," he said and kissed her cheek.

Oshun stood and closed her car door. Jaylah held her breath until he was halfway across the street headed back to his family. When she exhaled, she felt the small goosebumps prickle her skin.

Oshun David Lacoste.

Just how the fuck was she going to get the truth up out of him now? She wondered. Her head shook and she pulled away not sure what her next move would be. She was like a chicken with its head cut off. She had no clear direction of where to go from there.

CHAPTER 6

Omelly: Jaylah Imani Cole. Age 30. Birthday May 15, Mother Lisa Ann Cole. Father Jayson Cole. (Street name Clay) Parents are still married. Twin sister Jael Iyanna Cole. Jaylah works for HLN20 in Baymoor Falls. Bachelor's degree in broadcast journalism.

Oshun bit down hard onto his bottom lip while reading over the message. He clicked on the link and was blessed with a more extensive background check. Jaylah was clean. She'd never been to prison. Was smart as shit only her presence didn't make sense.

Oshun loved pussy. Craved it day and night but was never blinded by it. He was smart enough to know something was up. To run into Jaylah in Baymoor Falls was fate but to see her at his brother's home going service wasn't coincidental. It also didn't help that she was a news reporter.

Before he could put his phone away his cousins' friend Omelly hit his line.

"What's good with you?" he answered semi-faded, he'd been smoking since he left Malik's repass.

"Aye, she works for this fat motherfucka named Jerry Hegler. He's in the same fraternity as Officer Polk. Shit looks fishy as fuck," Omelly replied.

Oshun sat up on the freshly plotted dirt and his brows knitted together. He now saw why his people trusted Omelly to handle their paperwork. He was smart and quick with his shit. The niggas turnaround time was like thirty fucking minutes.

"Is that right?" he asked feeling his body coil with anger.

"Yeah and that fat nigga been online saying slick ass shit too. Not enough to get called out for it but I know a racist joke when I see one. I wouldn't trust her," Omelly advised. "Send her ass back where she came from," he told him.

Oshun smirked. He could do that, but then he wouldn't know just why she was there. Plus, there was something intriguing by the fair-skinned beauty with the pretty lips and slanted eyes.

"Thanks for looking out. I got it from here and keep this between us. I don't want the fam to worry," he replied.

Omelly coughed into the phone before agreeing.

"Enough said," he replied and ended the call.

Oshun went to Jaylah's name and sent her a text as the wheels in his head started to spin.

Send me your room number, love.

He put his phone away certain that she would, and soft hands rubbed up and down his pants leg. His hooded dark honey eyes drifted over to Latoya as she sipped her own bottle of brown liquor. She'd been his friend when they were kids. His first fuck as a teenager and now she was back to being the homie that was sometimes more than a friend when the liquor hit strong.

"You good?" she asked in her light syrupy voice.

Oshun shook his head. He would never be okay again.

"That was nothing," he said with his eyes inspecting her closely.

Latoya was the type of woman that never looked bad. Oshun was certain that at any moment of the day she was decked out in makeup wearing nothing but the best while wearing a smile. She was tall with a thickness to her that men could appreciate. Her hair was cut into a blunt bob while her round face was decorated with thick lips, doe shaped dark brown eyes, and a straight nose. Latoya liked diamonds and was always rocking some even in her small nose and pointy ears. She was gorgeous and he knew that one day she'd be a great wife to some man.

"I need to be up in a minute," he said feeling his phone vibrate in his pocket.

"I do too, Tamara blowing me the fuck up but let's finish this bottle first," Gio said with a crestfallen look on his face.

"Yes, let's do that," Latoya agreed once again placing the bottle of brown liquor to her lips.

"Remember when we went to the Virgin Islands? Malik was scared as fuck to jump off the yacht and go swimming. His silly ass almost drowned," Gio said and shook his head at the memory.

Latoya blessed them with a light giggle as Oshun thought back on the moment. He took a long swig from his drink as his eyes drifted down to the ground.

"I had to jump in and save him," he added lowly.

Latoya leaned her head onto his shoulder and Gio grabbed her hand. The threesome sat in silence at the cemetery thinking of Malik.

"He was smart," Latoya whispered holding onto Oshun's arm tightly.

Gio smirked as he held in his tears.

"He was stubborn as fuck," he co-signed.

Oshun and Latoya laughed.

"He's gone," Oshun couldn't help but say, and when his pain felt like it would spill from his dark honey-hued eyes, he clamped them shut.

"He's with us right now. I can feel his amazing presence. We love you, Malik, forever and always," Latoya said softly.

"Rest up, young king," Oshun said and swallowed the lump that was in his throat.

Everyone stood and collected their liquor bottles. Once the sun had settled and the repast was over, they'd retreated to the grave. The cemetery was closed but with money came power and there they were. For hours Oshun sat with his people thinking of his youngest brother. It felt odd with him not being around. Already his presence was missed.

"Gio I'm driving because you are fucked up. Oshun are you going home?" Latoya asked.

Her question was light, and her eyes weren't even on him still he felt the intent. She wanted to clock his moves and he was never with that shit.

"Not right now, ma but you are. Come here," he said turning to her.

Latoya let go of Gio's arm and quickly went to Oshun. She hugged him tightly while pressing her face into his dress shirt.

"I want this to be a bad dream," she whispered sadly.

Malik was like her baby. Latoya quickly found a liking for the young man and whatever he needed from her she obliged. She was his unofficial big sister and her heart ached the same as Oshun and Gio at the loss of him.

"I've known him since he was a kid. I don't want to wake up and not see him, you know? I don't want to prepare for his baby and not have him here. It isn't fair. He should be here with us," she cried.

Oshun swallowed hard. Hearing the pain in Latoya's voice was gutting him.

"I feel the same way, ma. This shit cut deep. Y'all head in and I'll fuck with you tomorrow," he told her.

Oshun placed a kiss to Latoya's forehead and when he went to pull away, she held him tighter.

"Or—"

"Or nothing. Go get some rest, beautiful," he responded and let her go.

Oshun made sure Latoya and Gio were safely in Gio's truck before going over to his white Urus. He slipped inside and checked his messages.

Cute ass Jaylah: I thought we agreed that I was in control. I'm at the De'Loines hotel, room 435.

Oshun smirked and started up his truck. He rode in silence to the hotel and when he was at the front door, he sent Jaylah a text.

Come down, I'm in the white truck love.

Oshun then sat back and commenced to rolling up another blunt. He usually wasn't so careless but at the moment he didn't give a damn. He wanted a cop to stop him and give him a reason to go ape shit on their ass. If they knew what was best, they would let him mourn in peace.

"I've never been inside of one of these before," Jaylah purred pulling the door open.

Oshun sealed his thick blunt and his eyes gazed over at the woman occupying a small amount of space in his mind. Like before she was outlandishly beautiful. That was not up for debate. Jaylah was bad as fuck. From her pretty little head that housed jet black long hair to her small toes that were painted white at the time. She wasn't as thick as he liked his women to be, but she had a slim thick body that was very alluring.

She had it looks wise now he wanted to see what her mental was like. Was she there to play him or was she really on some love for Malik shit? He didn't know but something in Oshun was telling him that the woman who pussy that tasted sweeter than fruit was on some bullshit.

He was a good judge of character and off bat he could tell that Jaylah wasn't what she claimed to be.

"Then I'm glad to be your first," he said smoothly, and she blushed.

Her skin was so light that he could see the green veins in her neck and on her hands. For the night she wore skinny jeans with a black spaghetti strap cami and six-inch black pumps. She was the kind of woman that didn't need to do it over the top, but her wig had thrown him for a loop. It was sexy on her giving off some Onika Maraj vibes, but he didn't feel like it was Jaylah's style.

"You smell good as shit. What are you wearing, sweet-heart?" he found himself asking as he lit his blunt.

Jaylah's pretty eyes stared at his hands, his blunt then the bulge in his slacks. Oshun smirked as he watched her assess the fuck out of his looks.

"Did I pass?" he asked.

Jaylah frowned as she put on her seat belt.

"Pass what?" she asked avoiding eye contact with him.

Oshun sat up and took a strong hit of his weed. He allowed for the gorilla strain to sit in his lungs before expelling it through his nose. His right hand went to her soft thigh as he licked his lips.

"When you talk to me, please look me in the eyes love. At all times I want to see that pretty ass face. And I asked you two things. What are you wearing, and do I look good enough for you? I saw you staring at me and shit," he told her.

Jaylah's skin flushed once more, and she nibbled nervously on her bottom lip. Oshun struggled to keep his monster at bay as he pulled away from the hotel. Jaylah didn't respond and he chose to let it slide. She didn't know any better and if he decided to keep her around, she eventually would.

"Where are we going?" she finally asked as he pulled onto the freeway.

"To this spot called The Hive."

Oshun turned on the radio for Jaylah and smoked his blunt

while heading to his jazz club. One of his first loves was music. He'd wanted to go into the industry but had chosen the BOC instead. When he'd told Malik that family came first, he meant that shit. He'd always put his family's wants in front of his own.

He loved jazz and even played the guitar. Not many people knew that about him besides his mom and Gio. For Oshun music was one of his escapes from the harsh world that he was living in. As he turned into the blue light district in downtown Detroit an area known for its live band bars, he lowered the volume in his truck.

"Jaylah, I need to rap with you about something very serious, love," he said pulling into his designated parking spot at The Hive.

Oshun relaxed in his seat and turned to Jaylah. She looked at him with a neutral look on her pretty face but in the crescent of her eyes, he could see nervousness brewing in them.

Good.

He wanted her to know and feel how serious he was about his family. Oshun sat up and opened his glove box. He pulled his wallet from the glove compartment and placed it on his lap as Jaylah's leg began to bounce. Her nervousness grew more intense as he followed her line of sight and he was able to see why.

His FN pistol sat in the glove box on a stack of papers. Oshun quickly shut the compartment and looked at her.

"Jaylah, I think you're very beautiful. I think your smart

and I think you are on your way to your destiny. Just from checking out your background, I can see you are a driven woman and I like that shit. I love smart women. To me, that trumps everything else because there is nothing I can do with a stupid pretty bitch. You're none of those two things, however," he said taking his time with saying how he felt.

Oshun scratched his beard as Jaylah shifted in her seat. His dark honey eyes slid down her legs in appreciation then up to her stunning face. He really didn't want the beauty to be on any shady shit, but all signs were pointing to yes.

"I love my family, Jaylah. That's a feeling you might not relate to because I remember you saying you wasn't fucking with yours anymore, well your pops at least, but I'm different. For my blood, I'll give my life. Throw it all away to keep them safe. So, when a beautiful ass chick from up north pops up like shit sweet it makes me wonder if this will be the moment, I have to place my freedom on the line," he told her.

Jaylah inhaled a sharp breath then shook her head. Her eyes wandered over to where she knew the gun was and she cleared her throat.

"I would never do anything to harm you or your family. I see this was a mistake coming here. I'm leaving tonight and you will never see me again," she promised quickly.

The little color Jaylah had drained from her face. Oshun had never killed anyone, but Jaylah didn't know that. He wasn't even threatening her life. However, he wanted her to know that severe things would happen to her pretty little ass if she brought bullshit to his front door.

"No need for all of that. I'm just letting you know, that I know who you are, and as long as you one hundred with me all is well. Let's be up," he said and exited his truck.

Oshun met Jaylah on the other side of the Urus and his hand went to the small of her back. She shivered before placing some space in between them.

"Relax, beautiful. The last thing I want to do is harm you," he whispered leaning down while making sure to press himself into her.

Oshun led Jaylah into the building that had a rustic look on the exterior and a vintage, House of Blues vibe on the interior. The stage was small but large enough for a full band. Round tables with two chairs filled the center of the building with a bar that took up the entire right side of the wall.

"What's good King?" the bouncer, a tall, brawny bald man asked dapping up Oshun.

Bruce. He was cool and good people.

"I'm good. Did everything get worked out with your problem?" he asked looking at him.

Bruce nodded and dapped him up again. Recently his home had been hit with a plumbing disaster and his insurance didn't cover the damages. Oshun laced him with a check that would get him straight.

"Aye, man look even while in mourning you was there for

me. I'll forever owe you because of that," Bruce said appreciatively.

Oshun shook his head as he kept Jaylah close to his side.

"I don't do it for that. Just whenever you can, pay it forward and be a blessing to the next man. Did she come on yet?" he asked referring to his homeboy's wife that had chosen to sing his favorite Nina Simone song just for him.

"Nah, they been waiting for you. Draco had everybody drop off their phones and shit at the door. You know that man loco," Bruce laughed.

Oshun chuckled. Draco was the Diddy of his generation. He owned a successful music company. His youngest brother Draye was a popular rapper and Oshun had known him for years.

"I see him," Oshun said and led Jaylah over to a round table that was near the front of the stage. He watched his friend Draco stand and his eyes shifted to a nervous Jaylah. "This Jaylah, my new friend," he told him.

Draco smirked as he peered down at her.

"Nice to meet you. How do you deal with this pushy ass nigga?" Draco asked smiling.

Oshun chuckled as he watched Jaylah visibly relax. Her pretty ass timid eyes shot up to him briefly before she shrugged.

"I don't. I keep telling him that I am the one in control," she replied.

Oshun pulled out Jaylah's chair and as she went to sit

down his eyes admired her round ass. Jaylah was stunning and he hoped for her sake, not on no bullshit.

"The man is supposed to lead. Don't let this Miss Independent shit fool you. Men and women both have a purpose together and whoever is by my side will know that only one of us can wear the pants," he said before dapping up Draco.

Draco smirked and when he looked at him his face fell into a frown. Oshun watched Draco's eyes grow sad and he shook his head. He didn't want that, and Malik didn't either.

"I'm good homie," he told him before taking his seat.

Oshun relaxed his big frame in his seat and pulled Jaylah's chair closer to him. His hand caressed her back then her thigh as he looked at his boy.

"I appreciate you and the wifey popping up on me like this. That's love for real."

Draco had not only attended the funeral but hopped on a jet to handle business in New York then come right back so his wife Hill could sing for Oshun.

Draco smirked at him as he lit up a blunt. In Oshun's club, you could indulge without having to worry about people complaining.

"You know how Hill is about your ass. She's gone stay so she can have lunch with Latoya tomorrow too," Draco explained.

Oshun smirked. Slick ass Latoya. She'd known all along where he was going and was probably in her feelings about not being invited.

"Is that right?" he asked lowly.

Draco looked at him and smirked.

"I'm just the messenger," he replied smiling.

Oshun turned to Jaylah as she text on her phone. His head dipped and he read over her message to someone named Kylie as the waitress brought over his favorite drink and appetizers.

"Who that?" he whispered.

Jaylah shivered. She put her phone away without replying.

"My best friend," she said softly.

Oshun nodded. He poured Jaylah a glass of brown liquor hoping to relax her some as Draco lit his blunt.

"You see the cops just hit a father of three in Cali with five bullets the other day. Said he was wanted for breaking into a gas station. Now he's gone and his family is mad as fuck. He was only twenty-five," Draco said.

Oshun shook his head. Being black in America wasn't safe. People of color didn't have the privilege of living a life without the worry of what the cops would do to them.

"Damn," he muttered not being able to think of anything but Malik. "Shoot me their name, I'll pay for the funeral."

Draco blew smoke from his mouth while shaking his head.

"Draye already handled it. Every time I hear some shit like that it makes me think of him and Malik. They took your brother and at any minute they could take mine. That wouldn't be smart for them though," Draco added and Oshun believed him.

Draco lived a life that wasn't legal before turning a new leaf and going legit. He was missing marbles and if anything were to happen to his brothers, Oshun was positive he would make the police pay in blood. Even with money, he was a hood nigga. He didn't fuck with the laws. He handled shit the street way.

"I feel you but it's not always that simple. Especially when you got a lot on the line," Oshun explained not wanting to say too much in front of Jaylah.

Draco looked at him.

"I wasn't trying to be funny. You know I would never do no shit like that. You are your own man and however, you handle this I support it. The right or the wrong way, I'm with the shits. You know a nigga like me run towards the smoke," Draco clarified.

"Oh, nigga I know," Oshun mumbled thinking of all of the times he witnessed Draco act a fool. It had been too many times to name.

Oshun sat back and drunk some of his liquor. His eyes ventured over to Jaylah and he cleared his throat. She was so quiet, and he wanted to hear her beautiful voice.

"How do you feel about the way cops handle black people? I see your news station rarely reports on that type of shit."

Jaylah's eyes widened and she quickly regained her

composure. She sat up straight with her hands on her lap. She looked so stuffy, almost out of place inside of the bar.

"I feel like when the cops stop you, you need to listen to them and all will be well," she said carefully and flashed Oshun a nervous ass smile.

Draco's face fell into a frown as Oshun peered deeply at Jaylah, getting a glimpse of who she really was. Her response was flawed as fuck and he couldn't stop himself from being turned off by her reply.

"Is that right?" he asked cocking his head to the side.

Jaylah's stance never changed and although she was saying something that was ignorant as hell, he appreciated her for not backing down.

He was a firm believer in standing by your word.

"Yes, Oshun. If the cops stop me then I'm going to adhere to what they're saying. I'm not going to argue with them and dismiss the fact that they are law enforcement. They have their badge for a reason. Protect and serve," she said with narrowed eyes.

The little hardness his dick was holding onto while sitting beside Jaylah deflated at her words. Draco chuckled lowly as Oshun peered at her with his jaw tightening. *Was she really that blind to the ugliness of the world*, he wondered.

"So, when the cops stop you for no reason other than the fact that you're being black you should still do as they say? Because doing anything else will justify in them killing you, right?" he found himself asking her.

Jaylah's brows pinched together as she looked at him.

"Do as they say and if you know its harassment get a lawyer and file a complaint. I don't see what the issue is," she replied.

"My, my, my. I need to go take this call," Draco said standing.

He walked away holding his blunt, phone, and drink as Oshun chewed on his bottom lip. If Jaylah was for the police then why the fuck was, she in Detroit at his brother's funeral?

"So, my brother deserved to be killed because he didn't immediately follow the commands that was given to him?" he asked sitting up.

Jaylah's skin flushed. She quickly shook her head, but he didn't believe her ass.

Fuck no, he didn't.

Oshun brushed a hand over his hair as he smiled. He needed to be rid of Jaylah before he said something that would hurt her pretty little feelings.

"Aye, this is a mistake. I'm all for a good debate but today is not the day for that shit. I just buried my youngest brother all because he was reaching for his inhaler and the last thing, I want to do is sit by somebody that feels like he brought that upon himself. It was nice knowing you, love," he told her and went back to his drink.

Jaylah gasped and when she tried to grab his arm he jerked away. His jaw tensed and his eyes narrowed.

"I'm trying to keep it respectful sweetheart but you

pushing a nigga. Have a safe ride back to Baymoor Falls," he told her.

Oshun ignored her presence as she took her time standing. As she walked away to leave, his mind couldn't stop replaying the shit she'd said. She was right winged as fuck even if she didn't know it and that wasn't a good look for him. He was lowkey pissed he'd even tasted her pussy because no bitch that believed the law had a right to kill a man because of color should know what head from him felt like.

"Gots to do better," he mumbled before finishing his drink.

CHAPTER 7

"I'm confused. I thought you were there to find out the real tea behind his family being drug dealers. Why does it matter if he's upset with you or not? I need you to get what you need from those people and leave Jaylah. Weeks have gone by and I miss you," Kylie whined.

Jaylah stared at her twin on the laptop screen with her heart pumping wildly. For the last three weeks, she'd been trying to bounce back from Oshun's dismissal of her. He refused to answer her text or calls, and she was at a loss on what to do. The days were drifting away while she sat with nothing to take back to Brooke. Jaylah was ready to call it quits until she checked the BOC's social media page. A flyer alerting every one of the neighborhood cleanup day was at the top of the page and she was grateful. She had one last chance to make a better impression and get what she needed on Oshun and his family. She was anxious to get the story over with and return home. The last talk she had with Oshun wouldn't leave her mind. His conversation sparked an interest in her to seek out the full truth.

Because of Oshun and Charise, Jaylah found herself googling images, reading up on topics, and seeing gruesome videos. She'd placed herself in a huge bubble since college. A bubble that was damn near impenetrable making only her life issues important and now she felt bad because she couldn't decipher the real from the fake.

She was even sad to read up on Malik. He'd done so many things in his young life and from everything she saw he appeared to be a regular young man trying to find his way. Even the other countless minorities that she read about being gunned down by the cops were good people. To read up on case after case of police shootings towards people of color made her uneasy. Downright sick to her stomach.

She couldn't help but wonder when her blinders were placed on her face to the ways of the world?

"Is not about that Kylie. I need him to trust me for me to be able to get close to him. That won't happen if he believes that I'm not on his side. I'm exhausted from all of this," she admitted.

Jaylah scrolled over her twin's social media page and when she saw that her twin had close to 500,000 follower's she clicked off the screen.

Jael had come along way and while she was happy for her

twin her anger didn't allow for her to miss the other half of her. Jael was toxic and foolish. Her attack was proof of that.

"I'm still confused on why he got mad in the first place. It didn't sound like you said anything wrong to me. Those people are bringing pain and strife onto themselves. I'm so over the narrative that slavery is holding us back. That's a crock of shit and an excuse to be lazy. I'm not on welfare using a bridge card because of slavery so they shouldn't use that excuse either," Kylie snapped.

Jaylah sat up on the bed with her face scrunching up.

"But you were born into money Kylie. Your advantage to making it in this world is different from a lot of people's," she told her.

Kylie was silent for a few minutes before snorting.

"I never thought you would try to use my wealth against me. What does that have to do with anything, Jaylah? Poor people make something out of themselves every day. Look at Jesse. He was homeless for half of his youth," she said speaking of her NFL player husband.

Jaylah rolled her eyes becoming frustrated with the conversation. Kylie didn't get it and it made her think of herself.

Had she sounded as crazy as Kylie did?

She wondered.

"Then he was adopted Kylie by a family that owns a chain of grocery stores. It costs money for sports. I was looking online last night and most of the kids in the inner city aren't able to do programs such as football and softball because of money. I guess coming from the Northside then moving to the Southside, I still hadn't grown up there so I didn't know how bad it could be for someone with low income. I can now see that people born into poverty are at a disadvantage in life. My views have been jaded by ignorance. My mom had a way of making it, where we still had a few things from our good life so I had no clue how bad it could really get. Looking back now even while being in the projects we were blessed."

"Yeah and then you had an incident that forever changed your life, right? Those same people that your trying to take up for, freaking raped you!" Kylie snapped aggressively, and her words jarred Jaylah into a vivid flashback.

The walk home wasn't far. After leaving the library Jaylah was tired. She missed her daddy and refused to take his call. Speaking to him made her depressed so she pretended that he was away on a business trip. That was the only way she could cope with not having her hero around.

"Aye, good twin! Come 'ere!"

Jaylah stopped walking down Fourth St. and turned to her left. Leaning against the cracked-up stairs that led to an abandoned home was Greedo. He wore all black with his Girbaud hoodie over his head still his masculine beauty shined. Unlike the boys surrounding him, he wore designer threads with high top black Air Force One sneakers.

As Jaylah advanced on the young hustler she smelled his cologne and sighed.

"My daddy wears that cologne," she said softly.

Greedo grabbed her hand and pulled her close. Jaylah ignored the glare from his friend Wooh who had been the guy to speak to her rudely. Wooh carried a disposition to him that was uninviting, and Jaylah didn't want to be anywhere near him.

"Its Issey Miyake, ma," Greedo said and flashed Jaylah a smile that made butterflies fill her small belly.

Jaylah blushed and Greedo licked his lips. His hands went to her waist as Wooh sucked his teeth.

"Nigga we need to be running down on the boys that took our shit. Fuck chilling," Wooh snapped.

Greedo's eyes narrowed and he gently pushed Jaylah to the side. He walked up on Wooh and stepped into his personal space.

"You the one that let them take your stuff. So, if anything you need to be running down on them. Don't ever in your fucking life tell me what the fuck I need to be doing. Fuck wrong with you," he growled and finished his words with a thump to Woo's peanut head.

Wooh recoiled and backed up while staring at Jaylah. She lowered her head not wanting to be on the receiving end of his anger.

"I got you, my bad," Wooh said and turned to walk away.

"You need to watch that nigga. He buggin," one of Greedo's friends told him.

Greedo walked over to Jaylah and grabbed her hand. He pulled her close while shaking his head.

"Nah, he in his feelings because the prettiest girl in Baymoor Falls is going to be my future wife. That's all the fuck that is. I'll be back," Greedo said and pulled Jaylah away.

Slowly they walked down Fourth St. as Jaylah held his hand tightly. She ignored the stares of the older girls that looked at them with screwed up faces.

"If that nigga ever says something to you let me know. Your beauty really got that nigga in his feelings," Greedo said before shaking his head.

Jaylah nodded. Being on the Southside still felt odd. She missed the calmness that came from being on the Northside. The streets were serene like while the Southside wreaked of havoc. Every other day it was some kind of drama and Jaylah was counting down the days for her to be out of the ghetto.

"Yeah, I guess," she replied nervously.

Greedo walked Jaylah to her projects and into the building. They quietly stepped onto the elevator still holding hands.

"Jaylah you wanna come out with me for my birthday?"

Jaylah's surprised eyes shot up to Greedo and she slowly nodded. Yes, he lived a dangerous life, but his presence gave Jaylah comfort. He spoke to her nicely. Made her feel good and most importantly he made her smile the same way her father used to do to her mom.

"I guess," she agreed and Greedo chuckled.

"Swear you the only female to curve me in the sexiest way," he smiled.

Greedo walked Jaylah to her apartment door. Jaylah quickly unlocked the door and turned to him. Greedo stared down at her with an intensity that she could feel.

"I like you. Don't ever let nobody make you feel like it's a bad thing to be smart," he said.

Jaylah took a step towards him and grabbed onto his long black hoodie.

"Okay."

Greedo dipped his head and kissed her forehead.

"It's some gang shit popping off later tonight. Stay indoors and make sure to tell your bad twin that. Goodnight Jaylah," he kissed her forehead again and he was gone.

"You want to fuck Greedo," her twin sang walking up behind her.

"Jaylah are you there! What the hell!" Kylie yelled.

Jaylah took deep breaths while her chest heaved up and down. Her sad eyes shot to the wall in front of her as she regained her composure.

She was losing her damn mind.

"Kylie, don't you ever in your fucking life bring that up again. I never told you that, so that it could be used against me."

Kylie gasped.

"I would never! I'm simply trying to remind you of how

brutal those people can be. You're making me out to be the bad guy. I thought we were on the same side. You need to stay offline. You're reading all of this pro-black shit and it's changing you. That's what that movement does you know. It brainwashes black people. That's why my dad never told us about that slavery stuff. He didn't want us walking around like we were victimized. I'm going to need you to come home, like now because I need the old Jaylah back. You didn't give a shit about those dusty ass people and their issues," Kylie said humorously.

Jaylah was insulted by Kylie's words. She'd always been smart. Had excelled at everything she ever did in life. The last thing she planned on doing was acting blind to the things she now knew.

Now that she was aware of what was happening, she couldn't stop thinking about it. It made cases like Malik's and so many others real. She saw the inhumane way they were treated, and it was something to be said about that. She was on the news. A place that was supposed to report what was happening in the world and for so long she had no fucking clue to the things happening to her people.

Her people.

Wow, she was changing.

"Kylie, I'm a college-educated woman. The last thing I'm going to do is not think for myself. I'm seriously starting to question if being here is the right thing for me now. I mean the things I saw and the stories I read are horrifying. Aren't you worried that something like that could happen to your son?" she asked.

Kylie sighed.

"And on that note, I'm going to end this call. My son is a good kid. He won't ever be in a position for the cops to harm him. He wouldn't be on their radar anyway. He knows right from wrong and he's only four. There are grown-ass black men that don't know how to take simple directions. You can allow for the media to make you think black people are being mistreated and then you can watch all of your blessings walk away. You and I both know no one wants to be around a *woke* black woman. We're all living our lives and being happy. Speaking on things like racism and police being unfair is just not my kind of party. Enjoy the rest of your day Jaylah," Kylie replied and ended the call.

Jaylah sat her phone down and checked the time on the clock by her bed. She had two hours to get ready before she was thrust back into a world that she was fearful might swallow her up.

After taking a relaxing bath while making sure to use her Sereneglobutter products she listened to the bible. It was something Jaylah hadn't done in months and instantly it made her feel better. Her past and her present were somehow colliding, and Jaylah wanted clarity. For so long she'd been green to the hatred consuming so many people in the world. She'd chosen to ignore the racism, conform to what the world wanted her to be and now she was angry at that.

Charise's words made sense. In some ways, she was a sell-out, but it hadn't been on purpose. Jaylah had no one. She'd hustled hard to get to where she was and had simply put herself first. But in the process of doing that she'd shun the black community. That anger towards black people started with her dad and was heightened after her attack. She saw all black men to be cruel and in many ways wasn't different from a racist person. She'd grouped all black people together as ruined people because of the unjust acts of a few black people.

Jaylah was confused, tired, and anxious. A strange mixture of emotions to feel and as she pulled her car into the BOC her eyes ventured over to the sign that was on the corner.

Welcome to a Black Owned Community

Jaylah snapped a photo of the sign with her Nikon camera and turned down the street. She parked in the first available spot she saw on the residential block. After putting her camera away and applying a coat of lip gloss from the brand Too Much Gloss she looked at herself in the mirror. If she said she hadn't been getting dressed with Oshun in mind, then she would have been lying.

Jaylah knew it was a great chance that he would send her away, so she wanted to make it hard for him to do so. She wore a royal blue Off White & Nike workout set with black sneakers and her Nike pouch around her waist. Her face was void of makeup outside of the one layer of face powder that she wore. Jaylah didn't know what to do. She could continue with the ploy and try to find something out that she wasn't sure was even there or she could call it quits and potentially lose her job from not doing so.

"God, what should I do?" she asked feeling closer to the Lord after listening to the word earlier and praying.

Jaylah found the strength to exit her car and her eyes bounced around the BOC. The houses were freshly painted two-story homes with manicured lawns and flower gardens. Kids played up and down the street on their bikes and scooters while young teenagers cleaned up the streets while holding trash bags and laughing.

Jaylah had never seen anything like it. Not even in the suburbs. Everyone was like a family. It was truly a sight to see.

"Hi! I love your fit girly. I wish I could find that in my size but the way this ass is set up," the pretty brown-skinned woman said walking over to Jaylah.

Jaylah looked at the brown beauty and smiled. The woman wore ripped jeans that hugged her thick legs with a white cami and designer slides. The woman's blunt cut bob was styled in loose curls while she wore a natural beat to her face. She was stunning and Jaylah was lowkey pissed she hadn't done more of an extravagant look for the day.

"Forget this outfit, you have me wishing I put on some real clothes," Jaylah laughed lightly.

The woman smiled as she advanced on her bringing with her a sweet floral scent.

"Hey, I'm Latoya, welcome to the BOC. Are you a new resident?" she asked.

Jaylah shook her head as she held out her hand.

"No, and I'm Jaylah. Malik's story brought me here," she explained.

Latoya's eyes saddened as she maintained her smile. She pulled Jaylah into a quick embrace and let her go.

"Girl we're family around here, so we hug. I can show you around," Latoya offered.

Jaylah nodded, discreetly looking around for Oshun.

"Sure!"

Well, this was the first block that the Lacoste's purchased. The homes back then were falling apart and abandoned. The brothers actually grew up in this home right here. It's now used for the neighborhood watch meetings along with other things," Latoya explained stopping in front of a two-story home that was white with red trimming. The home was beautiful with new windows and doors.

A peace blanketed the community and Jaylah wondered how nice life would have been if when she left the Northside, she'd been able to move somewhere like the BOC.

"This is amazing. I've never seen anything like it," she said truthfully.

Latoya smiled with pride.

"I know. It's unreal to see all that the family has done for this place. No gangs, no drug dealers, no loitering. This is like a fake town or something," she laughed.

Jaylah laughed in agreement with her. The block was something you would see out of a movie.

"Latoya let me see your keys so I can grab some more trash bags?"

A handsome man asked walking over. Jaylah looked at the stranger and automatically knew he was Oshun's brother Gio. While he was darker than Oshun and sported a bald head, he was still good looking. He wore black jeans with a white Billionaire Boys t-shirt. His eyes like Latoya's held a sadness to them that Jaylah knew Malik's death caused.

"Yep, here you go and don't forget what King said, no liquor today," Latoya said passing Oshun's brother her fob.

Oshun's brother frowned as he took the fob. His eyes briefly shot to Jaylah before going back over to Latoya.

"I'ma grown-ass man. I don't need you or Oshun clocking my moves."

Latoya placed her hand on her hip and smiled.

"Boy, I'm not trying to clock shit that's for your girl Tamara to do. Where is Oshun at anyway?" she asked.

Oshun's brother looked back to Jaylah once more as he responded.

"He at Willie's store playing chess, again. And I just remembered Ms. Rebecka is looking for you. Who this?" he asked.

Latoya peered over at Jaylah and smiled.

"This is the beautiful Jaylah. She heard about Malik's story and wanted to come check out the BOC," she replied.

Jaylah waved shyly and Oshun's brother smirked. He took a step towards her and Latoya punched his arm.

"Nigga you are *very* taken! Jaylah it was nice to meet you, I have to handle some things, so I got to go. Enjoy the BOC," Latoya said and pulled Oshun's grinning brother away with her.

Once Latoya was gone Jaylah wandered down the block and stopped when she came across the woman from the funeral that had her confused with her twin. The woman Pinky was wearing leggings like her with a sports bra and her braids pulled into a bun. She smiled wide and gave Jaylah a hug before squatting back down to plant the flowers.

They were in front of a two-story home that was being repainted.

"This is my granny's place. Wanna help?" Pinky asked.

Jaylah nodded. Not minding. She sat on the mat beside Pinky on the grass and watched her plant a few flowers before doing so herself.

"It's really good to see you again. I saw your sister at the bar the other day and I told her I ran into you," Pinky said breaking the silence.

Jaylah stopped planting the flower and peered over at Pinky. She was irritated that Pinky would do such a thing but also low key eager to see how her twin responded to the news that she was in town.

"And what did she say?" she asked.

Pinky grabbed another flower to plant while smiling.

"She didn't say anything. She grabbed her drink and walked away. I could tell she was surprised by it though. She's doing good too. When we were leaving, she hopped into a new G-Wagon. I remember in school she would always show me pictures of it on her phone's vision board. I'm glad to see her blessings are raining down on her," Pinky replied. "And that baby of hers is gorgeous with those grey eyes! My God!" she gushed.

Jaylah smiled but it was now awkward as fuck. There she was sitting beside a stranger that knew more about her twin than she did.

That stung.

Slowly she cleaned off her hands and rose to her feet.

"It was good seeing you, Pinky," she said ready to be away from the friendly lady that didn't know how to mind her own damn business.

Pinky stood and looked at her with furrowed brows.

"My momma always says I do too much, but I felt the need to tell her about you. I hope you're not mad about that. I promise I only did that with good intentions. My boutique is opening back up next weekend. You should come out it would be fun."

Jaylah looked at the pretty woman and sighed. Pinky was doing the most by talking to her twin, but she was sweet, and Jaylah didn't get any bad vibes from her.

"Sure, if I'm here I will definitely stop by. As I'm sure my twin told you I'm from up north."

Pinky nodded pulling out her phone from her bra.

"Yep and I think it's beautiful up there! Put your number in and I'll send you the invite," Pinky replied.

Jaylah grabbed her phone as Pinky's hand went to her hip.

"God is really showing favor on me today. How are you doing, king?" she asked smiling.

Jaylah's hand started to shake as she put her number in Pinky's phone. She smelled his cologne and felt his presence demanding her attention as she passed Pinky back her white device.

"Just chilling Pinky. Trying to keep things on track. Is everything good to go with the boutique?" he asked.

His voice seemed deeper and the rumble of it made Jaylah's nipples harden. She discreetly rubbed the pebble of them away with her arm while shifting from one foot to the other. Pinky looked at her strangely before smiling Oshun's way.

"It is and thank you again for the help. I don't know what we would do without you. Swear you need to run for mayor or some shit," she smiled, and the sultriness of her tone wasn't lost on Jaylah.

Oshun chuckled as his hand went to the small of Jaylah's back. His touch made her shiver.

"Nah, my only goal is to look out for my people. Politics is a corrupt game that I don't want to be a part of," he replied.

"Yeah, I feel you. You know Jaylah?" Pinky asked finally looking back to Jaylah.

Oshun's fingers pressed into Jaylah's lower back as he took a step closer to her. Jaylah remembered what those tattooed fingers did to her body as she looked at Pinky.

"I do, excuse us," he led Jaylah away from Pinky and silently they walked down the street. They bent the corner and Jaylah saw that several mom and pop convenient stores sat on the corners. They were, like the homes in stellar condition. "My parents were never rich, but they had love. The kind of love that made us feel like we were, you know? My pops had a heart attack and died a year after Malik was born. It was then that shit got real for us. We were struggling and my mom that had never worked a day in her life enrolled in school to become a nurse. She needed all of her money for that so we was left with nothing but she gave us all that she could. Eventually, she graduated and when she got her first job that shit felt like Christmas day," he smiled. The happiness in his deep tone warmed Jaylah's heart. "Them checks was hitting, and we were able to move to the suburbs. My mom made it clear from the start that being anything less than exceptional in life was not acceptable for her. It wasn't an option to not make it. We had to get a degree," he explained.

Jaylah nodded. His life sounded like the American dream. Nothing like what Jerry claimed his family was.

"This place needs to be talked about. What you and your family is doing needs to be discussed. It's rare to see something of this magnitude. Your mom succeeded with her job as a mother because you are everything but ordinary," she told him.

They stopped walking and Oshun peered down at her. Jaylah finally turned her eyes onto the man that was implanting himself into her thoughts and she swallowed hard.

Damn, he was fine for no reason.

Oshun looked mouthwatering good in his white designer short-sleeved polo that he'd paired with grey Amiri tapered jersey sweatpants along with white Balenciaga Triple S sneakers. His bushy beard was neatly trimmed while his burst fade was freshly lined up. The way the polo hugged Oshun's muscles made it hard for Jaylah to not stare. He was a sight to behold. His eyes a dark honey shade peered over her body slowly and she wondered if he felt what was brewing between them?

"What's good, Jaylah? You keep coming around like you want me to keep you. Is that what you looking for because I'm not sold on that other story you telling since we both know you for the law," he said.

Jaylah's fair skin warmed under his gaze. Her eyes slid to the right and she shrugged. Was this still work? Shit, she needed for it to be or her ass could possibly be without a job. She'd worked so hard to get to where she was at. She didn't want to throw that all away. She also wasn't into making up a story either.

Despite what people thought of her she wasn't heartless.

"Truthfully I don't know why I'm here. I should be back home, but something has me staying."

Oshun fixed his diamond Cuban link chain that was tangled because of his polo collar then placed his hands into his pockets.

"For weeks though, love? I need for you to make it, make sense," he told her.

Jaylah took a deep breath and exhaled. She stared up at him nervously not sure of what to say.

"The truth is, I ran into you at the club. We enjoyed our night and I found out later that your brother was Malik. I came down with the intention of seeing you and your family. All of the media attention that Malik's story has gotten has me intrigued by the BOC. So, I did want to see it for myself. After you made me leave that bar," she said, and when he smirked at her she continued. "I went home again but it didn't feel right. I couldn't stop thinking of the conversation we had," she replied.

Jaylah broke Oshun's intense gaze and rubbed her arms.

"I'm all over the place right now so yes I did come back down here once more. I took the chance on you shunning me but here I am."

Oshun licked his lips. He rubbed his hand up her back as he stared down at her.

"Jaylah right is right and wrong is wrong. What I could never do is chill with anybody that justifies racism. I want to believe all of this nice shit that you're telling me, but I can only go off what you've showed me. So far, I've seen a side of you that makes my dick shrivel up. Ignorance isn't appealing to a nigga like me," he let her know.

Jaylah pulled away from Oshun. She hated that he could pull emotions up out of her. Just from a couple of encounters he'd changed her viewpoints on life.

"I'm going to go because I'm not here to plead a case to you. I'm far from perfect Oshun. I have been shown privilege and I can admit that. I was stupid to think that the cops were being just when they've killed so many colored people. I've been blind to a lot of shit but I'm trying to change it. I am, and no matter what you think, I am sorry about what happened to Malik. —Goodbye."

Jaylah's eyes watered as she walked away. Oshun caught her before she bent the corner and he hugged her from the back.

"All I wanted was to see a real person that wasn't blind to the bullshit we're dealing with in this world. I can see your stressed, shit I am too. I can also feel your realness this time around. I can't do that fake shit and the second I feel like your back on it, you gone, and it will be for good this time," he told her.

Jaylah swallowed hard. The comfort she felt from being wrapped in Oshun's arms was unnerving her.

"I am tired but being here around you is giving me peace," she said softly.

"When you turn a corner and run into yourself. Then you know you have turned all of the corners that are left," his deep voice rasped to her.

Jaylah pulled away from Oshun and looked up at him. She knew it was a poem, but she wasn't sure who it was by. Her brows lifted and he smiled showing off his straight white teeth.

"Langston Hughes, love," he told her.

Jaylah simply nodded.

"Oh," she muttered trying not to blush.

"Come on, my people on this block," he said and led her away from the corner.

They walked down the second block owned by the BOC that housed another set of beautiful homes and Jaylah saw that a few of the homes were being re-painted. The street was filled with people handling the lawn care and planting flowers as Oshun led her over to a set of white Porsche trucks. On the side of the pricey vehicles were young attractive people pulling out painting materials.

"This man here always trying to out dress me and shit," a tall overly handsome man said walking up.

Jaylah found herself smiling as she watched Oshun embrace the man that was dripping from head to toe in designer.

"This shit comes easy to me," Oshun chuckled and

embraced the rest of the people. He turned to Jaylah and grabbed her hand. "This my friend Jaylah, Jaylah this the fam," he said pulling her close.

Jaylah offered a small wave while smiling.

"Hi," she said ignoring the penetrating gaze from the beauty with the light eyes and full lips.

The woman stood beside a man donning two long braids to the back and while his face was sexy his disposition told you he wasn't someone you wanted to fuck with.

"I'm Sayeed, the nigga he gets his swag from," the man spoke to Jaylah who had been the one to crack on Oshun's style when they walked up.

Jaylah smiled at him then looked at the stunning woman that was by his side. She stared at the woman until she remembered where she knew her from.

"Egypt? I did a story on you, or well more like I recapped your documentary on drugs. I've heard nothing but great things about it," Jaylah said to her.

The woman hugged Sayeed's side while cheesing at Jaylah.

"I like her already Oshun. Thank you that was from the heart. I'm working on something new. What news station do you work for?" Egypt asked.

"HLN20" Oshun said and Jaylah was reminded of the fact that he knew a lot about her.

Even the things that she felt weren't so glamorous.

"Well it was nice meeting you; I have a small screening

coming up where I show the first half of the documentary to close family and friends. I would love for you to come. Any kind of publicity I can get on it would be appreciated," Egypt told her. She pulled out her phone and once again Jaylah found herself giving out her number.

Back home she had one friend. Kylie. Here she was in Detroit not even a month and she was coming across friendly women with big things going for themselves. She liked it and wondered what was so different from her in the city than in Baymoor Falls.

She was the same person.

Right?

"What did you say your name was again?" a man asked with eyes so grey they could make a storm cloud jealous.

He too had the type of face that could make women go against their morals. Jaylah saw the resemblance in the man and Oshun. They both possessed the same nose and eye shape only Oshun was darker and his eyes weren't grey.

"Jaylah," she said holding onto Oshun's hand tightly.

The man nodded with his brows furrowed. He stared at her intently before walking away. He made it to his truck and peered back at her once more before pulling the door open.

"Deen ass bugging. Where should we start?" Sayeed asked Oshun.

Oshun chuckled.

"Shit that second house at the corner is a good place. I appreciate this, I really do," he told his family. He cleared his throat and Jaylah's hand had a mind of its own as it massaged his hand soothingly. "We have to go even harder for Malik. He would want that," he spoke with his head high.

Jaylah envied his strength wondering how he could speak of his late brother so calmly.

"He would, king," Sayeed said and patted Oshun's shoulder. "Baby lets head over there with your pretty ass," he said to his woman.

Jaylah watched her blush before following Sayeed down the street. Oshun then dapped up the man with the braids in his hair after he stepped up with the pretty woman by his side that wouldn't stop looking at her.

"Jaylah this my cousin Chevez. This my fucking guy right here," Oshun said proudly.

Chevez smirked as he looked down at Jaylah. His skin was a rich brown shade that was blemish-free. Tattoo's decorated his arms while his face held a masculine beauty to it that even his hard exterior couldn't take away from him. He nodded and his eyes went to the beauty by his side. It was then that his stance relaxed, and he smiled.

"This my lady, Sadie," he said in a deep tone.

Jaylah smiled placing a name to the face. The woman's colored eyes held a look of closeness in them that Jaylah wasn't expecting. The woman was gorgeous. She smiled at Jaylah before pulling her into a tight embrace.

"Satan causes chaos, confusion, destruction, and death. You have to be aware of his schemes. God is the author of love, not confusion, and when you know Him you know love. Real genuine love. Although things have happened to harden your heart do not let it continue to hold you back. I feel deeply that if you do it will be your own destruction. God's telling me to tell you that He hasn't forgotten about you. That even through the pain, He was there holding you while you cried. He was there when you felt the lowest and He will be there when you are at your highest. Find yourself and you will find true peace. It was very nice to meet you," the woman said after whispering in Jaylah's ear.

Jaylah nodded repeatedly as her eyes stung with tears. She swallowed hard and when she blinked, they slid down her face.

"Excuse me," she said softly and walked away.

"Aye, she wasn't trying to hurt your friend. That's just what she does nigga," Oshun's cousin Chevez said as Jaylah walked briskly across the street.

Jaylah found a tree to lean against and she slid to the ground. She pulled her knees up to her chest and almost like time was working against her, the personal cell she had in her pouch started to vibrate. Jaylah pulled the phone out and peered down at the screen. When her father's jail number slid across, she nervously answered the call.

Jaylah's eyes closed as she accepted the collect call then pressed the phone to her ear.

"Jaylah, baby," her father said in a hoarse tone.

Jaylah's lip trembled and her tears fell fast as her heart pumped wildly in her chest.

"I miss you so much, baby girl. I'm sorry for everything that happened. Your mom is sorry, and your sister is too. We love you baby and we are tired of not having you in our life. It's been too long baby. Please forgive us," he begged with pain taking over his tone.

A warm hand brushed against Jaylah's leg and her eyes shot open. She peered up at Oshun that was leaning down towards her and she ended the call with her father. Jaylah placed her phone into the bag that was on her body before she stood up.

"Hey!" she chirped trying to sound happy.

Oshun stared at her strangely. His big hands wiped away her tears as he peered into her eyes.

"That's my cousin Chevez's, woman. When I met her, she read the fuck out of me too but it's all love. She's honestly one of the nicest women I ever met," he explained.

Jaylah nodded as she looked away from Oshun and back over at his family that was across the street talking. They'd began to clean up and help out however Sadie was still looking her way with worried eyes. Jaylah waved to Sadie wanting her to know it was all good and it was only then that Sadie was able to grab a bag off the ground. Jaylah looked back up at Oshun and sighed.

"I heard about people like her, but I didn't know they were real. What she said was very true and it scared the shit out of me because I wasn't expecting it," she confessed before laughing lightly.

Oshun smirked as he looked down at her.

"I can assure you love that she doesn't do it every time you see her. I think even she knows that would be too much for someone to handle. Do you want to meet my mom and see Malik's girlfriend?" he asked.

Jaylah took a deep breath and nodded before exhaling. Oshun grabbed her hand and they headed towards the main street. Cars drove by honking as they walked.

"This was the first store we bought. My mom had worked overtime and saved for a year to get it. We struggled because at first vendors didn't want to work with us because we were black," he said as they stopped at a small candy store that sat on the corner.

Jaylah smiled as she looked at the cute tan and white store that was neatly painted and artfully decorated. She entered the store and gasped. The interior was a kid and candy lover's dream. Any type of candy you could think of lined the walls of the store in plastic containers similar to a vending machine. Only you didn't need money to garner the candy. At the bottom of the plastic tubing, you could dispel the candy into one of the plastic clear bags that were on the table beneath it.

The inside was also colorful, and Jaylah knew that the store was the holy grail for the young kids in the area.

"This is so cool," she whispered looking around.

Oshun pulled her close and his fingers brushed against her lower back causing her body to tingle.

"Yeah, my mom loves candy as you can see. The woman that runs it is in the hospital. She had to get her foot worked on," he explained. "My mom is up this way. She can be intense, but it comes from a good place," he said leading Jaylah to the front of the store.

"What's good young lady?" Oshun asked and Jaylah smiled as she looked at Oshun's gorgeous mother Angie. Besides Angie was Malik's pregnant girlfriend Tiffany. Both women wore smiles on their faces only when Angie peered over at Jaylah her smile dimmed. She pressed her lips together tightly and passed the young girl in front of her some candy that was in a clear plastic bag.

"How was your chess game with Willie? Who won son?" Angie asked ringing up another customer.

Malik's girlfriend Tiffany moved quickly around the counter. She pulled Jaylah into a quick embrace before giving Oshun a tight hug.

"Welcome to the BOC. It's really nice to meet you. I'm Tiffany," the young woman spoke.

Jaylah again wondered how Oshun and his family were so damn strong? It was baffling to her.

"Jaylah and it's very nice to meet you, Mrs. Lacoste," she spoke up.

Oshun's mother nodded. She finished ringing up the young boy before placing her attention onto Jaylah. She held a youthful look to her with her short hair, smooth brown skin, and slim physique. She wore loungewear with a bare face and Jaylah could tell that she wasn't sold on her being in the store with her oldest son.

"How does Oshun know you Jaylah?" she asked.

Jaylah swallowed hard. She clasped her hands together as Oshun leaned against the counter. His gaze was on her and oddly she expected him to help her with the meeting of his mom, but he did nothing of the sort.

"I met him in Baymoor Falls. I work for a news station and I saw online what happened to your son. The story intrigued me and here I am," she said maintaining eye contact with Angie.

Angie frowned at Jaylah as she came from behind the glass counter that held up the register along with a few knick knacks like pencils and notebooks.

"Intrigued you *or* angered you?" she asked.

"Both," Jaylah replied.

Angie went over to Oshun and hugged him tightly. She whispered something to him that made him chuckle. As she pulled back her eyes drifted back over to Jaylah.

"My son is a real person. Not an animal on an exhibit. I don't want anyone fishing for a story be it real or fake young lady. Malik's legacy won't be tarnished. No matter how hard the media tries to defame it," she told her.

"And I would never do that. I'm only here to see this

amazing place. I met Oshun not knowing that he was even Malik's brother," Jaylah explained.

"So, you're here for my son instead? How old are you? Tell me some things that would make you stand out on your resume," Angie said folding her arms across her chest.

Tiffany offered Jaylah a comforting smile that she appreciated.

"Um," Jaylah's eyes narrowed, and she struggled to hold in her scowl. She wasn't used to mothers interrogating her. In actuality, Angie was the first mom she'd ever met. "I graduated from college at the top of my class. I have two degrees, one in journalism and one in social work. I've never been married. I have no kids. I work for one of Baymoor Falls leading news broadcast shows," she said confidently. "I've also never been interviewed by a mom before," she said light-heartedly although she wasn't joking.

Oshun smirked as his mother's eyes pinched together.

"Then you've never met a mother that only wants the best for her kids. I'm Angela Lacoste, it's nice to meet you," she said and held out her hand.

"Jaylah Cole," Jaylah greeted her warmly shaking the small hand.

Oshun's mother gave Jaylah a pensive gaze before smiling.

"She's very pretty Oshun," Angie said before going back to the register.

Jaylah sighed with relief glad the interrogation was over

as Oshun stepped beside her. He passed her a bottle of water with the cap already twisted off. Jaylah stared at the opened water bottle briefly then cheesed up at him.

"You didn't put your mouth on this did you?" she questioned allowing for her tongue to swipe slowly across her bottom lip.

Oshun stepped closer to her and he leaned down. His warm breath that smelled of the spearmint gum he just chewed kissed her exposed neck.

"I can put my mouth on anything that you own love," he whispered.

Jaylah's skin flushed as she remembered Oshun's thick lips caressing her sex in ways that she had never imagined.

"Hey king, I've been looking all over for you," a light voice said walking up.

Oshun pulled Jaylah close as she turned to the voice grabbing Oshun's attention. Her eyes landed on the gorgeous, beautiful Latoya and she smiled wide.

"Hey again," Jaylah waved.

Latoya stopped smiling when her eyes landed on her. She peered down at the hand that held Jaylah close to Oshun and she frowned. She looked up at Oshun with a questioning stare.

"Gio and I were looking for you. Did you forget that you have to speak about the protests?" she asked with an attitude.

Jaylah studied Latoya closely as Oshun responded.

"I didn't but did you forget who you were talking to?" he asked Latoya.

Latoya's pretty face shifted into a tight-lipped smile.

"I didn't, king. Who is this you have here?" she asked finally looking Jaylah in the eyes.

Jaylah's brows pulled together as she stared at the woman.

"We met earlier?" Jaylah reminded her.

Latoya shook her head and hummed to herself.

"Don't think that we did. I would remember meeting someone as pretty as you. I love that outfit but that wig, sis it's lifting in the front. Might want to get that touched up. Gio is at the surplus store waiting on you Oshun," she said and walked away.

Jaylah's body tensed as she watched Latoya head towards the back of the store taking with her that big ass of hers. Jaylah looked up at Oshun and saw that he was already staring down at her.

"It is lifting sweetheart, but you still look good," he said lowly.

Jaylah frowned before stifling a laugh. Oshun leaned down and kissed her cheek as his arms went around her waist.

"Still look beautiful as shit," he whispered. "Good enough to eat," he added. "Now I need to see if you are deserving of the tongue lashing I wanna give your pretty ass," he said lowly.

Jaylah's walls clenched in anticipation. She pulled back from Oshun and licked her dry lips. He was a storm. A category fucking five. She had no choice but to get wrapped up in him. The real question was when it was all said and done would she survive or be torn apart?

"I should head out," she said not wanting to cream through her leggings. She peered back at his mother and Tiffany. "It was really nice meeting you all."

Tiffany smiled while his mom stared at Jaylah intently.

"You too," Tiffany said.

Oshun's mother simply nodded and began to ring up another kid that was looking to buy candy. The mercurial mood of Oshun's family wasn't lost on Jaylah.

"Well okay," Jaylah muttered and exited the store with Oshun.

"Why didn't you tell me my hair was messed up?" she asked.

Oshun smirked. He placed Jaylah closer to the sidewalk so that he was near the street and he chuckled.

"Regardless of how it looks, you still beautiful. With or without the wig."

"It's not a wig, it was sewn down," Jaylah defended feeling silly as fuck.

She'd been around Oshun, his friend, and family with a lifted wig. She couldn't wait to call up her stylist Miesha and tell her about herself.

"That's irrelevant, love," he replied.

Jaylah stopped walking and looked at Oshun.

"But is Latoya irrelevant?"

Oshun reached out to grab her hand as the cops pulled up to the curb where they were standing. Their lights cut on and they stepped out of their vehicles with their hands on their guns.

"Hands in the air! We received a call about a break in occurring at this candy store," the shorter officer yelled with his green eyes narrowed on Jaylah and Oshun.

Oshun pushed Jaylah behind him as he looked at the police officers.

"And just how the fuck am I breaking into something I partly own, motherfucka?" he asked calmly.

"Stop resisting and raise your hands in the air!" the taller cop yelled with eyes hard as flint.

His skin was flushed beet red as if he'd been insulted and Jaylah was truly perplexed by the situation. They'd done nothing wrong to warrant the behavior from the police officers. She moved around Oshun and looked at the two cops in bewilderment.

"Officers, he owns this store. We've done nothing wrong and I know my rights. No call was made and no break in is occurring however an unlawful police stop was made by you two officers when you all could have been out fighting real crime. My lawyer would be on this in five seconds and have your boss so far up—"

"Hands in the air! I won't repeat it again!" the tall officer yelled pulling his gun.

Jaylah's heart dropped. She looked at the cop that was

dead set on thrusting his weapon her way with her blood boiling. Oshun slowly raised his hands while peering over at her.

"Jaylah put your hands in the air, sweetheart before I have to make the news tonight. I need you to calm down and listen to these motherfucka's," he said calmly but she couldn't.

She'd done nothing wrong for a cop to pull a fucking gun out on her. She was insulted and felt disrespected.

"Aye, not again! He owns that store!" a young man yelled running up with his phone out.

"I said put your fucking hand in the air girl!" the cop hissed.

Girl?

He'd said the word like Jerry and his insistence to belittle and scare Jaylah only added fuel to her fire. She shook her head defiantly not caring what happened. To be treated like an animal for simply trying to do right was incredulous to her.

"Are you fucking kidding me? I wish I would allow for you or this fucking puny ass piece of shit partner of yours to make me raise my hands in the air. You would never get that out of me," she said defiantly, and the cop smirked.

"You are under arrest for resisting an officer! Anything you say, can and will be held against you!" the taller cop called out putting his gun away.

Jaylah's arm was grabbed with force and she was slapped with handcuffs so tight they dug into her wrist. Her eyes connected with Oshun's as the rest of his people pulled up onto the scene.

"When you can't get to me or my family, you arrest the woman by my side? Y'all know that shit is on camera, right?" he asked the tall cop arresting Jaylah.

"Just be lucky it isn't you," the tall cop snarled and when his eyes connected with Oshun's narrowed gaze he stopped smirking. "Keep your eye on him, James," he told his partner.

"You'll be okay, sweetheart," Oshun told Jaylah.

"I know because I did nothing fucking wrong," Jaylah snapped.

"Just don't say anything else to provoke them baby and do as they say," Angie said walking up with Latoya and Tiffany.

"I did nothing wrong!" Jaylah yelled trying to pull away from the cop.

"Calm down!" the cop based glaring down at Jaylah.

"Oh Lord, please relax sweetie," Oshun's mother said holding onto his arm.

Jaylah's eyes connected with Oshun's angry gaze and when he nodded at her she was able to calm herself down.

"Be cool, Jaylah," he told her.

Jaylah sighed in defeat. She could see the anger brewing in his gaze as he stared back at her.

"I'm fine," she lied not wanting him to fall for the bait of the officers.

She flashed him a small smile before the cop pulled her away while reading her the rest of her Miranda Rights.

Five hours later after sitting in a holding tank with women of all ethnicities Jaylah was released from jail. The cop that brought her in looked happy as he pulled open the cell for her.

"You are good to go," he said moving to the side.

Jaylah's brows pulled together as she walked by him. She looked down at her wrist and saw the marks from the cuffs bruising her fair skin. She walked slowly with the cop as he chuckled softly.

"I spoke with your boss and your all good. Everything in the system has been wiped clean. Your *friend* is here to retrieve you so don't tell him about our set up. I programmed my number into your phone. In a few weeks, I will meet up with you and give you the drugs to plant. I need time to be able to take it out of an inventory that's big enough to take them down. We appreciate what you're doing," he whispered before walking away.

Dumbfounded by all that the cop Jefferson told her, Jaylah walked from the back of the jail area and into the waiting room. Her eyes landed on Oshun as he leaned against the wall with one of his legs touching the paint. His eyes landed on her and he rushed to her side. Jaylah's tiredness with the situation hit her like a brick and her eyes welled with tears.

"I'm tired. Like really tired," she whispered while hugging him.

His presence brought her comfort and peace. Jaylah was relieved to be back in his space after sitting for hours in the jail.

Oshun picked her up bridal style and carried her out of the station. He took her to his Urus and placed her into the front seat. His lips, soft and warm brushed against her forehead before he strapped her in. He was next to slip into the truck before pulling away. Jaylah rested her head against the window while massaging her wrist. She felt low and the entire situation was draining her. She'd evilly walked into a place with malicious intent and now she was reaping what she sowed. She hated the feeling of helplessness that came over her while being arrested and never wanted to feel that again.

The cop hadn't known who she was at the time and he'd treated her like she was trash. She done nothing but walk down the street and that had been a crime? Her mind traveled back to the thousands of stories she read about online concerning racism and she felt her stomach grow uneasy. Yes, some things had been provoked but a large number of other cases started because of race.

The darker the skin the harder the law came down on you.

She groaned realizing her error as blue and red lights flashed in the truck from the back.

"These niggas on one today. Don't say anything and do what they ask love," Oshun said pulling over onto the side of the street.

Jaylah closed her eyes as her breathing picked up.

"This is insane, Oshun. Is it always like this for you?" she asked above a whisper.

Oshun lowered his window. Pulled his license and registration out and sat it on his lap. His eyes narrowed as he peered over at Jaylah.

"They hate the BOC and they want to take us down by any means necessary," he replied.

Jaylah sighed and sat her hands onto the column in front of her. Her eyes swelled with angry tears as two African American cops approached both their windows.

"License and registration," the officer at Oshun's window told him peering into the truck as he kept his hand on the top of his gun.

Oshun passed the officer everything he asked for as the officer at Jaylah's window looked at her with narrowed eyes.

"Your license as well," he said in a stern tone.

Jaylah wanted to keep her mouth shut but she couldn't. The will to be quiet wasn't inside of her at the moment. She looked at the cop beside her window with disgust.

"What exactly for? We literally just left the fucking police station and already we're being harassed again! Just wait until I call my lawyer!" she hissed pulling out her license.

"Relax," Oshun said as she shoved her license at the police officer.

The officer smirked as he walked off with her identification. Jaylah's leg started to rock as she sat angrily in the passenger's seat. Her mind wouldn't stop going back to the news stories she heard on various black men and women being harassed by cops. She'd casually shrugged off the stories chalking it up to black people looking for sympathy when all along they'd been real events. Real accounts of individuals being singled out by police because of the color of their skin.

She felt foolish.

She felt sickened at what she'd turned her head too.

And she was now ashamed of her actions.

Baymoor Falls was far from perfect but the thing about living in smaller places was that everyone knew you. Even with her father being a known hustler she'd never experienced him being harassed by the cops or maybe she'd been too blind to notice. For the most part, the police always left her family alone. The only time they'd come knocking was to arrest her father and even then, it had been the federal police not local.

"You did a stop and roll when you were leaving the police station. You can either pay the ticket online or at the courthouse. You, two lovely people, enjoy the rest of your night," the officer said passing Oshun back his license and registration along with Jaylah's license.

Oshun passed Jaylah her license and put his personal things away before pulling off. Silently they drove down the street and when Oshun pulled up to Jaylah's hotel she peered over at him with weary eyes.

"Please come up with me. I don't want to be alone," she

admitted sounding the most vulnerable she had in a long time.

Oshun nodded looking as tired as she felt.

"Of course, love," he replied and his willingness to comfort her made her more emotional.

Jaylah quickly slipped out of the truck and waited for Oshun to receive his valet ticket. Then together they entered the five-star hotel. Jaylah held Oshun's hand tightly and when they stepped onto the elevator she leaned on his arm as if they were a couple. She'd never needed a man. Not since her father let her down but being around Oshun had her needing his presence. He brought with him things that everyone wanted in a spouse. He was strong, smart, and comforting. He made her feel like not being perfect was okay and for Jaylah that was scary because all she'd ever wanted out of her life was perfection.

"It's down this way," she said hoarsely leading him down the floor by hand. Jaylah unlocked the hotel door and while Oshun went into the seating area and took off his sneakers Jaylah went to the bathroom. She thought of the day's events and wished she could call her mom and her twin, but it wasn't that simple. She'd shunned them years ago and now with so much time gone by she wasn't sure if calling them up was the best thing for her to do.

Jaylah looked at herself in the mirror and when her eyes fell onto the lace unit, she wore laughter fell from her pretty lips. Her stylist fucking owed her because her wig was lifting up so bad that her real hair was showing.

"Wow, I look and feel a hot fucking mess," she muttered bending down to retrieve an eyebrow razor from her makeup bag.

Jaylah took her time cutting the weave from her hair making sure to be mindful of her braids. She then took her braids out and gave her body a deliberate wash before going into the bedroom.

Hours passed and when she spotted Oshun asleep on the bed her body relaxed. Jaylah known for sleeping naked grabbed her black silk robe and placed it on her body before joining him in bed. She faced Oshun and stared at his handsome mug as he peacefully rested.

She saw so many things when she looked at his face. He was at peace and had no clue that the world was still trying to take him down including her. Jaylah hated what she was doing because he didn't deserve that.

"I'm sorry," she whispered softly and kissed his lips.

Oshun stirred in bed but didn't wake up. Jaylah kissed him softly again loving the feel of his lips before turning onto her back. She stared at the wall straight ahead and thought of the decisions she needed to make until sleep came looking for her.

CHAPTER 8

A MONTH LATER

"I called everyone here that I felt I needed for this project. This hospital for me and my team has been a long time coming. With losing my cousin my focus has been and will stay on us getting justice, but I felt this meeting was needed. Now more than ever. We are all affluent black men that can be the change this city needs. And I know the world needs the change too but like my momma always said. You can't help anybody else until your own house is clean. My brother Sayeed has his boxing gym for the youth, and I felt like we could use that as a starting point but why not do more? Because shit I'm a larger than life kind of nigga," Deen said and smiled.

Oshun smirked warming up to his people. They'd stuck around and were genuinely trying to rebuild the bond. He appreciated the effort they were putting in, so he was meeting them halfway.

"Yeah, okay Diddy," Oshun's cousin Chevez grumbled looking at Deen.

Deen shook his head as his grey eyes peered over at Chevez.

"Never wanted to be anybody but my damn self and that's facts. I fuck with Diddy but I'm building my own legacy. Oshun and Gio along with auntie Angie started the BOC and I feel like we can play off that. We can start our organization for young black boys under that title. Our goal is to save as many young black men that we can. If we can put them into college or trade school, then America can't put them into jail."

"Amen to that," Sayeed said with his hands in the praying position.

Deen rubbed his waves and smiled.

"We will help them out in any way, that we can as long as they stay out the streets and do good in school. I need y'all on board for this because we all can bring something to the table. It would be one thing if we didn't have the funds for this shit, but we do. The same way we can bust down the mall and drop bands on these designer labels that don't give a fuck about our black asses is the same way we can invest in our youth. I am also looking for benefactors and I will expect you niggas to do the same. The more money we have for this organization the more we can help, feel me?" Deen asked.

Oshun nodded as he peered around the room at the men occupying the round table in Deen's Westside office. He knew almost everyone there and was comfortable with the setup. It was a good idea what his cousin was proposing and anything to help the youth in Detroit he was onboard with it.

"I'm in," he was the first to say.

"Me too," Gio mumbled and Oshun stared at his younger brother wishing he could lift his spirits.

"I can also hit up a few of my people too that would be interested in this," Oshun added thinking of his friends Ameer and Brando that he knew could help out.

"I'm in too and I'm sure Grady would be down with it," Deen's friend Huss replied.

Oshun sat back as all of the people his cousin invited agreed to starting the organization. *And they think we can't do shit but kill each other. Fucking dummies,* he thought proud to be surrounded by such strong ass black men.

"I'm in too," Deen's friend and financial advisor Qwote said looking up from his phone. "I'm sending out messages right now, I should have some money on the floor for us by midnight."

Deen rubbed his hands together like Birdman the rapper while grinning.

"Well shit let's make some history than in this bitch," he chuckled.

Everyone laughed and Oshun and his family stayed back

after the meeting was over and talked shit with one another. Oshun was playing it close with Gio not wanting his brother to fall deeper into a depression. He studied Gio sipping once again on liquor and an idea came to him.

"Aye, let's come up with a date to go to the cabin up north. The family could use some downtime to get our mind off everything that's going on," Oshun suggested looking at his cousins then finally his younger brother. "You can get on the jet skis and shit," he said and Gio's visage shifted.

Gio nodded and gave him a crooked grin.

"Yeah that would be cool," he agreed.

"Shit, I'm down. Egypt's been working hard lately and could use the break," Oshun's cousin Sayeed said standing. "Just hit me with the address and the time we can come through. I'm out," Sayeed said before leaving the office with the rest of the family.

Deen looked over at Oshun and chuckled.

"Your mom is at church with my mom right now. I dropped them off earlier today. They were gossiping about everybody in that bitch," Deen told him rolling up a blunt. "But it's good to see they finally over that family shit."

Oshun nodded feeling the same way. For years he watched his mom cry over the treatment her father's side of the family laced her with. His mother's family wasn't close and were all down south. They rarely reached out to Oshun's mom, so it had always just been Oshun, his mom, and his siblings. To have his mother's people on her pops side finally take her in was a relief. Because while he didn't give a shit about it, he knew it meant the world to his mom. She wanted the acceptance and acknowledgment of who she was to them and he could understand that.

"I asked my mom one day why they gave us all the Lacoste last name even though they all had husbands and shit," Deen said rolling up a blunt.

Oshun smirked. He'd always wondered the same thing. His pops never complained about it but as an adult, he didn't get that because any kids of his would carry on his name.

"And what auntie say?" Oshun asked smirking.

His cousin looked at him with his grey eyes and chuckled.

"She said that because they didn't have a brother, they pops drilled it into their head as kids that it was up to them to keep the name alive. I can see he told auntie that shit too," Deen replied.

Oshun nodded.

"Yeah, I guess it makes sense but still. My kid will have to carry my last name. Fuck all that," he replied.

Deen smiled.

"No, I feel you and this the last thing I'ma say about this shit because it's past us. My granny was bitter no lie, but I remember even as a kid hearing our grandad talk about your mom. He loved her a lot. Even days leading up to him passing away he talked about her," Deen said to him.

Oshun swallowed hard. He appreciated his cousins' words, but they weren't needed. His mom was good and as long as he was breathing, he would ensure she stayed that way. He sat up in his seat and like she'd been doing for the past month, Jaylah crossed his mind. Oshun couldn't shake the feelings that were building for her and he wasn't sure how to feel about it.

Jaylah was there when he handled business in the BOC and she even helped with the Boys and Girls Club in his community. When she wasn't trying to be perfect was when he liked her the most. Oshun got a kick out of hearing her laugh and staring at her beautiful face. She was finally letting her guard down around him and he liked that shit.

He wasn't ready for her to go home but he knew eventually she would leave and now his mind was trying to find reasons on how he could get her to stay.

"How long do you think it takes to fall in love with somebody?" he asked Deen and chuckled at the shit coming from his mouth.

"Forget I said anything. I'm fucking tripping," he said pulling out his fob.

Deen shook him off and passed him a bottle of cognac and a glass from his nearby bar.

"Men have feelings too. Don't be ashamed to talk to me. We're family and that's what we here for. Honestly, men don't talk enough and that's why we be mentally breaking down and shit. What's up?" Deen asked looking interested in how he felt.

Oshun made himself a drink and took a few sips before responding.

"Jaylah will probably be leaving soon, and I don't like that idea. I want to tell her to stay but that's her life up there. We're not a couple or no shit like that for me to be sprouting out demands."

Deen blew weed smoke from between his lips before responding.

"What I know from personal experience is that love can happen at any moment and that's real. I also know that sometimes you have to let shit be what it is. If it's real, it'll come back. You lay it out on the line what you want from her and what you can offer her. She can either accept it or move on but don't drag your feet. Don't be that nigga," Deen told him.

Oshun chuckled.

Slacking was never his style.

"Nah, I'm far from a slacker. I want her in my life. I want us to keep getting to know each other. It's hard because this Malik shit is gutting me. I don't even feel right being happy while he's dead. Shit just don't seem fair."

Deen sighed and Oshun pulled his vibrating cellphone from his pocket. He looked at the screen and saw Latoya was calling him. He finished his drink and stood from his seat while looking at his older cousin.

"I appreciate the talk though. I'll send out a group text

within the hour with details about the cabin," he told him and dapped up his cousin before leaving his office.

Oshun hit back Latoya as he got into his car.

"I'm on the way, ma," he said not giving her time to speak once she'd answered the phone.

"Oh okay, no worries king," she said sweetly and ended the call.

Oshun relaxed in his seat and before his thoughts could play on what Latoya wanted to speak to him about, he called Jaylah. He'd sent her to the spa that morning on him and was wondering if it had been worth the $300 that he'd spent on the shit.

"Oshun, I feel so good. My body is so freakishly soft that it's unreal," she cooed answering the call.

Oshun grinned to himself as his member thickened. He was horny as fuck and with his sex buddy back in town blowing his line down, he was tempted to answer but so far, he hadn't. He was interested in seeing where things could go with Jaylah and he didn't like to fuck on different women while courting another one. That wasn't his style.

"I'm glad to hear that, love. I made plans for us tonight. I want us to eat at Mon Amour. Its owned by Draco that you met at the Hive. He opened it up for his wife and its nice as fuck. I love the lamb chops from there. My cousin and his girl are coming with us. Chevez and Sadie. She really wanted to talk to you again. Is that cool?" he asked not wanting Jaylah to be uncomfortable.

"Uh, sure. What time should I be ready?"

Oshun pulled up to Latoya's favorite bakery in Detroit and parked near her red Telluride.

"At eight, love. I'll see you then," he replied before ending the call.

Oshun exited his car and went into the bakery. He found Latoya at her favorite spot by the window and he sat across from her after kissing her forehead. Latoya looked beautiful like always in her workout gear with her hair pulled into a loose bun. She wore a smile on her face as she slid a pink folder across the table towards Oshun.

"I love you and I'm going to always have your back. You know I make a living with my spyware company, so it was nothing for me to look into Jaylah. She is who she says she is Oshun, but she has a jaded past. It's a vibe that I get from her that I don't like," she told him.

Oshun opened the folder and was met with a police report dated back fourteen years ago. He quickly read over the report with his heart racing.

The young woman was found in the Southside area in the housing projects. Her twin sister alerted the cops that she felt her sister was okay until she heard screaming coming from the bathroom in the two-bedroom apartment. It was then that she was held down and forced to be quiet. Once the group of four men left unknown to the twin sister she rushed to the bathroom and saw her sister naked on the floor with her chest bleeding along with her private area in the vagina region.

Oshun closed the folder not able to read anymore and his fist balled as he looked at Latoya. He felt like her intentions were good but what she did wasn't a play he would have called. He sat back and chose his words wisely as he processed what he now knew about Jaylah.

"First let me say I appreciate you, ma. I know it's been you and me for a while and to see me with someone new could be difficult for you. But this wasn't your call to make Latoya. I'm not a fucking kid. I don't need you to check up on the women I spend time with. I used to knock down Nene that owns that nail salon you like, and you didn't give a fuck so why the interest now? This wasn't your business to tell and I feel fucked up for knowing this," he told her.

Latoya's face fell into a frown as she looked at him.

"Please just look through the rest of the folder. Her father was some drug Lord in Baymoor Falls that's still in prison as we speak. She comes from a corrupted family and she has a sketchy past Oshun. She isn't good enough for you and that's why I'm trying to put you up on game. She has some secrets that you need to know about. You see her, the light skin and pretty eyes and you forget about your standards. You don't even like stuck up bitches, like this is crazy to me! She's a grown-ass woman with bills yet she's been here for how long just because? That isn't alarming to you? She's using you and this family and time will soon tell on why she is. So yes, I'm going to ride for you because I love you and shit being honest. If you're going to be with someone it should be me. Just a few months ago I had your dick on my breath and now I'm your friend again? I mean how is that right?" she asked with her eyes watering.

Oshun rubbed the back of his neck as the room grew warm. With other women, he could cut straight to the chase and feel no remorse, but Latoya wasn't other women. No matter what he fucked with her the long way so he would always handle her with care.

He sat up in his seat and grabbed her hands from across the table as she held back tears.

"You will always be special to me but that doesn't mean you're the woman for me. Sex isn't love. It's not and you're smart enough to know that. There is no us in that kind of way anymore and who I pursue is my business. I do what the fuck I want and that's not changing. If you got a problem with that then we might need to reevaluate this friendship we have," he said in a tone reserved for her ears only.

Latoya let his hands go and pulled her bottom lip into her mouth. Slowly she shook her head while staring at him. Oshun knew she was hurt and upset but he would never apologize for wanting Jaylah. He had the fucking right to and just because Latoya knew what his dick felt like didn't mean she owned him. It wasn't that kind of party and he knew that doubling back to her could never happen again because she couldn't handle it.

"I'm glad we have an understanding. I'll call you later, enjoy some of your favorite muffins on me," he said and dropped a fifty onto the table before standing.

Oshun grabbed the folder and left the bakery with his brows pulled together. Simply thinking of someone taking advantage of Jaylah had him seeing red. He wanted to pull up on her sooner than their date time but opted out of calling her up. Instead, he went by Malik's gravesite and perched a seat against the headstone.

The warm breeze brushed against his skin and when he closed his eyes, he saw Malik. He envisioned his laugh and his heart expanded. Oshun swallowed hard as he felt his body began to vibrate with pain.

"We won't let them get away with it and this shit is hard for me. I'm trying to be patient, but the DA is still allowing for these niggas to work. The lawyer said to trust him, and he would make sure they go down, but the shit isn't happening fast enough," Oshun shook his head. "This sitting and doing nothing makes me feel weak and it doesn't help that Gio keeps reminding me of the fact that we haven't run down on them. I'm conflicted Malik," he confessed lowly.

He pulled at the beard covering the lower half of his face as his eyes narrowed.

"If they don't get arrested soon, I will be forced to take shit into my own hands. I love you and we got your girl. She's holding up so good too. She's strong and I can see why you loved her. I'm sorry I wasn't there. I'm sorry I didn't protect you from them. We always had that target on our back but if keeping you alive meant walking away from the BOC I would have. I would have ended that shit just to have you here with us," he let Malik know before leaving the cemetery.

Oshun got into his car and after driving for forty minutes pulled up on his friend Ameer at one of his many warehouses. Ameer had hit his line while he was spending time with Malik and said he needed to speak with him about something urgent, Oshun just wasn't sure what it was.

Oshun parked and made sure to grab his phone before exiting his truck.

"I'm real sorry about Malik. I can't say that shit enough man," Aamil who was Ameer's younger brother said standing in front of the large building.

Oshun had known him for over ten years and had always respected Aamil. He was a laid-back nigga that minded his own business.

"I appreciate that, where Kasam crazy ass at?" he asked referring to Aamil's other brother that was also a well-known rapper.

"Shit, on the road. He's gearing KJ's lil ass up for a tour. Time flying like a motherfucka," Aamil replied and shook his head. "Just know we got your back. No matter what we do and this shit with Malik has pulled a side out of Ameer that I haven't seen in a long time. We don't take this shit lightly because we know that if it happened to Malik, it could happen to any of us," Aamil told him.

Oshun's dark honey eyes shifted to the ground. He gritted his teeth hating that everything Aamil said was true. If the cops could gun down Malik without thinking twice, they could do the same to any of them including the younger men that were in their family.

"Yeah that's facts," Oshun agreed. "Let me see what this nigga talking about," he said and went into the warehouse.

The vast space was dimly lit but Oshun could make out Ameer in the back of the nearly empty warehouse. Ameer stood by a chair along with his right-hand Luke. Oshun quickened his steps as he headed their way.

"I'm not trying to overstep. I just couldn't let this nigga walk around like shit was sweet. His stepping fletcher ass has to pay," Ameer said as Oshun walked up.

Oshun frowned in confusion until his eyes landed on the man before him. Tied to a chair beaten to the point that his right eye was closed was the African American officer that was involved with Malik's shooting. Officer Milton peered up at Oshun with one eye open and he struggled against the zip tie.

"I'm sorry, this happened. I swear on my family I'm so sorry! I asked if he was okay and Polk didn't respond at first. I was on the other side with the girl. I didn't know what was going on, on that side of the car," he pleaded.

His words meant nothing to Oshun. He was a black man

that had gone along with killing one of his kind. The hell that was waiting on him would be hot for sure.

"And I should spare your life because you were blind to the ignorance my nigga?" Oshun asked with his jaw tensing.

The officer shook his head.

"No! No, I'm just saying that I never signed up for killing innocent people. I never did, shit got out of hand. For so long you all have been a pain in the police side. Trying to start your own government and shit, and they didn't like that. After hearing about you all and the bad shit you were doing for so long, I started to believe it myself. They beat that shit into my head," he cried.

Ameer sucked his teeth as he held a pistol in his left hand. He smacked Officer Milton in the face with the gun and made him cry out in pain.

"You a grown-ass man. You think we gone feel sorry for the weak shit you allowed for them to do? You lucky as fuck because I swear on my life, I really want to make all of y'all niggas bleed out, but they won't let me. If the police wanna play God then so can we," Ameer told him coldly.

He passed Oshun his pistol and Oshun grabbed the weapon. He slowly raised the steel as his body grew warm. Oshun's heart pumped to a beat he'd never felt before. The blood rushed through his veins rapidly and out of nowhere Malik appeared inside of the warehouse. Malik wore the clothing he'd last seen him in the day of his shooting. Worry sat on his face as he looked at Oshun.

This not you man. The reason why I respect you so much is because you not like everybody else. You showed me that you don't have to be a killer or sell drugs to get respect. All you have to do is be the kind of man that people want to show love to. God will handle them brah, because this is beneath you.

Malik's words jarred Oshun. They made his eyes prickle with tears. He dropped his head and quickly reigned in his emotions. Luke grabbed the gun from Oshun and patted his arm.

"It's cool, man. Alex David Milton, resident at 2200 Lincoln Dr. in Southfield Michigan that's married to Jessica Milton maiden name Cross, whose kids attend Learning Write academy in Beverly Hills Michigan with a teacher by the name of Luisa Moore. With parents that live five miles away from you in a home at the address of 1233 12 Mile RD. It's best for you to keep your mouth fucking shut about this shit, right?" Luke asked menacingly.

"Yeah! Yeah, I swear I will!" the officer screeched nodding as hard as he could.

"Cool," Luke said and Oshun turned.

He bypassed Aamil that was leaning against the wall and exited the warehouse. He was mad that his boy had placed him in such a position. He respected Ameer for all that he stood for but what he would never do was want Ameer to make decisions for him.

Ameer grabbed his arm before he could make it to his truck, and he glared back at him as he snatched it away.

"Look, I had to do it. We shouldn't let this nigga walk away," Ameer said breathing hard.

This was not only someone he trusted but someone he looked up to as well. He hated that his boy had overstepped his boundaries because now he didn't see him in the same light. Oshun wasn't a follower. He didn't need help with shit. If he wanted that man dead, he could have killed him months ago. He didn't need for Ameer to do it for him.

"I lost my brother, not you. You my nigga, always been that, but don't you ever in your fucking life make a play like that again! That was my decision to make not yours. This shit not about you, cause trust you not hurting how I am. I know you may see me as that same young ass nigga looking to hustle for you but that's old shit. I can hold my own now and if I decide to do anything to them it will be on my terms."

He walked off and Ameer grabbed his arm again. Oshun took a deep breath to calm himself down. He didn't want shit to turn completely sour between him and his boy, but Ameer was really pushing it.

"I'll just fuck with you whenever," he said trying to relax.

Ameer let his arm go and Oshun walked away before he could reply. He slid into his truck and sped out of the warehouse parking lot. He was so angry that his fist gripped the steering wheel tightly. Ameer was like family to him but the play he'd called was wrong. Ameer knew that Oshun wasn't from the same background as him. Oshun didn't hustle or kill people. His lifestyle wasn't set up like that. He may have looked the part, but in reality, he was a black man trying to peacefully live in a world that was set up for him to fail.

Now he felt like half of a man because while he'd done the right thing it felt wrong as fuck in his soul to leave the same man breathing that watched his brother take his last breath.

CHAPTER 9

"I can't believe you were arrested. I heard my granny and her girlfriends talking about it yesterday. They said it happened awhile, ago in the BOC. Why didn't you tell me when you came to the boutique? I swear I hate the cops and it's not all of them. I even have a few people in my family that are law enforcement and they too don't like how things are going with the police and minorities. Still, it is a lot of people with a badge that don't like or trust people with skin that has some color to it," Pinky fussed.

Jaylah sat on the hotel bed nodding. After receiving a WYD text from Pinky she'd decided to call her up. She was currently waiting for Oshun to arrive at the hotel so they could enjoy their night together. Jaylah had been dodging calls and texts from Jerry and Brooke. A decision was to be made and she was still on the fence on what to do.

"Your boutique thing was for you. I wasn't going to make that about me and thanks again for inviting me. It was fun. I was arrested though girl, and I don't regret it. Oshun told me to be quiet but I just couldn't do that. They were harassing us for no reason then when we left the police station, they stopped us again," she replied.

Pinky gasped.

"Wow! Is it like that up north?" Pinky asked.

Jaylah shook her head.

"Not really. Everybody knows everybody so it's more of a family vibe. I can say it was different living on the Southside though. Now looking back I do remember the cops stopping guys for being black. I just never thought anything of it," she confessed.

"Hmph. Well, down here we've always dealt with that. I mean when I was younger, I used to hate going to the suburbs. Good license or not I knew the cops would harass me. We were scared to cross 8-mile road girl. It's like second nature here and it's even harder for the men. They have to be a Steve Urkel kind of dude to not be harassed but even then, they get a lil smoke. However, if you look like king, you really gone be stopped," Pinky told her.

Jaylah's eyes went to the clock inside of the room and she saw it was thirty minutes passed the time Oshun was supposed to retrieve her. She sighed hoping he was okay.

"Hey, why do you all call him king?" she asked lowly as if someone beside Pinky could hear her talking.

Pinky laughed loudly.

"Girl why the fuck you whispering? And before my granny moved to the BOC, I heard about the Lacoste brothers. Even their cousins Sayeed and Deen is the shit but when I saw Oshun—I knew. I knew he was the one they called king. He naturally handles business. He is a born leader. He's there for everybody girl. I mean *everyone.* His crown is visible as hell to me. Royalty is flowing through his veins and if he likes you then you better do what Cardi said. *Wrap your legs around that nigga make him give your ass a child,*" Pinky joked rapping the end.

Jaylah snorted before laughing. Cardi B wasn't her cup of tea, but she did know the song that Pinky was referring to.

"Nah, it's not that serious," Jaylah claimed shaking her head.

"Bitch! It better be. This is fucking Oshun Lacoste we're talking about! I know a bitch that wanted him so bad she went to a witch doctor and the nigga still curved her. That's how godly he is. You can play if you want twin and let the realist nigga in the city get away. That's on you," Pinky said and smacked her lips.

Jaylah smiled as her phone vibrated. Without looking she knew who it was.

"And who is Latoya to him?" she asked quickly as she stood.

Pinky giggled.

"She's like their sister but I do think for a minute she

was fucking Oshun. She's cool, I guess. I never hung with her, but I can say that he's never looked at her the way I see him looking at you. She is fine as hell with that body of hers but for a man like Oshun, you will have to make him fall in love with more than pussy. He seems like the kind of man that likes a challenge. I guess that's why he's fishing up your pond, enjoy your night twin," Pinky said and ended the call.

Jaylah looked at her phone and smiled at the message waiting on her to be read.

Oshun: I'm outside.

No love or sweetheart still the message made her feel good on the inside. She slipped on her black Fenty cowgirl heeled sandals, grabbed her black clutch, and rushed out of her suite. She giddily went to the first floor and before exiting the sliding doors she walked slower with a strut to her subtle curves that weren't as much as Latoya's but still packed a mean punch.

For the date, she'd worn a black slip dress that was so tight she first feared she would bust through it. Jaylah had gone to the mall and found it inside of Allure Boutique. The store was nice with custom pieces that she didn't mind spending money on. Plus, the store was black-owned. Jaylah was happy to learn that after meeting the owner, a pretty woman by the name of Mickey.

She felt like if she could shell out thousands on white designer labels, she could do it for one of her own.

Her own.

There she was again feeling that way only this time it didn't scare her.

Instead, it made her smile.

Jaylah exited the smoked glass sliding doors of the hotel and sucked on her bottom lip as she watched Oshun lean against the passenger door of a white McLaren 570S. Jaylah eyed the expensive car with her heart racing. Her eyes once again connected with Oshun and her lids navigated their way up and down his tall frame slowly.

Oshun was wearing black slacks with a cream collared silk Balmain shirt that was unbuttoned at the neck. Black loafers sat on his feet while black jewels decorated his wrist and neck. Those hooded dark honey-hued eyes of his looked sad as Jaylah advanced on him.

"Are you okay? What's wrong? Was it the cops again?" she asked ready to act a fool.

Oshun's chin lifted. He shook his head as a smirk came over his face.

"Relax, love and you look so sexy my dick feels like it's about to break off. Give me a hug," he told her.

Jaylah walked into his embrace and hugged him tightly. She closed her eyes as she rested in the peace that he carried with him.

"Let's be up, baby," he said pulling back.

Baby.

She loved that word falling from his lips. It was her favorite term of endearment from him. It carried with it a softness that caressed her heart.

Oshun opened the car door for Jaylah and gently tapped her ass as she slid into the sports car. The inside was luxurious and while the car sat low to the ground Jaylah didn't mind. She watched Oshun get in and as he pulled away, she turned her body to face him.

"Your late," she scolded him softly.

Oshun peered over at her and smiled.

"Today has been hectic on me mentally love. I apologize. I'll make it up to you," he swore, and his words made her nipples harden.

"You promise?" she asked wanting him to make it up to her that night.

Oshun nodded as he weaved in and out of traffic at an even pace.

"My word is bond, pretty girl."

Jaylah cheesed.

Jaylah your acting like a fucking schoolgirl. What are you doing? Are you willing to give everything up for this man?

She asked herself.

Nothing was making sense but being with Oshun felt good. It gave Jaylah a happiness that she hadn't felt in a long time.

"What happened today? Maybe I can make you feel

better?" she probed wanting to know what was going on in his life.

Oshun sighed and his big hand slid over to her left hand. He caressed it while staring straight ahead.

"Talk to me some more so I can hear that sexy ass voice. Has your boss called for you to come back home?" he asked.

Jaylah's skin prickled at his question. She tried to remain calm as she stared down at his tattooed hand.

"Not yet, why? Are you ready for me to go?"

Oshun shook his head while frowning.

"If that was the case, I wouldn't be paying that high as hotel bill," he replied.

Jaylah smiled as relief fell over her. She'd been surprised when she checked her card and saw that the hotel had stopped charging her. Oshun took it upon himself to place his American Express card on file and while she didn't financially need him to do that, she respected that he did.

"You said you wanted me to keep you so that's what I'm doing love," he said breaking the silence.

Jaylah blushed. She smiled to herself as she looked out of the car window. Oshun's hand went to the split in her dress and he caressed her bare thigh before sliding his hand up. Jaylah willingly opened her legs and allowed for his mannish fingers to caress her silky, clean-shaven folds.

His brows rose as he peered over at her. "No panties?" he asked.

Jaylah shook her head. She wanted to say it was because

none worked with the dress, but she knew the real reason why.

"No, *sir*," she said softly.

Oshun's breath hitched. He pulled up to the red light and his eyes drifted over to her. Two of his fingers found their way into her love box as he stared into her eyes. She was slippery wet for him and her moan vibrated inside of the car as he fingered her tight walls.

"I wanna taste your pussy again, love," he professed.

Oshun pulled away as Jaylah opened her legs wider. His fingers felt like dick as they thrust into her walls searching for her orgasm.

"I want that too," she moaned trying to talk through the pleasure. "I've never met anyone like you Oshun. I know that eventually, I will have to go back home and that makes me sad because then I'll be apart from you. I'm trying to figure this out. I really am—I mean, I really need to cum sir," she begged no longer able to hold off.

Oshun pulled up to the restaurant's valet. He shut the car off and hit the locks. He leaned over and kissed Jaylah's neck sensually as if it were her pussy.

"I want you to wait. The next time that pussy cum it will be on my dick. Let's be up," he said and removed his fingers from her sex.

Jaylah's chest heaved up and down as she pouted. She got herself together and patted her coochie dry with a napkin that Oshun gave her. Together they entered into the Mon Amour restaurant hand in hand. Oshun called off the Lacoste name and they were immediately shown to a booth in the back of the place. The restaurant was retro chic with its black and white wallpaper and Andy Warhol style pictures of great Hip Hop and R&B legends.

Jaylah grabbed Oshun's hand as they approached the booth with his family. The woman Sadie that read her like a book stood and pulled Jaylah into a hug.

"I'm happy you all could make it," she said rubbing her back.

Jaylah smiled praying Sadie didn't feel the need to read her again.

"Sorry about us being late," she offered as Sadie let her go.

"I called them already baby," Oshun said dapping up his cousin.

Jaylah gave Oshun's cousin a timid smile and he returned with a head nod. They all sat in the booth and Oshun pulled Jaylah to his side. His eyes peered into her intently as she looked up at him.

"You look so beautiful, baby," he whispered.

Jaylah blushed.

She appreciated his words. He seemed to like her any way that she came. She'd heard about women being with men that only preferred them one way but Oshun didn't seem like that type.

"We ordered the chef's meal for everyone. Oshun said that was okay," Sadie said looking at Jaylah.

Jaylah nodded. That was fine. There wasn't anything she was allergic to that she knew of. She wasn't a big meat eater, preferring fish instead but if Oshun wanted to feed her some filet mignon she would scarf that shit, down for him without giving it a second thought.

"Yes, that's fine. How have you been?" Jaylah asked.

Oshun and his cousin sparked up a conversation as Jaylah smiled Sadie's way. Like before Sadie was stunning. She wore a black jumpsuit with her sandy brown hair pulled into a sleek ponytail. Her natural beauty was on display as she wore no makeup with nude glossy lips.

"I've been okay. My spirit has been down lately. With everything happening with Malik and the world in general I've struggled with being fully happy. I have peace because of God, my man, our kids, and the family but this chaotic world we're living in is draining me," Sadie admitted.

Jaylah nodded. Sadie carried a light to her that Jaylah had never seen before.

"Has He been talking to you about me? I've been all over the place as well," Jaylah laughed but was dead ass serious.

Sadie smiled. She sipped some of her lemon water and shook her head.

"He hasn't. I see somethings but I don't want to scare you. I'm a firm believer in people finding their way. Sometimes we have to run into the wall to acknowledge that it's there."

Jaylah nodded.

So, it's a wall in front of me. Just great.

She thought.

"Well can I get a hint then I promise to leave you alone about it," Jaylah begged shamelessly.

Sadie sat up and reached across the table for Jaylah. Jaylah eagerly met her hands.

"Trust in the Lord. Stop leaning on your own understanding. Stop trying to do His job. I don't know your life Jaylah, but I can see that for so long you've done things your way. Why not try it His way and see just how He can shift things for you in your favor? Whatever the devil is using to hold over you can only work if you allow it so speak your truth," Sadie told her.

Sadie let Jaylah's hands go as Jaylah's mind went to work with what Sadie could possibly be talking about.

Holding over my head? Jerry? The job? Plotting on Oshun is for sure up in there somewhere.

She said to herself.

Jaylah made sure Oshun and his cousin weren't paying them any mind before she responded.

"Thank you," she said softly.

Sadie waved her off.

"I only did it because He told me that you needed to hear it. Let go and let God handle it. And Oshun I heard about you getting on board with Deen's hospital. Are you having a wing named after Malik?" Sadie asked.

Jaylah's eyes shot to Oshun. The waiter brought out salad

along with a bottle of wine and Jaylah chose to go for the wine over the food as she waited for Oshun to respond.

"For him, I have to. The hospital is a good look for Deen. I'm glad he brought me on board with it then we're creating a program for young black men to join so we can keep them out the street. Last I checked we had five businesses on board that is willing to give them jobs. We still need benefactors for scholarships and shit like that though," he replied.

Jaylah's jaw nearly dropped from her pretty face. She held her glass mid-air while staring at Oshun. She knew about the BOC and the other businesses he owned but this was next level. It was a fucking hospital. It seemed unreal but Oshun wasn't the type to fib for clout, so she knew it wasn't a lie.

Oshun's dark honey eyes peered over at her as his cousin began to talk with his woman.

"Don't drop your glass, baby. Didn't I tell you I would make you have faith in black men again?" he asked and tapped her chin.

Jaylah's mouth clamped shut and she turned facing forward in her seat. Oshun pulled her closer to him, kissed her neck tenderly and for several minutes everyone ate in peace. They were soon served the main course which was a rack of lamb with rosemary, asparagus, and a yogurt sauce. Sadie blessed the food, and everyone dug in as the waitress brought out dark liquor for them to drink.

Oshun's disposition was once again shifting as Jaylah

noticed his jovial mood fade away. She rubbed his leg and squeezed his thigh to garner his attention.

"Everything okay?" she asked in a whisper.

Oshun nodded pouring up a drink.

"Yes, baby," he said lowly.

Sadie looked their way and smiled.

"Isn't black love beautiful?" she asked.

Jaylah and Oshun stilled at her words while Chevez smirked. He kissed Sadie's cheek as she popped her hand over her mouth.

"I know eventually you will just want to stay the hell away from me, Jaylah. I wasn't trying to make you all uncomfortable," she apologized smiling.

Oshun shook his head.

"If love is what happens to us then I'm good with that," he said coolly as if he were discussing the basketball game.

Jaylah's alarmed eyes shot to Sadie and Sadie winked at her before they began to discuss something else. An hour later they were stuffed and slightly intoxicated as they stood to leave. Sadie pulled Jaylah close as they walked out of the restaurant.

"Can you meet with me later this week? I need to talk to you about something very personal," Sadie said quietly.

Jaylah nodded. She called off her number to Sadie and they exchanged hugs once again before departing at the door. Oshun placed his hand at the small of Jaylah's back and led her to his car. They slipped in and Jaylah sighed. Her body was feeling right off the good wine she'd drunk all through dinner.

She brushed her thighs together, licked her heart-shaped lips and peered over at Oshun. He drove with a small frown marring his face.

"Oshun will you please talk to me?"

Oshun glanced over at her and his eyes did a quick sweep of her alluring body. He looked back at the road before speaking.

"It's nothing love. Let's listen to some music," he said.

Oshun turned on the radio. One song was ending as the radio host spoke into the speaker.

"Okay, so I'm low key heated right now! The chief of police just released a statement and said that he is going to allow for the officers involved with the shooting of Malik Lacoste to remain on the job. Like they haven't done anything wrong and I feel some kind of way about that bullshit. Just twenty minutes ago this was released to the public and I'm sure it was done to support the police departments fucked up ways. I don't want to play it but the way the media is set up they will just play the shit anyway so here you go," the woman radio host said.

Seconds later a clip began to play and when the deep voice broke out inside of the car Jaylah's eyes shot over to Oshun.

"Look its always fuck the police to me. Them motherfucka's can't tell me shit to do. I'll handle all of them bitches and

if I can't I know my brah can. They need to be scared of a nigga like me. I'm black, strong as hell and smarter than them bitches," the young man said with a laugh. *"Aye, pass that blunt my nigga!"*

The recording stopped and Jaylah closed her eyes. This was the media deflecting. She'd even done it plenty of times on her news station.

"The chief of police released this statement after this audio of Malik Lacoste was released earlier," the radio host cut in to say.

"As a man that has been sworn in to protect the public, hearing such an audio breaks my heart. There is no doubt in my mind that this young man was a criminal. He has said from his own mouth that he hates the authorities. The dashcam from the shooting is ruined due to technical issues on the police departments' end but it is safe to say that the shooting was authorized. If it wasn't wouldn't the attorney general be prosecuting the officers involved?" the chief of police said snidely.

Oshun turned the radio off before the clip was done playing. Jaylah reached for Oshun's right hand and inhaled a sharp breath. It was hard as steel as she gripped it softly.

"Please slow down. I don't want them to stop us," she said worriedly.

Normally she was with the smoke but with how angry Oshun was she could see the officers shooting him down out of fear that they would be beaten to death by him.

"I wish they would fucking stop me right now," he gritted out.

Oshun took Jaylah back to her hotel and hit the locks on his car. She reached for the handle but stalled when her eyes ventured over to him.

"Please come up," she begged softly.

Oshun stopped frowning to peer over at her.

"In a minute, I need to smoke, my love," he told her.

Jaylah relaxed and slowly she nodded.

"Okay."

She exited the car and went into the hotel with her mind racing. Jaylah took the elevator up to her room and took a quick hot shower to pacify the ache in her sex before having a glass of wine from the minibar. Jaylah turned on Nina Simone remembering that she was one of Oshun's favorite old school singers and she waited for him at the foot of the bed in nothing but her black silk robe.

She knew it was lust. It had to be. Because truly it was insane to love someone you just met still the emotions, she felt for Oshun were real. So palpable that they frightened her. She was over her job, done with the scheming. The Lacoste family was hurting. What the police had done was wrong as hell and they were still fucking with them. Oshun wasn't a drug dealer. He helped his community, gave back to anyone that he could, and invested in hospitals. He was shit, her dream man, not Americas most wanted.

She needed to change that narrative and was willing to do anything to show the world the real him.

Jaylah jumped up from the bed and grabbed her cell. She ignored the texts she'd received from Jerry, Kylie, and her MLN connection. Jaylah checked the savings on all three of her accounts and sighed.

The one good thing about it being just her was that she was able to save. Her $300,000 savings was proof of that.

"So, if they fire me, then they just do," she murmured putting her phone back onto the charger.

"Why would they do that?" Oshun asked stepping into the room.

He wreaked of cannabis as his arms went around her waist. Oshun kissed her neck sensually before pulling back and taking a seat at the large black chair that was in the corner of the bedroom. Jaylah turned to him and finished her drink. Nina Simone's "Don't Let Me Be Misunderstood" began to play and damn wasn't the song on point. Jaylah dropped her robe as Oshun pulled on his beard hairs sitting at the bottom of his handsome face.

His hooded eyes were red-rimmed, and she could tell he was upset. All she wanted to do was take his pain away.

Baby, you understand me now?
If sometimes you see that I'm mad
Don'tcha know that no one alive can always be an angel?

"What you know about Nina, love?" he asked lowly while smiling.

Jaylah grabbed the silk belt from her robe and smiled sexily at him.

"Nothing until you came into my life. Let me take your pain away even if for a moment," she begged.

Oshun didn't reply as she advanced on him, robe belt in hand. Jaylah sat the belt onto his lap and held out her wrist with her palms turned up. She pushed them together as if they were about to be cuffed and Oshun cleared his throat.

"I'm not ready to fuck you yet sweetheart," he said lowly.

His words crushed a piece of her happiness, but she quickly shook it off. Jaylah dropped to her knees in front of Oshun with her wrist still extended out.

"Then let me pleasure you, sir."

Oshun licked his lips as his eyes slid over her oiled-up body. He tied her wrist tightly before standing. His belt was soon unhooked and as he slid his boxers down freeing the beast that swung between his legs Jaylah's sex clenched together.

She wanted him so bad she was about to lose her mind.

"Who runs the show, Jaylah?" he asked grabbing her face.

His hand stroked her cheek as she peered up at him.

"You do sir."

That easily she submitted.

Oshun stared down at her lustfully as his dick bobbed with his movements.

"I want some clean head tonight, Jaylah. If spit fall you better, make sure you catch that shit and when my nut shoots out, I want you to hold out that pretty little tongue of yours and allow for all of it to drip in your mouth. Okay?" he asked.

Jaylah moaned eager to suck his dick.

"Okay."

Slap.

His hand lightly popping the bottom of her face made her moan. Damn, she'd never been into this type of freaky shit but doing it with Oshun made her wetter than an ocean.

"Okay, *sir*," she corrected herself and happiness brushed across his face.

"Good girl. Open your mouth," he commanded, and like his love slave, she did. Her eyes admired his beautiful brown shaft that was blemish-free. It was thick like a sausage and veiny with its large mushroom head. Pre-cum slipped from the opening and she licked at it as he rubbed the tip around the front of her mouth.

"No teeth, no gagging, and no lazy shit. Now suck me off love, let me feel that warm ass mouth you got," he said to her.

With her hands bound Jaylah sucked in as much of Oshun as she could. She peered up at him lovingly as she used her jaw muscles to suction his penis. More saliva filled her mouth and slowly it started to slip down his rod. Jaylah allowed for his penis to plop out of her mouth and she caught her saliva as it slid down his balls. His penis smelled so fresh and clean that she couldn't get enough of it.

Jaylah sucked on his balls taking them in two at a time. She heard him groan and his pleasure gave her pleasure. She stopped pleasuring his sack to slide her tongue back up to his shaft. She gently sucked on the head then grew more aggressive as she whirled her head to allow more of his member into her mouth.

"Damn, baby right fucking there. Suck that shit," Oshun groaned.

Simply thinking that she was giving him the pleasurable escape he needed made Jaylah moan. She went harder on his dick taking in so much that she feared she might choke on it. He pulled back almost sensing her discomfort and jerked the base of his shaft while she sucked on the head of his penis.

"There you go, suck that shit," Oshun groaned and his words of encouragement were enough to make her go harder.

Jaylah suctioned his penis until his legs did a slight shake.

"You taste so good, please cum in my mouth sir," she begged wanting him to release his fluids onto her tongue.

Oshun's breathing hitched as he looked down at her. He grabbed a handful of her straight strands and pulled harder as he pumped into her mouth.

"If you want me to cum your gonna have to suck that shit like you mean it. Take it all, love," he coached her.

Jaylah nodded obediently. She breathed through her nose and took her time deep throating his cock. She'd never sucked a dick so big. Fear of the unknown made her nervous while wanting to please Oshun made her anxious. Jaylah's tongue slid around the base and she sucked his dick so far into her mouth that when she swallowed, she squeezed his fat mushroom head. Oshun's grip on her hair loosened and she knew she had him where she wanted him.

Jaylah peered up at him and she commenced to sucking the life from his body. She wanted him to remember her head then go to sleep and dream about that shit.

"It's coming, Jaylah. *Fuck* here it go!" Oshun groaned and pulled out his member. He jacked it fast as she held out her tongue.

He emptied his release into her mouth, and she swallowed it all. Oshun pulled himself together and untied her hands. He then fell back onto the bed and before Jaylah could ask if he liked the head he was lightly snoring.

The next day Jaylah talked with Kylie as she waited for Pinky at a nearby breakfast spot. Oshun was gone from her bed and she couldn't stop thinking about how fat and long his dick was.

She couldn't wait to feel it inside of her.

"Jaylah, what's going on down there? Months have gone by and you're still in Detroit. Like damn, come home! I miss you and I need you around. You're even ignoring my calls and texts like were not best friends. Are you still mad at me?" Kylie asked.

Jaylah sighed upset that she'd finally taken Kylie's call.

Their talks didn't carry the same vibe as before. It seemed like everything Kylie said got on her damn nerves.

"I've been busy Kylie," she said rolling her eyes.

"Then you send me a text about you being locked up and you go missing again. I was worried sick! I couldn't believe that you were arrested. Like you have a fucking record now because of this mess," Kylie said in astonishment.

Jaylah nodded.

"I know all because of the cops," she replied.

Kylie snorted.

"The cops? Um mam I was speaking of you. If you would have done what they asked none of that would have happened. I saw a video online of the entire thing on that damn BOC page. Jaylah you were provoking them," Kylie told her.

Jaylah's face twisted in anger as she shook her head.

"Provoking them? Kylie, they stopped us for no reason. We literally were walking down the street!"

"I know and all you had to do was comply. They said they heard about a break-in, so they had a right to stop and frisk. Their job is to protect and serve. Old boy is fine, like so fine I would fuck him on me and Jesse's bed, but he isn't fine enough to take a bullet for. You must have slept with him for you to be doing all of this. Tell me what that dick looks like?" she asked giddily.

Jaylah's eyes rolled in irritation. She watched Pinky walk up and the person beside Pinky was none other than Greedo.

Jaylah dropped her phone as she was catapulted into another memory from her past.

"This is different," Jaylah said stepping into the deserted park.

Greedo chuckled as he walked behind her. He hugged her from the back, and she struggled to remain calm.

"Don't tell nobody about this. They gone think a nigga soft," he said chuckling.

Jaylah looked at the picnic that was laid out for her on the large plaid blanket and she blushed. Seeing Greedo put so much effort into the park date made her feel special. They'd been dating for a few months and she could see herself seriously falling for him.

"I love it! I mean this is something my dad would have done for my mom. Very thoughtful," she told him.

Greedo let her go and smacked her ass appreciatively.

"Glad you like it," he said smiling.

Jaylah slipped off her flip flops and copped a squat on the blanket. She cheesed like a giddy schoolgirl as Greedo pulled sandwiches from the cooler along with a bottle of champagne. He popped the Moet as Jaylah took small bites of the sandwich. They were in a deserted park on the Northside of Baymoor Falls. The scene was movie like as roses sat on the blanket along with a black gift bag. Jaylah eyed the gift bag as she watched Greedo take the Moet to the face.

"I'ma be a rapper one day Jaylah and you gone be my wife," he told her.

Jaylah smiled wider.

"I am?" she asked.

Greedo nodded. Instead of his usual designer hood gear, he wore black pants with a designer button-up. His fade was freshly trimmed along with his goatee. Jaylah had never seen anyone as fine as him ever.

"Hell, yeah you are. You will be on the news while I'm on the road making that paper. I already got money put away for it," he said passing her the bottle.

Jaylah didn't want to seem green to drinking so she chugged down the champagne and burped when she set the bottle down. Her cheeks burned with embarrassment as Greedo stretched out onto his side.

"Excuse me!" she yelped beyond embarrassed.

Greedo waved her off.

"Stop it. Nothing you could do would make me not like you. Check the bag," he told her.

Jaylah looked into the blue gift bag and pulled out a small box. She opened the box with a jittery stomach.

"I had to have my aunt help me out with the shit. She said she eventually wants to meet you," he whispered.

Jaylah blushed as she peered down at the heart pendant that was a stunning rose gold. She allowed for Greedo to place it around her neck and as she touched the necklace his lips brushed against her skin.

"I wanna lick on you, can I?" he whispered.

Jaylah closed her eyes and her body warmed to his words.

She never done that before but wasn't scared of it. She just had never met anyone that piqued her interest until she met Greedo.

"Yes," she conceded.

Greedo placed Jaylah onto her back and hovered over her body. She was able to peer up into his chestnut almond eyes as his hand fondled her breast.

"I like you and if you stick with me, you will be good. I'll never hurt you," he swore kissing her lips.

Jaylah moaned into his mouth as he made her body feel a way it never had before.

"Damn you so pretty, I just wanna make you feel good," *Greedo whispered before sliding down her body.*

"Omg, that's Greedo! Can you sign my shirt! *Ahhhh!*" a woman screeched from a nearby table.

Pinky sat down rolling her eyes as Greedo stood planted to the floor in front of the table. Jaylah stared at him as her leg began to shake. He looked better. More mature with his full beard. Long gone were the days of his even fade. He now rocked a curly taper and while his clothing was designer and he smelled of a nice cologne none of it mattered.

Jaylah rushed to grab her things as her heart thundered in her chest.

"Jaylah, this is my brother on my daddy side. If I knew you hated rappers, I would have made him stay home but he's in town just to see me. Is everything okay?" Pinky asked raising her brow.

Jaylah ignored Pinky and rushed out of the bakery. Greedo caught her by the arm as she walked towards her car.

"Let me go! Don't you ever in your fucking life touch me again!" she yelled so angry that she was shaking.

Greedo quickly dropped his hand and walked up behind her. His hand went to her waist as Jaylah closed her eyes. She didn't want to cry. Shit, she didn't want to feel anything however the onset of fresh tears was too hard to ward off. They came in a flood blurring her vision.

"My lil sis was talking about you. She said that you were from up north and I might know you. I came just to see if it was you, ma. We need to talk. I need to know if she's—"

"Don't! Don't you dare say it. Leave me alone and if you ever come near me again, I'll go to the cops and tell them your harassing me. Stay away from me," she told him and unlocked her car door.

Jaylah got into her car and hastily pulled away as Greedo stood in the middle of the parking lot with his hands on his head. Jaylah started for the hotel and changed her course as she thought of Greedo. Seeing him had her feeling vulnerable. Oshun was in Chicago handling business with his cousin and she needed comfort. She wanted someone to talk to that would understand her pain. Only the person she was going to see was also responsible for some of the tragedy that happened in her life.

After using her GPS to navigate her way through the city Jaylah pulled up to her twin's beauty bar. Because of social media, she was aware that Jael was working that day but wasn't sure if she was still there. Jaylah pulled up to the J-Spot Salon and parked on the side of the building. She wiped her face and sat in her car for several minutes not sure what to do.

Her mind went to Oshun once again and when she pulled out her phone to call him. Jerry's call came through. Jaylah declined his call and seconds later she received a text message from him.

Jerry: The pickup has been ready. Not sure what's going on with you Jaylah, but I saw something in you that no-one else did. I chose you out of all of the new hires. Together we're an unstoppable duo girl. I hope you're not forgetting about the one person that always had your back. Call this number and do what you have to do so you can come home. This has gone on long enough.

313-200-3221

Jaylah read over the message before going to Oshun's number. She dialed him up praying he answered the phone.

"He's busy," Latoya answered then ended the call.

Jaylah's jaw dropped before she nodded. She wasn't in the mood for Latoya's shit. Oshun made her believe he was taking a trip with his cousin Deen for business but now she knew better. He was keeping secrets and although she was too it didn't sit well with her how he was playing shit. Jaylah put her phone away and took a deep breath. She exhaled, said a silent prayer, and got out of her car. Her feet felt heavy as bricks as she walked around to the front door.

"Welcome to the J-Spot, do you—"

Jaylah smiled at the receptionist that was probably caught off guard by her resemblance to her twin.

"Is Jael here?" she asked nervously.

The receptionist with the big brown eyes and small button nose nodded slowly.

"Um, yeah. Jael! Your twin literally just walked in!" she yelled.

Jaylah smiled and sat down on the blush nude leather sofa in the waiting area. She ignored the curious glances from the receptionist as her leg started to shake.

"Lele, I don't have time for the games. Diamond is ready to go home and so am I. I still have two faces to do before—" Jael stopped talking when Jaylah stood up. Her lip quivered as she dropped her makeup brush, she was holding. "Is this for real? Are you really here right now?" she asked.

Jaylah swallowed hard. She nodded as her eyes watered. Her sister was so beautiful. She'd blossomed into everything she was meant to be and instead of feeling anger, Jaylah felt complete being in her presence.

"Hey," she said softly.

Jael rushed over and pulled her into a tight embrace as the women from the back of the salon came to the front to witness the reunion.

"I'm so sorry they did that to you. I swear I am and if I could go back and trade places with you, I would!" Jael cried hugging Jaylah.

Jaylah hugged her twin while inhaling her scent. It was strange because for so many years she told herself that she was fine. That she hadn't needed her for anything but as she held onto the other half of her, she felt it. The wholeness that she'd been searching for. She'd held onto the past for so long and she was tired. Jaylah was fed up with being alone and she didn't just want any old body in her life. No, she wanted her family back. She wanted the people in her life that at one point in time she couldn't live without.

"Give them space you guys. Jael deserves that," a makeup stylist announced, and all of the women and kids went back to their respective spots in the salon.

Jaylah and her twin went over to the reception area and seconds later Jaylah's twin was given her daughter. She was a chunky four-month-old beauty with a face similar to Jaylah's. Jaylah smiled hard as she peered down at the beauty that wore pierced ears already with a gold bracelet on that read Diamond.

"She's gorgeous twin, can I?" Jaylah asked.

Her twin smacked her lips as she continued to cry.

"I mean she's half your baby too so yeah. Diamond, this is your auntie, Jaylah," her twin said passing her the baby.

Jaylah held Diamond securely and her mind couldn't

help but wonder. Her twin looked at her and rubbed her arm with knowing eyes.

"I know and it's okay," she whispered.

That was why she was there. They just got each other.

"I saw Greedo today and I freaked out. I haven't seen him since the hospital all those years ago. I can't run from it anymore twin. I mean if I do, I'll be jumping off a bridge soon," she spoke truthfully.

Jaylah's twin shook her head. She was thicker than Jaylah with more ass and breast. Her skin was also covered with a few tattoo's and her beauty, it was still there. More vibrant than ever before. She'd grown into a stunning woman.

"Don't say that. Daddy told us that you finally picked up the phone and we knew. I could feel it then I saw Pinky and she told me you were in town. We've missed you so much. Mommy and daddy are very sad without you. I am too," she expressed.

Jaylah felt guilt wash over her as she gently bounced her niece.

"Work brought me here and I'm at a crossroads in my life. I need you and I can't ignore that anymore. Like I need you in my life again," Jaylah said becoming more emotional. She dropped her head as despair washed over her.

"It's fine, twin. I'm here and you can count on me from here on out. Even when you felt like you couldn't I was there. I got your back," Jael told her, and the thing was she believed her.

Two hours later Jaylah sat with her twin and beautiful mom Lisa inside of her sister's high-rise condo in downtown Detroit. Jaylah couldn't get over how young her mom still looked. She hadn't aged a bit and was now running her own home health business. The reunited family had gone shopping and out to eat and were still catching up as the day was nearly over.

"I missed you and I love you," her mom whispered as she rested her head in her lap. "I don't want us to ever go without speaking and when you go back home, we'll be up there every other weekend," she promised.

Jaylah smiled.

She loved the sound of that.

"That would be nice," she whispered.

"And I want you to forgive your dad," her mom said softly.

Jaylah swallowed hard. Instead of responding to her mom's words, she looked over at her niece that was asleep in her white and pink bassinet. Her sister went crazy with lavish gifts for her daughter, but she understood it.

"Diamond is so pretty," Jaylah whispered.

Her mom smiled as she played in her hair.

"She is. She is the spitting image of you two. I just need for you girls to speak your truths and be happy. That's all I want," she replied.

Jaylah frowned not sure what she was talking about. As

far as her mom knew she was there for work and nothing more.

"Mom, what truths?"

"Momma your husband is calling you on that secret phone of his," Jael said stepping into the room.

Her mom stood and looked from Jaylah to her twin with a big smile on her face.

"God is so good," she whispered before walking off.

Jaylah waited until her mother was out of the room before she looked at her twin.

"What secrets are you hiding, twin?" she asked her.

Jael sighed. She placed her hands onto her thick hips and Jaylah couldn't help but laugh. Like giddy kids they wore matching pajamas and just being in the same space with her twin gave them both such joy.

"Let's go talk before your nosey momma get off the phone," her twin said pulling her away.

They retreated to her sister's bedroom and Jaylah sat on the large bed. Her twins' condo consisted of white and gold furniture. Everything was nice and Jaylah could tell it was also expensive. She was happy to see that her sister was living such a nice life.

"You go first," her twin said joining her on the bed with her baby monitor in hand.

Jaylah sighed.

"No."

"No?" her twin repeated.

Jaylah snickered.

"Stop doing that. You go first," she insisted.

Her twin took a deep breath and sighed.

"Mom is upset that I haven't told Diamond's real father about her. Now you go," she said quickly.

Jaylah shook her head. It wasn't right but she didn't feel like she was in a position to judge anyone.

"Well after college I started working for the news station back home HLN20. Jerry asked me to come down here for work like I said earlier," she explained as her phone started to ring.

"Okay," her twin said smiling. "Keep going."

Jaylah could feel the room grow warm.

"He uh, he wanted—" Jaylah trailed off as she looked at a message from Oshun.

King O: Pick up love, I miss you.

"Who the hell is King O!" Jael yelled snatching the phone.

Jaylah's cheeks burned with embarrassment as she sipped her wine. She watched as her twin read over the message thread and soon Jael's fair skin was darkening.

"Wow, this man has some big dick energy to him. Who the fuck is he? What happened to Garris?" her twin asked.

Jael's brows knitted together.

"You know about Garris?"

Her twin dropped her phone onto the white duvet and sighed.

"Sort of. Me and mom stalked you online. Your IG page was hella dry, but you did just enough to make us feel like we had a piece of you with us," her sister replied.

Jaylah nodded feeling even more fucked up.

"Oh. Well, Garris left me for another woman before I came down here."

Her twin looked at her and smiled.

"Like you care! This King nigga sounds like he is a better man anyway. He talks to you so smooth with that love, and sweetheart. Like daddy does mom," her twin replied grinning.

Jaylah smiled.

"Yeah, I guess he does. The thing is you know that guy that was killed by the cops here? Malik Lacoste?"

Her twin stopped smiling.

"Yeah. What does he have to do with you?" she asked Jaylah.

Jaylah fidgeted with her silk gown as she looked at her twin.

"Jerry wants me to help the cop who pulled the trigger. They share the same fraternity. He's been in the army. He's a hero, Jerry said," she spoke rambling on.

Her twin's almond eyes a greenish hazel shade looked at Jaylah skeptically.

"Spit it out," she said with a tight mouth.

Jaylah cleared her throat.

"I have to get close with the Lacoste family. The original plan was to find out if they sold drugs and exploit that to the media. In return, I would get a pay increase. That then turned into me getting a side deal from someone I know at a major network. I would be the first black primetime news anchorwoman if I handed over information on the Lacoste family. And now Jerry wants me to plan drugs on the family," she revealed.

Her twin stared at her with narrowed eyes.

"I don't know what to say," she admitted.

"Well I do," their mom said stepping into the room. In her arms was baby Diamond as a fierce scowl sat on her beautiful face. "You two girls will not be the death of me. I'm going to need both of you to get your shit together immediately. Jael you will tell Diamond's father about her or I will and you young lady," Jaylah's mom said looking her way. "I know the past fucked you up. I can't imagine the nightmares you have or the feelings that being around a group of black men can evoke out of you but does any of that justify you doing this? This family has lost their son and instead of you covering that story and encouraging the state to lock up the cops you instead set the family up? It's not right sweetie," she said to her.

Jaylah fell back onto the bed and placed her arm over her eyes.

"I'm not going through with it. I would never do that. I mean I won't do that now mom," she said sadly.

Jaylah's mom nodded.

"I know you won't. You don't get a pass to harm other black men because your attackers were never caught, sweetie. I'm not playing baby, make this right."

Jaylah sat up on her shoulders to look at her family.

"I will and I'm scared because even doing that means I lose someone that I care deeply for," she confessed.

"Well, that should give you even more of an incentive to do the right thing. Black men need to be held down. The worlds already kicking them in the back. I hate to see that you're out there helping them. You need to fix this, then pray to God for forgiveness. That's the only way," their mom said and walked out of the bedroom.

CHAPTER 10

THREE WEEKS LATER

Chicago

The white Pyer Moss dress shirt that he'd paired with black slacks fit his upper body so well he told himself that for the next week he would go even harder in the gym. His designer loafers tapped casually on the black shiny floor as he sat beside his cousin and pastor. The inside of the office was fancy. With nice shit everywhere. From the floor to ceiling silver toned mirrors down to the minimalistic black velvet office furniture.

This was CJ Young. One of the highest earning attorneys in the country. With a retainer fee of 150,000 he could afford the opulence of the law firm that sat in downtown Chicago in a High rise building.

Oshun's patience with the police was running out. The last thing he wanted to do was commit a crime and take the law into his own hand, but damn they were trying him.

"Sorry about that. My newborn daughter is sick," CJ the lawyer said stepping into the office.

"Hope she feels better," Pastor Domani spoke beside Oshun.

The lawyer, a young black man that had graduated from a HBCU at the top of his class sat down while nodding. He was two years shy of forty and while his age was young compared to his competition, he had a fire inside of him that propelled him to the top of his game. He represented celebrities and politicians even regular folk like Oshun.

The thing was he only took on cases that called to his spirit. He wasn't your average lawyer. So being represented by him was a blessing.

"I'm glad you all decided to come see me. I'm not disparaging your other lawyer, but a lot should have been done by now. This case is huge, and a brilliant life was taken. We won't let them get away with this. In Simmons VS. Chung, the setup was similar and within three weeks I was able to get those officers suspended from their job which ultimately led to their arrests. I don't play when it comes to my career. This is why God put me here and even if you didn't have the money I would have taken on the case. That's how strongly I feel for you and your family. I've already set up meetings with the Attorney General from your state. He's sleeping right now so it's time for us to wake him up. Oshun I see your presence is big online and in your community. You have a calling on you as well. Something greater than even you imagined. I think it would be good for you to speak out. Do some interviews outside of your pastor, with all due respect. Show the world that you are nothing like what they make black men out to be. What you've done with the BOC is amazing. People should know about that. Right now, they're controlling the story. Even pulling up audio from Malik's old social media accounts to discredit him. I love how well your family is handling the media and the law. But it's time to come at them with everything that we have. I set up an interview with you in New York with the biggest radio show. I'm sure you've heard of the trio and they are eager to talk with you. Is that something you can do?" the lawyer asked.

Oshun nodded although he wasn't too sure. He wasn't looking to be in the public's eye. He wanted to take care of his family and his people. That was it but for Malik he would step out of his comfort zone to make shit happen.

"Yeah, I can," he replied after clearing his throat.

The lawyer looked at him and smiled.

"Perfect. Also, I've done some digging and the Officer Polk is connected to a well-known racist fraternity. The members are executives, lawyers even politicians. They have a strong hand in the way this country moves. That's not something to be ignored. I'm sure that's why he's still on the job. I've compiled a list of the members and I've passed it over to a few of my friends that work in the media. Tomorrow at noon they will post those members on all of their social media pages asking for them to tell Officer Polk to do the right thing. Just another tactic to let them know that we know who they are," the lawyer told them.

"I'm feeling that. You on your shit," Deen said looking at the lawyer.

The lawyer sat back and frowned as his eyes connected with Oshun's.

"I *promise* I will do everything that I can to make sure these cops spend the rest of their lives in prison," he said, and his words were spoken with so much conviction that Oshun actually believed him.

After meeting with the lawyer Oshun talked with his pastor outside of the building as his cousin and Latoya waited for him inside of their car.

"I appreciate you coming with us here," Oshun told Pastor Domani.

The pastor shook his head.

"Don't thank me just keep having faith that God will handle this. I know for a man like you that's been nearly impossible, but the Lord is working on it. He's also proud of you. He wants you to know that. Come here,"

the pastor said and pulled Oshun into an embrace. "*Blessed is the man that stands on faith*. If at any time you need me, you call. I'm not just a pastor. I am your family, your friend and your confidant. Stay safe," he said and let him go.

Oshun made sure his pastor was safely in his town car before going over to his cousins white Phantom. Their first stop was the hotel to change before heading to dinner at one of Chicago's newest steak eateries. Latoya sat beside Oshun while Deen talked with his lady friend Mickey. Oshun was uncomfortable with the setup because he hadn't known that Deen was bringing someone with him. Now the shit looked like it was a couples get away when it was everything but that. He'd come to Chicago for business and to talk with the lawyer. Latoya was along for the ride but that was them. They always hung out with no issues. However, he didn't want her getting any ideas because they weren't moving towards anything sexual ever again.

Especially now that he saw she couldn't separate the two.

"How did everything go with the lawyer, king?" Latoya asked scooting closer to him.

Oshun stopped eating his salmon to peer over at Latoya. In the dimly lit restaurant, her beauty shined bright. She wore a black pantsuit that hugged her curves with high heels. Her lips were painted red while she wore her hair in tousled curls. She smelled divine like always and he couldn't stop the smile from forming on his face. They'd been through a lot of things together. She had his back same as he had hers.

"I'm happy with changing the lawyer. This guy is really on his shit," he replied.

Latoya smiled wide. She grabbed onto his arm while grinning.

"For Malik," she whispered.

Oshun nodded somberly.

"Yeah, for Malik," he agreed.

His thoughts drifted back to when he was inside of the warehouse. Easily he could have claimed his revenge. While he knew that walking away was the right thing to do it hadn't made him feel good. He still felt fucked up about it and the only thing to lift his spirits had been Jaylah.

He missed her pretty ass and couldn't wait to get back home so he could see her. Between flying in and out of Chicago along with doing extra work in the BOC he'd been busy as hell. Jaylah was reconnected with her family and was catching up on all of the time she could with them. Oshun was happy for her and would never complain about that but damn he missed having her by his side. Originally, she was set up to be in Chicago with him, but she'd canceled at the last minute to stay home with her mom that was getting over a cold. The small time apart from Jaylah showed Oshun that he wouldn't be able to handle her going back to Baymoor Falls. That would fuck him all up. He was currently plotting on ways to keep her in the city for good.

"Excuse me, ma," he said and rose from the table.

Oshun went to the men's room and pulled out his cell. He leaned against the wall as he called her up. Like her phone had been doing since yesterday the call was automatically sent to voicemail. For her to be okay with not talking to him made him uneasy. He decided to send her a text as he chewed on his bottom lip.

What's good beautiful? I pray your still in Detroit when I get back. Are you mad at me and if so why? Without talking about it, I'm at the disadvantage. I can do a lot love, but mind reading is not a skill a nigga like me has. Hit me back baby.

Oshun exited the bathroom and bumped into Latoya in the hallway. She possessed a coy smile on her face as she stood in the center of the floor.

"What's good?" he asked surprised to see her standing there.

Latoya shifted from one foot to the other.

"Nothing I'm just happy to be here with you. All that's missing is Gio and Malik. I know things got heavy with that girl, but we're back on track. I want you to know that I will always be there for you."

Oshun's brows rose. He wasn't a funny style nigga and he was far from simple minded. He didn't play dumb because he fucking wasn't. The last thing he would ever do was let someone disrespect the woman in his life.

"That girl? She looks like a whole ass woman to me, ma. Show respect because I wouldn't let her disrespect you. Stop with the shits Latoya. You're smart, beautiful and cool as hell. Give one of the niggas chasing you down a real chance."

Latoya's smile dimmed as she gazed up at him.

"Anyone but you, huh? Just how did this woman come along in such a short amount of time and grab your attention?

What's so special about her, like I really want to know?" she asked.

Oshun tugged on his beard as he thought of Jaylah. She was beautiful but it was beyond that. She had flaws. Big ones that she didn't think even he could see but he did. Her beliefs were jaded, and she was green to a lot of shit however her heart. He could see that past the ignorance was a beautiful soul. That was what kept him wanting more of her. Oshun could see the potential in the beauty. It was nothing for someone to love a person that spoke, looked and dressed perfectly. But it took real strength to love the sides of a person that wasn't so appealing. He wanted to help her find the beauty inside of herself because then he knew that she would really be a dream come true.

"With her I don't have to try. The chemistry is just there and that's not no dig against you. We vibe all the time but it's not the same. And I would never lie about that to save face. My mom always told me that when love is real you don't have to try hard to feel it. Let's go finish our meal," he replied and pulled Latoya away.

Latoya and Oshun re-joined Deen and his date before calling it a night. As they walked out of the restaurant Deen pulled him to the side. His grey eyes were troubled as he looked at Oshun.

"You good?" Oshun asked.

Deen sighed. He rubbed his waves while looking out at the heavy traffic flowing up and down Michigan Ave.

"Yeah, man. Mickey's pregnant," he said lowly.

Oshun took a step back with wide eyes.

"Damn, congrats," he said dapping up Deen.

Deen nodded. He looked at him worriedly before peering over at the car Mickey was sitting in.

"I'm guessing you not happy about that," Oshun noted.

Deen smirked. He chuckled as he looked back at him.

"It's not that but you know me. I want a wife not a fucking baby momma. And its just—I'll get up with you later and watch Latoya. She was looking *different* tonight," he replied and walked away.

Oshun shook off his cousins' words and went to the car Latoya was waiting in. They went back to the penthouse suite they were sharing and while Oshun read over another article that was written about Malik with false content Latoya passed him a drink.

His angry eyes lifted to her as she stood over him inside of the vast bedroom.

"You need it king, goodnight," she said softly and kissed his forehead.

Oshun nodded and she exited the room. He downed the dark liquor in one sip. Almost instantly the liquor invaded in his system. For another hour he read over articles about Malik before he lost the battle with being awake.

Now it was two days later, and the weekend was upon him. All day he'd been lowkey hyped as fuck because he got to spend some time with Jaylah, but she didn't share the same sentiments as him.

She was mad.

That much he knew but he wasn't sure on the cause of that anger. However, she played it off well. Despite Latoya being there, she still shined like the rare diamond that she was.

Oshun couldn't stop staring at her as he sat on the back of their family's lake house smoking a cigar. His family was able to finally agree on a time to go to his lake house and he was getting a much needed break.

Oshun watched Jaylah swim in the pool with Tiffany and he smiled. Tiffany had been stuck to Jaylah like glue since they'd been there, and he was glad that everyone was getting along.

The lake house was large and had more than enough space for Oshun and his family with its ten bedrooms and five baths it possessed. It also came with a pool that everyone was loving.

Oshun blew smoke from his mouth as his eyes slid up and down Jaylah's curvy body. She was more of a slim thick frame but damn she still stacked. Her ass sat up begging for a spanking while her perky C-cup breast pleaded for a licking. Oshun adjusted his dick not wanting that lil nigga to wake up as his cousin Deen joined him at the glass patio table.

"How long you been knowing her?" Deen asked while staring Jaylah's way.

Oshun looked at him and smirked. Damn his family just didn't want to give Jaylah a break.

"A few months, why? You know her?" he asked.

Deen shook his head. He sat back as he pulled out his ringing cellphone.

"Nah, I don't," he replied then took the call.

"It's time for spades and I want some real money on the floor!" Gio yelled walking up.

Oshun chuckled. He pulled some fifties from his pocket as his brother sat at the table. Jaylah came over seconds later wearing a black sheer skirt cover up while smiling. Her inky black strands were pulled into a hair clip while the black and pink one piece she wore stuck to her body. Oshun pulled her onto his lap never the coy type of nigga and he kissed her neck.

They'd been there half the day and she barely talked with him. Was even quiet on the ride up. He didn't like that shit because it felt like she was trying to pull away from him. He was expecting her to tell him at any minute that she was going home to Baymoor Falls.

"You good, love?" he felt the need to ask.

Jaylah tried to stand and Oshun placed his hand securely on her flat stomach.

"Relax. Did I do something to piss your sexy ass off?" he whispered.

Jaylah sighed. She shook her head again and Gio looked their way. He frowned as he pulled cards from his pocket.

"Let her breathe nigga. She can be your partner. Deen can be mine," he said with a slur to his words.

Oshun's eyes narrowed as he looked over at his brother.

"Didn't I say you needed to chill out with the fucking drinking? Even Tamara tired of that shit. Don't think she didn't call me complaining about your ass," he snapped.

Jaylah stood and sat across from Oshun while Deen pulled money from his pocket as well. Gio smirked as he looked at him. He grabbed his red cup and took a slow sip. Oshun sucked his teeth trying not to knock his silly ass out. Gio was slacking. He'd stopped doing work in the BOC and at his accounting company. His shit was falling apart and while he played in liquor searching for happiness that was at the bottom of the bottle Oshun carried his dead weight.

"You think this shit funny?" Oshun asked sitting up.

"Chill we family," Deen said looking at Oshun and Gio.

Gio smirked. The glazed overlook in his eyes told Oshun that he got a rise out of pissing him off.

"Nah, this nigga looking at me like he got a problem. Do you?" Oshun asked his brother. "Because I got a problem with your ass. We don't have time to drink our days away. We're not them type of niggas. You better tighten the fuck up," he warned Gio.

Gio waved him off but he didn't respond and Oshun was grateful for that because he didn't want Jaylah to have to witness him fuck his brother up.

A few of their family members came out of the house laughing while holding drinks.

"I got next and I'm hurt you didn't pick me as a partner," Latoya said carrying a slur to her words.

Oshun sat back and placed his dark honey eyes onto her. She was chill as fuck after the bathroom incident in Chicago. It was like the old days. They laughed and when he handled business, she shopped. Shit was good but now she was at the cabin doing too much and he didn't like that shit. He wasn't trying to axe Latoya from his life, but she was making their friendship awkward when it didn't have to be.

"Why don't you go get some water and sober up some and bring Gio out some water when you can," he suggested.

Latoya looked at him and smiled. She looked sexy in her white two piece that put her curvy body on display.

"Sure thing, *king*. I mean picking the wrong partner could have you rising real soon anyway," she said seductively and walked off.

Oshun's eyes shot to Jaylah. She stared at him with an indifferent look on her gorgeous face.

"How much longer you staying down here? Did you quit your job, baby? Shit you been here half the year and shit. What you take an administrative dick leave?" Gio said shuffling the cards.

Oshun grabbed the money from the center of the table and placed it in a glass bowl. His narrowed eyes shot to Gio.

"As long as you don't have to pay her bills it shouldn't matter to you," he told him.

Gio smirked. He looked at Jaylah and shook his head.

"Shits weird is all I'm saying. You pop up out of nowhere on some friendly shit and never leave. And what's even funnier is that nobody is saying shit about it," he commented.

Deen shook his head as Oshun tugged on his chin hairs. He had half a mind to knock his brother from his fucking seat.

"What the fuck is the real issue Gio? She isn't doing shit to you," Oshun snapped.

Jaylah sat up and smiled at Gio.

"I took some leave time and my job is okay with that. I knew Oshun before everything happened and he is the reason why I'm still down here but that is coming to an end very soon. It's time to head home. Just being here at this cabin is showing me that," she replied with a big smile.

Oshun's jaw ticked. He stared at the woman that was trying to infiltrate her way into his heart and he frowned.

What the fuck did that mean?

Was she trying to leave him already?

"Gio be nice and you better slow down on the liquor. I'm not Tamara or Oshun, I'll get a belt and whoop your ass if I have to. Now like I was saying leave Jaylah alone, I know a good person when I see one. Me and my sisters are about to head to town. We found a cute bed and breakfast that we couldn't pass up. We'll be back tomorrow afternoon," his mom said and smiled before going back into the house.

Oshun's eyes locked with Deen and Deen smirked at him.

"Mossberg will be with them, you can relax," Deen said speaking on his driver that was often his mom's security.

Oshun nodded he studied Jaylah closely while they played through two hands together. He'd never felt so far away from her. Her words, her mood was off. She was trying to walk away.

He didn't like that one bit and planed on rectifying the situation as soon as he could.

CHAPTER 11

Black Lake

"Thank you for finally taking my call. I had no clue any of that happened to you with my brother and I'm so sorry. He is as well but I won't mention it again," Pinky told her.

Jaylah sat near the pool with her feet in the water. Her body felt right after consuming three glasses of wine that carried with it an 18% alcohol level. She was ready to leave and mad with herself for being so dumb as to ride up with Oshun to the cabin after he'd spent two days in Chicago laid up with Latoya.

Latoya had taken it upon herself to send Jaylah several pictures of them out enjoying the city. Jaylah refused to let Latoya see her sweat but, on the inside, she was hurting. The pictures were proof that it was time for her to go. Being in Detroit with Oshun wasn't her life. Jerry was threatening to come down to the city if she didn't pick up the drugs from his fraternity brother that was a cop.

Jaylah was tired and for the first time in years afraid.

She knew that whatever the outcome was it would take him away from her in the end. Because even with Latoya sending the photos of her and Oshun it still didn't make Jaylah hate him. She saw that he was flawed. He wasn't smart enough to see through Latoya's games, but he was still a good man.

Hell, a great man that she was falling in love with. Jaylah sighed as she placed her attention back onto her phone call.

"I appreciate you not saying his name. I don't want to talk about it either. I've got enough going on with Oshun," she replied and brushed her left hand through her messy strands that had dried into curly ringlets on her head.

"I'm with Oshun and his family up north. I shouldn't have come. It's time for me to go home, Pinky," she replied.

Pinky sighed into the phone.

"Shit I thought you were moving down here. You've been here for so long. This feels right and that's why you're still here. Is Latoya fucking with you?" she asked.

Jaylah smiled.

"Something like that but it's not anything I can't handle."

"Okay well how about we have a girl's night when you get back? You look like you haven't gone to the club since high school and twin can come, I'm so happy you and she made up," Pinky said excitedly.

"That would be cool," she said quietly not sure if it would happen.

Jaylah was ready to wrap up her life in Detroit.

"So, it's set. Have fun and never let a bum hoe that wants the man you have, fuck up your time with him. That's rookie shit right there. You better pull some strength from your twin. She didn't play that shit. She was chin checking bitches for looking at her nigga too long, talk to you later!" Pinky said and ended the call.

Talks of her twin made Jaylah hit her up. She'd learned from her sister that through stripping she met an NBA player. They were on the rocks because of his cheating but Jaylah could sense her sister wanted to take him back. She rose from the pool as her twin's voicemail picked up. Jaylah closed out the screen on her phone and headed back to the house.

She yawned ready for bed although it was only nine at night. Light sniffling grabbed her attention as she passed a set of large bushes. She turned and sitting on the ground with her hands covering her face was Tiffany.

"Hey, you okay?" she asked walking over to Tiffany.

Tiffany lifted her head and gave Jaylah a small smile. She nodded as Jaylah sat beside her.

"Just missing Malik," she said quietly.

Jaylah felt compelled to grab Tiffany's hand. Tiffany rested her shoulder on Jaylah as she started crying again.

"I keep telling myself that everything will be okay. I have his family and his mom sent over his life insurance money for the baby so money wise I'm good. I know I'm one of the lucky ones but then my daughter does a kick in my belly and I'm reminded of the fact that she won't grow up with her dad," Tiffany stopped talking and Jaylah blinked to keep herself from crying.

"I want to die somedays Jaylah because being here without him is so hard. I love him so much and I don't understand why he had to go? Its killers and pedophiles in this world yet Malik was taken? It's just not fair!"

Tiffany broke down and Jaylah allowed for the heartbroken beauty to get out all of the tears that she needed to. Her heart broke for Tiffany. She couldn't imagine the pain the beauty was carrying with her.

"God will comfort you Tiffany," Jaylah whispered.

Tiffany shook her head. She wiped her face as she sat up.

"I don't need comfort Jaylah. I need my man back," she said and stood to her feet.

Tiffany rubbed her belly that was finally protruding as she walked away. Jaylah sat on the ground for several minutes before getting up.

Old school R&B greeted Jaylah as she stepped into the large cabin. Jaylah looked around the downstairs part of the cabin and her eyes connected with Latoya's. Latoya held a glass of wine in her hand while scowling her way. Her eyes were half-mast and Jaylah could see she was well past her limit.

"Tiffany you should get some rest sweetie, the baby needs it and so do you," Latoya said still scowling at Jaylah.

Tiffany nodded as she stood near the sofa holding a bottle of water.

"Yes, I need it, goodnight everyone," she said and walked off.

Once Tiffany was out of the room Latoya changed the music. Jaylah decided to make herself one last drink before searching for Oshun. She found him in the dining room playing chess with his cousin Sayeed. They were seated at a long oak table that housed eight seats.

Jaylah walked up to him, and he pulled her onto his lap as he made his move.

"Yes, please distract this man so I don't lose anymore fucking money," Sayeed grumbled.

His fiancé Egypt rubbed his back tenderly while grinning at Jaylah.

"I'm going to head up for bed. I'm tired and these dudes can hang all night. That's a dub for me, goodnight everyone," she spoke softly. She looked at Jaylah and shook her head. "I want to hook up with you in the morning to discuss my documentary lady. That's cool with you?"

Jaylah nodded. Being on Oshun's lap as he gently rubbed her exposed thigh had her mind thinking of sexual things.

"Sure," she said quickly as Latoya stepped into the dining room bringing with her negative energy.

It was as if Jaylah could immediately feel the shift.

"Great," Egypt said and kissed Sayeed on the lips before walking away.

Latoya sat in the available spot beside Oshun and continued to scowl at Jaylah. Jaylah ignored the heated looks she was pushing her way as Oshun slid his hand up and down her thigh slowly.

"We should play a game," Latoya suggested with a big smile on her face.

"Aye, you juiced as fuck right now. You need to play the sleeping game," Gio told her from the other end of the table sounding much sober than he did earlier that day.

Latoya giggled. She sipped on her drink while smirking at Jaylah.

"We should play never have I ever. I mean we're at the cabin, let's turn up," she replied.

Oshun ignored her still playing chess while Jaylah decided to look at Latoya. The evil way Latoya smiled made Jaylah's stomach knot up. Something about the chick wasn't right.

"I'm going to lay down too," Jaylah said not wanting to show her ass in front of Oshun's family.

Oshun stopped from making his move and held her close to him. His lips brushed against her neck before he kissed the soft spot behind her ear.

"Not yet love. You been spinning me all day. When it's time to lay down we gone do that shit together," he whispered.

Jaylah swallowed hard. He was so demanding and at times it irritated her soul then there were moments when it made her want to suck the skin from his dick.

"*Okay*," she said softly, and Latoya snorted.

"*Okay*, Deen you go first," Latoya said excitedly.

Deen sat up in his seat as his brows tugged together. Tiredness showed on his handsome mug as he looked at Latoya.

"Never have I ever not got to the bag," he said groggily.

A few people chuckled including Oshun. Everyone had to take a drink because making money was their style. The next person to speak was Gio. He looked up from his phone and sighed.

"This some kiddy ass shit," he grumbled. "Never have I ever licked ass," he commented.

The men chuckled while Jaylah's jaw fell slack. She was green to the game and caught off guard by Gio's words. She had no clue what she would say but was certain it wouldn't have anything to do with sex.

"I see all of y'all freaky ass men is drinking up beside Gio," Latoya added while smiling.

The question went from Chevez who refused to play to Sadie. Sadie smiled as she looked at Chevez.

"Never have I ever been in love like I am right now," she said staring at him.

Jaylah swooned at the beautiful couple while Latoya rolled her eyes.

"It's not that kind of game but whatever. Sayeed it's your turn," she told him.

Sayeed waved her off and kept studding the chess board.

"I'll pass on this dumb ass game," he mumbled.

Oshun smirked.

"I'm good as well," he said studying the board too.

Latoya looked at Jaylah and she smiled wide.

"What about you? Do you pass as well?"

Jaylah nodded.

"Yeah, this game is foreign to me," she replied.

Latoya rolled her eyes before snickering. She grabbed her drink and held it casually in her hand while looking at everyone sitting at the table.

"Uh gosh what can I say?" she laughed. Gio shook his head as he looked her way. Latoya sat up straight in her seat and grinned at Jaylah. "Never have I ever given a child up for adoption," she said slowly.

Latoya's eyes connected with Jaylah and she winked at her.

"You better drink up."

Jaylah couldn't stop herself from leaning over. With a death grip on Latoya's short hair she used her free hand to pummel her pretty face.

"Bitch! I tried! You just wouldn't fucking leave me alone! Now I'm going to show your ass! This what you wanted!" Jaylah screeched.

Jaylah jumped onto Latoya and they fell to the ground

falling out of the chair. Latoya tried with all her might to fight back but the anger inside of Jaylah was too strong to go up against. Jaylah saw her attackers on Latoya's face as she grabbed her head and smashed it into the hard wood floors repeatedly.

"Dumb ass bitch! Looking for my attention and now you have it! What, you mad that he wants me! Well guess what saying all of that still won't make him want you!" she yelled bashing her head in.

"Ayo, what the fuck!" Oshun remarked pulling Jaylah off Latoya.

Clumps of Latoya's hair was hanging from Jaylah's hand as he carried her away.

"I'm calling the cops! Bitch you're getting arrested again!" Latoya yelled while holding her head.

Oshun rushed Jaylah up the stairs and into his large bedroom. He locked the door and carried her into the bathroom. Oshun held her close as he turned on the shower. All four of the shower heads expelled hot water as he stepped inside. Jaylah closed her eyes ashamed to look at him.

Oshun sat her on the bench inside of the shower and she allowed for him to take off her swim gear then his own clothing. Naked he held her as the water sprayed against their skin.

"Don't ever be ashamed of anything in front of me love and I swear on my life you will never have to see her again. And don't hold your head down because of that. I mean how the fuck can your crown stay on if you're not holding it up high?" he asked.

Jaylah smiled sadly. She lifted her head and her eyes connected with Oshun.

"I have a daughter that I gave up for adoption when I was seventeen," she said and closed her eyes because it caused her great pain to say those words. Her lips quivered and Oshun silenced her cries with a kiss.

His tongue slid into her mouth as he held her bridal style. Together their tongues mingled in a sensual tango that comforted her heart. Jaylah pulled back not able to take the spicy tongue dance after a few minutes and looked at him.

"I need to lay down," she whispered.

Oshun kissed her forehead.

"Let me wash you up first," he said and like she wasn't able to Oshun did just that.

He sat Jaylah on her feet and took his time cleaning her body. His hands, tongue and even fingers massaged into her skin until she was thoroughly washed clean of the day's worries. Once he was done, he took her into his bedroom and dried her off.

Jaylah's eyes closed halfway through his oil massage and before sleep could overtake her completely, she heard Oshun whisper words to her that were so loving, so raw, so caring that they made her cry.

"I'm willing to love all of you, not just the pretty parts

that you want me to see. Get some rest sweetheart," he whispered.

And rest she did.

The next day Jaylah arose to Oshun hovering over her. Her body was tied to the bed with white silk scarfs. Her legs were being spread with a 20-inch spreader bar that housed leather cuffs that went around the ankles. Jaylah slowly tried to lift from the bed as Oshun peered down at her.

"I want to go home," she said in her raspy voice then cleared her throat.

Oshun's dark honey eyes slid over her frame slowly. Jaylah followed his line of sight and saw that honey trailed from the center of her neck down to the apex of her thighs. He licked his lips longingly as he nodded.

"I know love. Last night was some bullshit and you didn't deserve that," he replied.

Jaylah squirmed on the bed. The position was awkward, but she wasn't in any pain.

"So, you tie me to a bed to keep me here? Sex won't redirect my steps. I'm leaving Oshun," she told him.

Oshun's dark honey eyes filled with worry as he nodded.

"I know, the car is on the way to get us as we speak."

Jaylah opened her mouth to ask another question and Oshun lowered his head. His long tongue swiped across the honey coating her skin. He licked it up like a starving man as his thick fingers massaged the lips of her sex. His tongue trailed the honey across to her left and right nipple and he bit them both tenderly while peering up at her.

"Alexa, play *"Jaylah's About to Cum"*, playlist," he spoke in his deep ass voice.

His tongue went back to her body as *Butta Love* by Next began to play. Jaylah closed her eyes and allowed for Oshun to have his way with her.

"For staying so still I'ma eat this pussy until you cry," he promised and pulled a vibrator from a bag by the bed.

Oshun opened the new vibrator, a shiny rose gold device and turned it on. He licked the rest of the honey from Jaylah's center before placing the vibrator onto her clit. Jaylah's stomach dropped and her thighs shook from the immediate pleasure.

"*Oh*, God," she mumbled.

The pleasure was intense and instantly her body wanted to orgasm from the pleasure. Oshun used two of his fingers to massage her snug walls while using the vibrator to play with her clit.

"Don't cum until I tell you to. Okay, love?" he asked.

The lust in his voice was heavy as he stared up at her.

Jaylah's walls begged for a release as she opened her eyes.

"Okay, sir," she agreed knowing that if she did what he asked she would be rewarded for it.

"Good girl. I want to show you just what this tight lil pussy is capable of," he whispered and changed the speed of the vibrator.

Jaylah bit into her bottom lip as a thin sheen of sweat coated her body. Her head lolled from one side to the other as Oshun leaned up to suck on her nipples.

"Oh my gosh, this feels so fucking good!" she yelled.

Oshun rolled his tongue around her areolas while staring at her. He leaned in to peck her lips as more of her wetness coated his fingers. She was dripping in pleasure.

"Who making you wet like this?" he asked with his lips on hers.

"You sir," she whispered.

Oshun fingered her harder as he pecked her lips.

"Who got that pussy wet like this?" he asked.

Jaylah moaned and he bit her bottom lip.

"You sir!"

Oshun pulled the vibrator away from her clit and kissed her again.

"Who do you want to own this pussy?"

Jaylah looked at him as her chest heaved up and down.

"You sir," she conceded.

Oshun's eyes darkened and he lowered his head.

"When I suck on this pussy, I want you to cum all in my fucking mouth. You hear, me?"

Jaylah nodded very happy with those orders.

"Okay sir!"

Oshun settled between her raised thighs and wrapped his lips around her clit. He sucked on her throbbing bud with a passion and within seconds Jaylah's body bucked for him. His fingers went to work inside of her walls and between the amazing sensations her orgasm was reached. Her eyes grew wet as her mouth fell open. Orgasmic bliss washed over her body as Oshun ate her pussy with all that he had.

An hour later Jaylah hid out on the back patio as she waited for Oshun to load up their belongings. So far, she hadn't seen Latoya and she was fine with that. Jaylah was upset that she hadn't gotten a chance to really kick her ass and promised herself that when she saw the woman again it was going down. She'd use every trick in her book to put that bitch in her place.

"Hey, you," Sadie said stepping onto the back deck that was closed in.

Jaylah offered her a smile as she held her cup of Morning Glory coffee. Sadie set beside her and together they stared out into the backyard. The day was unusually quiet, and Jaylah knew it was because of Latoya's need to put her past on blast.

"What I love about the bible is reading Jesus parts. He's so amazing you know. When he entered the world, he was determined to show everyone that there could be a new way to living. That as man we can still be acceptable in the eyes of God. I also love how he made it a habit of healing the broken. Time and time again he showed that God is merciful. He's forgiving. If only you knew the hell I've endured in my life and He showed mercy on me. The same way He's showing it on you. Your story is being written as we speak. Don't be afraid of change. Don't be afraid to lose people, hell even lose things, Jaylah. There's something that God has shown me that we can't forget," Sadie said and finally looked at her.

Jaylah swallowed down her sadness as she peered over at the beautiful woman with the wise words and gentle smile.

"What's that?" she asked.

Sadie rubbed her leg.

"Everybody can't come with you. When you evolve into being the person you were placed here to be everyone won't be along for that ride. Let go of the pain, sadness, people and things holding you back from growing," Sadie told her.

Jaylah couldn't stop the smile from forming on her face. She leaned over and placed her head on Sadie's shoulder.

"Thank you for that. If only you knew the cluster fuck that my life is right now. The sad thing is my hands aren't entirely clean and I know that's why this is happening. What's even worse is that when it's all said and done, I might not even have Oshun," she revealed feeling safe enough to expose some of her truth to Sadie.

Sadie cleared her throat as she leaned on her.

"If it's in Gods will then he'll be with you in the end. Oshun loves you and real love can withstand anything that is thrown its way. Never forget that," Sadie replied.

Jaylah and Oshun said goodbye to his family and slid into Oshun's truck. Jaylah stretched out, tossed the black chenille blanket over her body and peered out of the window. Oshun turned on Atlantic Star's *"Am I Dreaming"* as he pulled off. The music cut on and Jaylah cut her eyes over at Oshun. She wanted to be angry with him. Everything in her being was yelling for her to end it now. Stop the train before it collided into the wall.

She needed to *derail* soon because if she didn't a head on collision into chaos was inevitable.

"You went to Chicago with her," she said lowering the music.

Oshun turned the volume back up and winked at her. He mouthed the lyrics to her as he rode on the highway.

Now I've heard talk of angel's baby
But never thought I would have one to call mine
See you are just too good to be true

He sung charmingly.

Jaylah looked down not strong enough to keep up the angry façade and he lifted her head.

"You stay trying to drop that crown. What I tell you about that? And I did take her. It was strictly on some friendship shit," he replied turning the volume down on the radio.

Jaylah shook her head. A regular man she could buy, the I didn't know act, but not from Oshun. He was too fucking smart to not know how Latoya felt about him.

"The last thing you lack is common sense so why would you think it's okay to be with her alone like that?"

Oshun's jaw tensed as she waited for a response.

"Since I was a teenager Latoya has been there. It wasn't

until we was older that we fucked around, but I never mentioned us being anything other than friends. Latoya asked me about you a few months back and I let her know that wasn't her place. I made it very clear love so in my mind I figured we was on the same page. Men don't over think shit the way women do sweetheart. If she and I agreed that it was a friendship, then to me that's what it was. Especially since she's never done no bullshit like this before," he replied.

Jaylah's brows rose as a thought hit her.

"Did she tell you about my daughter before this?" she asked narrowing her eyes.

Oshun briskly shook his head. He glanced over at Jaylah and cleared his throat.

"No but she did show me papers on your rape. I let her know then that shit wasn't to be discussed ever," he said quickly.

Jaylah swallowed hard. She shook her head as her eyes watered.

"Just stop," she muttered and turned up the radio.

Oshun chose to stay silent and she was grateful for that. Jaylah relaxed in her seat and closed her eyes.

Three hours later she opened them.

The streets.

The housing.

The area.

It was familiar. So familiar that it made her stomach knot

up. She peered over at Oshun and shook her head. *What type of shit was he really on?* She wondered.

"Why are we in Baymoor Falls?"

Oshun rubbed the back of his neck as he pulled up to the nearest gas station.

"Tomorrow we leave from here to take a small trip. The niggas that shot my brother is being charged with his crime. They haven't publicly stated it yet, but my lawyer hit me up last night after your fight and told me. Shits about to get tense and I could use a quick getaway," he replied.

Jaylah nodded. She could feel Jerry's anger from across town still she was relieved. Malik deserved justice.

"I'm really happy to hear that, king," she said honestly with a softness to her voice.

Oshun leaned over and pecked her lips.

"Hearing you call me King makes me wanna eat your pussy from the back love. You want anything from the store?" he asked.

Jaylah's cheeks darkened as she shook her head.

"But why are we here?" she asked again.

Oshun sat back and looked at her.

"We're here because before I go up in you, I wanna see where you come from. Is that asking too much?" he replied.

Jaylah's eyes diverted down to his thick print that was visible inside of his grey sweats. She shook her head and he smirked at her. Oshun exited the truck and Jaylah watched the Baymoor Falls women drool at the sight of Oshun. He wore sweats with white designer sneakers, a crisp crew neck t-shirt and a black Fendi baseball cap. The women had no clue that his attire for that day was light work.

Jaylah decided to check her phone quickly before Oshun got back into the car with her. She went to her text messages and Jerry's name was at the top of her list. She took a deep breath and sighed as she read them over.

Jerry: Are you okay?

Jerry: Where are you, you didn't pick up the drugs?

Jerry: the cop is waiting to give you the stuff to take them boys down. Where the fuck are you?

Jerry: I thought I could count on you. I'm very disappointed in you girl.

Jerry: they fired my frat brother! Where the fuck are you?

Jerry: is this how you do the person that has always looked out for you? How could you do this to me?

Jerry: Look can you still meet up with the guy? Please do this and I will forget any of this happened? We can't let them get away with this Jaylah.

Jerry: I had my brother check up on you because I feared you were hurt and guess what he sends me? Pictures of you laughing and shit. This better be for play! Call me now!

Jaylah closed Jerry's message thread and blocked his number. With a racing heart she sat back in the seat and closed her eyes.

"What am I going to fucking do?" she asked before turning on the radio.

"Hey what's up Baymoor Falls! You all are tuned in with your girl Swan! Today we are discussing fear. I talked with my homegirl and she asked why was I still single? I told her straight up, it's because of fear. She thought I was delusional and went on this whole spiel about how I was missing out on my husband because of fear and shit. Ladies do you agree? I mean we all know fear is bad but it's not easy to move past it. I know for me it definitely isn't. I want you all to call in and tell your girl Swan how you were able to overcome your fear? Shit give me some pointers," Swan said into the radio.

Jaylah sat up in her seat and listened hard as Oshun joined her in the truck.

"Baymoor Falls lets welcome Alena to our channel. Alena how did you overcome your fear?" the radio host asked.

Oshun pulled away from the gas station after placing a bottle of water and a muffin onto Jaylah's lap.

"For me it was all of the things that I missed because of the fear inside of me that helped me to let it go. I never went to the college that I wanted to go to because it was too far away from my family. I never left that sorry ass man of mine because I was afraid to be alone. Heck I waited years to do something as simple as going to the gym because I was afraid of how I would look in my workout clothes with my not so perfect body. I woke up one day and I was like fuck this. I'd wasted years of my life

because of fear. I had nothing to lose but everything to gain," the woman said.

Jaylah was so tuned into the radio station that it didn't register that she was outside of her Northside loft until Oshun was exiting the truck. Her jaw dropped in shock as the radio host responded to the caller.

"Honey you just said a mouthful," the host Swan said with happiness in her voice.

Begrudgingly Jaylah exited the truck.

"Damn her show is actually good," Jaylah said pulling out the keys to her place.

Not in the mood or even interested in how Oshun knew where she lived, Jaylah unlocked her front door. Hell, he'd known her other darkest secret, so she was sure getting her address was a piece of cake to a man like him.

"I checked your license when you were asleep last night love," Oshun said stepping up behind her.

Jaylah smirked.

Of course, he did.

"This is nice," he said breaking the silence.

Jaylah stepped out of her sparkly Golden Goose sneakers and smiled. She loved her place.

"Thank you. Are you tired? Hungry? I can go grab us something to eat," she said. She thought about the tender way he held her after her fight with Latoya and she sighed. "Or I can go get some food to cook," she suggested.

Oshun walked up behind her and kissed the back of her head.

"I would love that, baby. Point me in the direction of the bed and I'll see you in a couple of hours. I want you to show me around later then afterward we can have dinner and I can have dessert," he told her.

The heat from his body mixed with the heaviness of his words made her skin prickle in anxiousness. She nodded and held her breath until he walked away. Jaylah freshened up her place making sure to remove any remnants of Garris that she saw lying around.

She then took a quick shower and headed to the market for groceries. Jaylah made sure to dress incognito not wanting anyone to know she was back in town. She quickly grabbed what she needed from the store and was on her way. Then before Oshun's truck could take her back home, Jaylah drove to her usual stalker spot. She idled near the driveway with a heavy heart.

Never have I ever given a kid up for adoption.

That bitch.

Jaylah wished she could run into Latoya again so she could kick her ass some more. She closed her eyes as she thought back to the day, she gave Greedo her purity.

"How did you get this?" she asked looking around the king suite in the Queen's Hotel.

It was one of the most lavish hotels in Baymoor Falls and Jaylah was impressed. She was also excited because it was one of the hotels that her parents once frequented and now that she was there, she could understand why her mom loved the place so much.

"My man's Tuna got it for us. You like it?" he asked leaning against the wall.

Jaylah turned to him and smiled. Greedo looked like the best thing she'd ever seen in his rustic denim jeans with his black Polo hoodie and black high-top Air Force Ones. His fade was freshy cut while his growing mustache was neatly lined. The look of lust sat in the crest of his eyes as he peered at Jaylah longingly.

"My boy thinks I should do a city to city run to promote my music. He says that shit could really hit. Maybe even bring in some real money," he told her.

Jaylah walked over to him in her black Tommy Girl halter dress and hugged his waist. She smiled as she peered up at him.

"I think that's a very good idea. This could be your way out of the hood," she whispered.

Greedo shook his head as his hands went to her hips.

"Nah this could be our way out of the hood. It's you and me good twin. My momma never loved me. She put that hoe ass nigga before me, and my pops is too busy making babies all over the fucking world to see how I'm doing. All I ever had was myself. And now I got you," he said.

Jaylah's heart expanded. She leaned into him while grinning.

"Do you really mean that? I hear the rumors about the other girls and—"

Greedo silenced her question with a kiss. In one swift motion he picked Jaylah up and carried her over to the large bed inside of the suite. He laid Jaylah on her back and removed his hoodie. Then there was his black beater and as he stepped out of his kicks, he licked his lips.

"You the only female that has my love and my trust. Never forget that and I'm far from perfect but what I have with you is, and shit like that can make people jealous. Even some of my so called niggas hating on us but it's all good. Like you said we close to being out of this bitch. Fuck 'em."

Jaylah nodded loving the sound of that.

"Yes, forget them," she agreed.

Greedo slid off his jeans and grabbed the hem of her dress.

"I love you Jaylah and only you," he whispered.

She stared up into his eyes seeing her future. He was the light in her darkness. He'd become her everything in such a short amount of time. She couldn't see a world without Gavin who was known as Greedo. If he was driving, she was riding. That she knew for sure.

"I love you too," she whispered raising up so that he could slip off her white cotton Hanes panties. "Please don't leave me," she begged.

Greedo took off her underwear an assisted her with taking

off her bra. His dark eyes soaked up her attractive young body
with appreciation.

"I promise I will never do anything to hurt you," he swore
and took off his black boxers.

Jaylah smiled and opened her legs wide ready to give him
something that no other person had touched.

Tap.

Tap.

Jaylah pulled herself away from her flashback and her
eyes flew to her passenger's side window. Her throat clogged
up at the sight of the fawn colored woman with the bright
brown eyes, full lips and thick curly hair that was touching
the top of her shoulders. She gave Jaylah a gentle smile and
waved at her. Jaylah looked past the woman and saw the gate
was open. At the end of the driveway was a red bike with a
small boy attached to it. Jaylah looked back to the woman as
she lowered the window.

"Sorry, I didn't mean to block the driveway. I'm lost," she
lied with a nervous laugh.

The woman shook her head. She licked her lips and
cleared her throat. Elegance brushed off the woman in waves
as she looked at Jaylah.

"I know who you are. Up until about five or six months
ago, you came to my driveway and sat at least three times a
week. My security company notified me and my husband of
this years ago. Jaylah, we know who you are honey," she
said.

Jaylah placed her car in drive and as her breathing picked up. She looked straight ahead as the woman looked at her.

"I know that happened years ago. Emotions were high and you were very distraught, but I will never forget meeting your mom. She was very sweet, and Oakley is very much a part of you. Call me when you're ready to meet her, God bless you Jaylah," the woman said and handed Jaylah a business card from her Louis Vuitton pocketbook.

She gave Jaylah one more smile before heading back towards the boy waiting for her on the small bike.

Jaylah's watery eyes peered down at the business card in sadness.

Angelica Morrow, M.D.

Her name was as pretty as her smile. Jaylah put the card up and willed herself to drive off. Oshun was still asleep when she arrived back home. Jaylah put the groceries away then slipped into a white lace maxi dress. She pulled her hair into a sloppy bun and called her sister. She'd missed Jael immensely since being gone from the city and wanted to see what was happening with her.

"How is the cabins? I was calling you and you didn't pick up. I felt like something was wrong," her twin asked.

Jaylah smiled. The funny thing was she too could feel something was off with her twin. Since reconnecting their bond was strengthening again and she liked that.

"I can say the same for you. A lot happened at the cabin, but you go first," she replied.

Jaylah's twin groaned into the phone.

"I can't say too much because I'm at my business and these bitches are nosey, but I got into it with my dude and things got ugly," she replied in a low tone.

Jaylah sat the chicken to the side and frowned.

"Ugly like what? Did he hit you? Just because he plays ball doesn't mean he can beat on you," she snapped.

"I know and it wasn't that! But we did tussle and I ended up pulling my gun out on him just to make him leave. It was crazy but he's gone and I'm okay. I told him I need a break. He wants to get married and I just want peace," her twin clarified.

Jaylah nodded.

"I get that but even him pushing you isn't a good thing. You know men with money feel like they can use that to get away with anything."

Her twin sighed.

"I know and I would never let any man put his hands on me. I'm just dealing with a lot. Mom's also forcing me to contact Diamond's dad," Jael said angrily.

Jaylah smiled.

"And that's a good thing, I mean who is this man that you've been hiding?" she asked really wanting to know.

The line was quiet for several minutes before her twin responded.

"It's no one now what happened at the cabin? I divulged enough," she finally responded.

Jaylah snorted.

"You did?"

Her twin laughed.

"I did," she repeated.

Jaylah made sure Oshun wasn't coming into the kitchen and she exhaled. She replayed the story back to her twin as quickly as she could leaving nothing out. She even made sure to tell her about the run in she had with her daughters adopted parent earlier that day.

"Wow, I mean damn I thought I had a bad few days. You might need some weed, liquor or good dick to take them troubles away," her twin replied.

Jaylah laughed. Her sister really had no clue. Things were going to get worse before they got better for her.

"Twin can I ask you something and get the honest truth from you?" she asked.

Jaylah placed her chicken and vegetables into the glass dish ready to bake them.

"Sure, what's up?"

Jaylah closed the oven and turned. Her eyes peered around her kitchen as she thought about the child she'd given up for adoption.

"Did I do the right thing?" she finally asked.

She closed her eyes as she waited for her sister to reply.

Her twin sighed.

"That was the best decision for you. I could never tell you that you didn't. I don't have that right twin. Although she wasn't the product of rape you were traumatized. Badly beaten and heartbroken. You weren't in any shape to raise a baby. Mommy had just gotten fired from her job; I was running wild in the streets. Shit we had nothing to give a baby. She's where she should be," Jael replied.

Jaylah nodded slowly needing to hear that.

"Thank you, I love and miss you. As soon as I get back to Detroit, I will come see you. A lot is about to change for me twin. Please don't let any of the things people say turn you away from me," Jaylah said sadly.

"Jaylah, what's going on? Is this about the job?" her twin asked.

"It is. I have to go but I will fill you in on what I'm about to do as soon as I can. Oshun is here with me in Baymoor Falls. We're leaving in the morning for a small trip. I'll let you know where when I get there."

Her twin laughed.

"Um, I made you share your location with me a month ago so no need for all of that. I'll see for myself. Have fun, send pictures and relax. Whatever is about to happen won't be the end of you. You are so much stronger than you realize. And Jaylah," her twin called out.

Jaylah turned back to the stove and smiled.

"Yeah?"

"Please pick up the next time dad calls. He has something

very important to tell you. Love you lots, pretty girl," Jael said and ended the call.

Jaylah finished dinner, took another shower and got dressed before Oshun awoke from his slumber. As the sun started to set, she sipped on her wine while setting the table. His scent alerted her of his presence. She closed her eyes and smiled as he hugged her from the back.

"Who knew your sexy ass could throw down like this," he said and kissed her neck.

Jaylah beamed with pride as she watched Oshun salivate over the food she'd prepared for him. On her small glass dining table was smothered chicken with homemade corn-bread, yams, cabbage and a upside down cake. It was as if Jaylah couldn't stop cooking when she started. She thought back to how much joy it gave her mom and she now saw why. Cooking was therapeutic as hell.

They took their seats and Oshun bowed his head. Jaylah followed suit and her eyes closed.

"Father, we thank you for life. Even before Malik left us, we knew how precious it was but to watch you take him back showed me that time is of the essence. We can be here today and gone tomorrow. That's why I'm sitting across from this beautiful woman now because I don't want to miss out on any blessings that you send my way. I need your help though, God. I need to be at peace with you handling the cops that killed my brother. I need to be able to rest in that Lord without feeling like I should have done more. Don't stop working on me or this beautiful lady across from me, amen," he prayed.

Jaylah swallowed hard.

"Amen," she whispered lifting her head.

With the white Tiffany plates in front of them Oshun hastily made his plate. Jaylah made a much smaller plate and pushed the food around while staring at Oshun. He was dressed down again for the night in a dark blue Dolce and Gabbana logo's sport jacket with the matching trackpants. On his feet were a pair of designer sneakers as two Cuban link chains sat on his neck. His beard looked freshly trimmed and as Jaylah sat across from him, she basked in the peace he provided. Her time with him had really been something. The highs and the lows were life changing. She'd never felt the things she had for a man not even Greedo until she met him. He was truly one of a kind.

"We should talk about what Latoya told you," she finally said.

Oshun nodded. He finished the rest of his chicken and sat back in the seat. He rubbed his belly as he stared at her.

"Whenever you ready love," he replied.

Jaylah cleared her throat as her chest tightened. She placed her hands onto her lap and stared at the man that changed her for the better. That's what was so amazing about him. Jaylah knew that people either brought out the good in you or the worse. Oshun pushed her to be better and made her want more for herself. He showed her that money and good looks didn't mean shit if you had a bad soul attached to you.

"Shortly after moving to the Southside me and my twin met Greedo who is now a well-known rapper," she said nervously.

Oshun's jaw tensed and she smiled at his protectiveness over her.

"I heard of him," he stated lowly.

Jaylah cleared her throat again. She was frightened to speak her truths because they were so ugly. It was always easy revealing the good parts of yourself to people. But not so easy with the flaws, however.

"My twin liked him at first. He was like the *it* guy in the hood. I was turned off because he was a hustler, but he showed me a softer side of him. He made me feel safe. The type of security I needed after losing my dad to the prison system. I fell for him after that. He was my protector, my friend and eventually my lover," she revealed.

Jaylah broke her gaze with Oshun, and her eyes slowly went around the room as she fought to remain calm.

"We were going to leave Baymoor Falls together. He would rap, I would attend school and we would be together. Like a perfect couple then things started to fall apart."

"How so, baby?"

Jaylah's heart warmed at how loving Oshun was with her. She blinked as her eyes began to water.

"I found out that he was taking girls with him on the road

trips he did to promote his music. There was even a video that was made of him having a threesome. I was very heart-broken because I trusted him, and he let me down."

"Like your pops did," Oshun said finishing her sentence.

Jaylah wiped her face and nodded.

"It was also around that time I found out I was pregnant. I was devastated because he was once again gone on the road. His name was getting bigger and with he and I not getting along he chose to keep taking the road trips. However, the last one he took he was stopped, and they found drugs in his car. Greedo and his DJ were locked up for it and after that I was back on my own. Only now, I'm pregnant so I had no choice but to do what I did," she said skipping over a major part of her story.

Oshun stared at her intently for several minutes before sitting up in his seat. His eyes held empathy in them as he looked her way.

"I'm very sorry that happened. I know my words do nothing for your pain, but I am, and I would never judge you because of anything like that. That's what you did to give your child a better life. It takes a courageous motherfucka to put someone else's needs above their own."

Jaylah closed her eyes. She grabbed her stomach and Oshun raised from his seat. He was at her side before a tear could fall. She envisioned her big belly. The nightly kicks, the heartburn and the weight gain. She'd hated it all honestly.

Even the birth and now she regretted it all wishing she could go back.

"I wish I would have been strong enough to keep her. I wish I could have been that brave," she cried.

Oshun leaned down and hugged her. She cried into his jacket as he rubbed her back.

"You were brave enough to know that she deserved a good life. Stop looking at the bad and acknowledge the good sweetheart. The devil has his hold on you with that shit but don't worry, I'ma hold you down and get that nigga off your back. If having another kid is what you want when the time comes it will happen for you. You can't hold on to pain like this beautiful. It could eventually ruin you. Did you ever tell Greedo about it?"

Jaylah pulled back so that she could wipe her face.

"I did. His mom didn't really care about him, so I had no real way to reach him. However, my twin found out his jail info and I wrote him a letter explaining what happened. He never responded but somehow when I was at the hospital ready to be released after having her, he popped up on me. He called me everything but the name of God for giving her away and left. I pretended that part of my life never happened, and I went to college," she replied.

Oshun kissed her forehead before stepping back.

"Thank you for sharing that with me, baby. I know that wasn't easy. Let's take a drive. Show me your hood and try to change the tone for the night. We won't let that pain hold you hostage anymore love," he said, and she smiled.

Jaylah wiped her face and stood.

"Sounds like a good idea," she said quietly.

Thirty minutes later Jaylah drove Oshun around Baymoor Falls. He rode shot gun smoking on a blunt as she pointed to the places that she held many memories at. Jaylah refused to take him by the projects on the Southside but when she drove by Crust Lust she had to stop. It was close to eleven and per usual the spot was packed. She pulled up to a personal drive through station similar to something you would see at Sonic or Hardy and she parked. Jaylah rolled down her window and peered over at Oshun.

"You want something to drink?" she asked.

Oshun blew weed smoke from between his lips.

"I'm good love," he replied and finished texting on his phone.

Jaylah looked at the menu and hummed.

"Welcome to Crust Lust how may I help you?"

Jaylah sighed.

"Can I have a tequila and watermelon slushie?" she asked.

Oshun leaned over and his eyes inspected the menu quickly.

"And a large 1738 on the rocks," he added.

Jaylah smirked.

"Now you want something?" she asked amused as she took off her seatbelt.

Oshun sent off a few messages, snapped several photos of her and put his phone away.

"I want everything you have to give me love."

Jaylah blushed. She pulled her license from her wallet as well as Oshun. They were soon served and relaxed in their seats as they sipped on their drinks. Oshun looked at the teenagers and adults hanging in and around the pizzeria.

"This a cool lil joint. We don't have shit like this in Detroit. I might have to build us one for the BOC," he said lowly.

Jaylah smiled.

"You could definitely do that. They would love it."

Oshun gripped her thigh as she peered over at him.

"How are we gone do this ma? You come down every weekend but see that's only gone hold me over for so long. Shit I'll open up a new station for you if that mean you can move to the city," he said staring at her.

Jaylah laughed lightly. If only it was that easy. Being home was a huge reminder of what she was doing and what she still had to do. She was certain that once she made her next move Oshun wouldn't want anything else to do with her.

"We'll see," she said softly not wanting to feed into a future that would never happen.

"I need more than that. I know this is your life, I love that you have your own shit going on. I also know you've been

gone for months from your home, but I don't like the thought
of you not being with me. Some type of way we have to make
this work," he replied.

Jaylah nodded while pulling the straw into her mouth.
She looked back out of her window and choked on her drink
at the sight of Kylie standing by the truck. Besides Kylie was
her husband Jesse. His olive toned skin was flushed as he
smiled at Jaylah. Jaylah slowly lowered the window with her
heartbeat increasing.

"He said this was you in this truck and I just couldn't
believe it. Like wow you come back home and not tell me!"
Kylie snapped looking offended as she stood in her skinny
jeans, black heels and white blouse outside of the truck.

"Babe calm down. Hey Jaylah, this is a nice ass truck. I'm
still on the wait list for mine. Is this your new dude?" he
asked.

Jaylah sat back and Oshun peered over at Kylie and her
husband.

"I am, Oshun," he said coolly.

Kylie's face stretched into a smile along with her husband.
Jaylah wasn't sure who was smiling harder.

Kylie worked her hands through her black glossy long
extensions and licked her pouty lips. Her hand went to her
small hip as she looked at Oshun.

"I'm Kylie, Jaylah's best friend and this is my kids' father,"
Kylie replied.

Jaylah frowned at Kylie's introduction.

"That's her *husband* Jesse," Jaylah elaborated staring at Kylie strangely.

Kylie laughed lightly and waved her hand in the air making the Rolex on her wrist sparkle when the streetlights hit it.

"Don't mind me I'm tipsy. You two should come with us to the bar on the Northside. We came down here for the pizza but now it's time to go! You know they start snatching purses around twelve and I will not let my Birkin be taken by some young thug," she laughed.

Jaylah, her husband and Oshun simply stared at Kylie. Kylie stopped smiling and adjusted her diamond choker that sat on her slender neck.

"But any who lets rollout, just follow us," she insisted and air kissed Jaylah before walking away.

Jaylah swallowed hard as Kylie and her husband went to their car. She looked at Oshun and plastered a fake smile onto her face.

"Let's go back to the house," she suggested starting up the truck.

Oshun's brows pulled together as he re-lit his blunt.

"Nah, lets kick it with your people baby. Besides she seems—interesting," he said and turned on the music.

Jaylah maintained her fake smile and drove around the lot until she spotted Kylie and her husband's Mercedes. She slid behind them and nervously followed them over to the Northside of Baymoor Falls. The bar that Jaylah followed Kylie to was Roxie's. It was an upscale bar that catered to the elite of Baymoor Falls.

Jaylah and Oshun did valet same as her friend and when Oshun placed his hand at the small of Jaylah's back a sonorous voice called out his name.

"What's good, King?" Mr. Roi owner of Club Luxure asked walking over.

Oshun dapped him up as everyone peered their way trying to see who Mr. Roi was talking to. Kylie's thin neatly arched brows pulled together as she stared at Oshun.

"What's good with you? I'm just in town for one night with my lady," Oshun said so casually that she almost missed it.

Almost.

Jaylah leaned into him making sure to keep her head down not wanting to see any of her co-workers. Jerry was more of a reclusive kind of man that rarely frequented bars or clubs but there were still a multitude of people that she wasn't looking to run into.

"Ms. Cole," Mr. Roi said as if he knew her before looking back to Oshun. "You know this is my spot too, I'll make sure that you are served with nothing but the best. Let me know if you need anything," he told him and walked away.

"Hey babe I think they're taking us up into the elite section of the bar. Fuck yeah!" Kylie's husband said excitedly and tossed his fist in the air while smiling.

Kylie kissed her teeth while staring at Oshun and Jaylah. She looked at her husband and smiled wide.

"They saw you and wanted to show respect. It's nothing we're not used to," she said snidely.

Her husband shook his head while looking at her.

"Nah, we come here all of the time and it's a free bottle of champagne and nothing more. They doing all this for Jaylah's new dude, shit I'm happy I came out. Let's head up there Oshun, oh shit my bad I mean King," he corrected Kylie and walked off leaving her behind.

Kylie turned briskly and headed after her husband. Jaylah was placed in a stupor not surprised by the treatment but shocked to see Kylie come second to anyone. The last thing she was trying to do was stunt on Kylie, but she knew her girl wouldn't see it that way.

"What do you do? How can you drive a Urus? How do you know Mr. Roi? Do you sell drugs?" Kylie asked dropping question after question.

The elite section of the bar was on the second level in a suite that housed smoked glass windows, with it's on bar and restroom area. Complete privacy is what it offered and while Jaylah appreciated that, the anger coming from Kylie's thin body was making her beyond uncomfortable and a little upset.

Oshun relaxed in the seat and pulled another blunt from his pocket. He went to lite it up and Kylie's eyes widened.

She opened her mouth to protest and her husband smirked at Oshun.

"Can I hit it next?" he asked eagerly.

Kylie snorted before looking at her husband with amused lenses.

"Are you serious right now? You would never smoke pot like some hoodlum. Wow, I need some tequila for the night I'm having," Kylie said and waved over a waiter. "Hi, I need a tray of tequila shots. I need a bottle of champagne. The best you have. That is all," she said and flicked her hand to dismiss the waitress.

Oshun smirked as he hit his blunt. He passed it over to Kylie's husband and his dark honey hued eyes fell onto Jaylah. Jaylah sat upright on the sofa with a stiff back and racing heart. She hated Kylie's behavior but what really fucked her up was that not too long ago she had behaved the same way.

"Relax love," he whispered and pulled her close.

Jaylah looked up at his handsome mug and smiled.

"I am, I'm also tired," she whispered staring into his dark honey orbs.

Oshun kissed her nose and her heart melted.

"Then we won't be long sweetheart. I've seen all I needed to see," he told her lowly.

Jaylah closed her eyes in shame and he gently bit her lip.

"Don't lower it for nobody," he reprimanded her.

"Jaylah are you back for good? We miss you so much and

I'm sure your job misses you as well. Have you heard back from MLN?" Kylie asked.

Jaylah's head shot to Kylie and she frowned at her. She was baffled by Kylie's uncouth behavior.

"Kylie, let me talk to you over there," she said.

Jaylah pulled away from Oshun and Kylie shook her head. Arrogance swam over her head as she crossed her legs. She looked at Jaylah and smiled.

"I was in Louis Vuitton earlier and I ran into the producer of your show along with his wife. They're worried about you, Jaylah. Even Jerry," she added.

Oshun's brows tugged together and Jaylah could feel his questioning stare.

"Why would her boss be worried about her?" he asked.

Kylie's lip tucked in and she waved her head.

"He simply misses her. You sir never answered any of my questions. That's quite rude of you. As for me and who I am. I'm a stay at home mom. My husband is an NFL player. I'm sure you've heard of him and we own one of the biggest jewelry stores here in Baymoor Falls with *legit* money," she said sweetly.

Kylie's husband passed Oshun the blunt he'd smoke half of and Oshun chose to put it out. He sat up on the sofa as rolling carts of food was brought out along with champagne.

"I didn't ask for all of this," Kylie said nervously eyeing the champagne and food.

"This is for Mr. Lacoste and his beautiful companion," the waiter replied popping the tabs on the champagne.

Kylie rolled her eyes as she grabbed a flute filled with bubbly. She watched the waiters leave the room and she looked at Oshun.

"And just how have you become this larger than life character? What do you do exactly?" she asked once again.

"Babe, relax. I hate it when you get like this," her husband whispered.

Kylie shrugged him off while staring at Oshun.

"No, I won't! This man shows up with my best friend—"

"Can you really call her that, sweetheart? You haven't seen my baby in months, and not once have you asked if she's okay? You too busy checking for a nigga that you never met before with your fucking husband by your side. What I do and who I am is no concern of yours because you mean nothing to me and I mean this in the most respectful way brah, but you need to get her ass together. She's disrespectful as fuck," Oshun replied cutting Kylie off.

Jaylah's jaw fell slack. She watched Kylie's husband smirk before looking at his wife with empathetic eyes.

"Let's just go honey," he told her.

He grabbed Kylie's hand and she snatched away from him while glaring at Jaylah.

"Are you serious right now? I don't care about you! I was only checking for my friend and that's what she is and will forever be. You are nothing more than a low life, drug dealing—"

"Just stop. What you won't do is disrespect him. I didn't even want to come to this place. He insisted we follow you and the short time we're here all you've done is question him. You are out of line and I shouldn't have let it get this far Kylie. Don't ever talk to him like that," Jaylah said looking at her.

Kylie's head snapped back in shock and her husband pulled her up. Jaylah held her breath waiting to see if Kylie would spill the beans on her scheme.

"You turned out to be just like your twin. A want to be Nicki Minaj bitch with a low life hoodlum and FYI you were *never* on my level. I just needed a backup singer. Somebody to hold my coat and tell me how pretty I am when I'm feeling down. You're a project bitch and I don't care how many drug dealers dicks you sit on you will always be that," Kylie said hatefully as her husband drug her out of the room. "Ramen Noodles eating whore! You weren't even woman enough to keep your kid!" she yelled.

"Kylie enough, damn!" her husband yelled pulling her through the door.

Jaylah grabbed the glass of champagne and smiled. She thought of Sadie as Kylie's harsh words bruised her heart.

Everyone won't be able to come with you on this journey to a better you.

Sadie had been so right that it was startling.

"I'm sorry that happened love," Oshun said rubbing her leg.

Jaylah looked at him and smiled.

"Don't be. I prefer the real hate over the fake love any day. It is what it is. Let's enjoy the night before heading in," she said and smiled although she wanted to cry.

Like she smiled so hard it stretched her face and before she could give him a fake laugh he leaned over. His lips brushed against hers as he looked into her eyes.

"She didn't deserve you as a friend. When the smoke clears love don't forget what she said out of anger because she meant that shit," he whispered before kissing her again.

CHAPTER 12

Her fingers moved slow as she watched the number slide across her screen. It had been a while. After reconnecting with her twin she'd blocked him by calling into the company the collect calls were through. However, the strangest thing happened while she was with Oshun at his family's cabin. She'd missed the irritating calls that she regularly refused to take so like a petulant child she'd called back and removed the block now there he was calling again.

Jaylah rolled over in the bed and looked out of the bay windows. A cool breeze brushed through the vast room as she accepted the collect call with Oshun snoring softly beside her.

"How are you?" he asked like it was normal for them to have the talk of how their day was going.

Jaylah closed her eyes soaking in his voice. She sat up on the bed and exhaled. Oshun made her so fearless. Almost like she could take on all of the pain from her past and handle her future without batting a fucking eyelash. She would miss him greatly when it was all said and done.

"I'm doing better—daddy," she finally responded.

Her eyes watered and she swallowed the lump in her throat. She didn't want the moment to be overrun by pain. This was for Jaylah a step towards the future.

"You don't know how long I've waited to hear that sweet voice call me that. I love you," he told her.

Jaylah smiled remembering the love she felt from her dad. It had been nothing like it.

"Love you too," she replied softly.

"And again, I'm sorry. For it all. I've been praying for years for you to forgive us. I know I let you down and I will die living with that hurt baby. I've made a lot of mistakes in my life, but God isn't done with any of us yet. I'm coming home soon," he revealed.

Jaylah's eyes widened at his revelation.

"You do?"

Her father laughed lightly, and she tried to imagine his smile but couldn't.

"Yes, baby I do. In a month I will be released to halfway house an hour away from Baymoor Falls. My time has finally come to be free. I have to go but I need to say this. I talked with your sister. Don't be mad you know she couldn't wait to tell me. She said everything that you're dealing with and it's been on me heavy since that call. I want you to be safe, Jaylah. Your only priority is you. One of my favorite quotes by Dr. Martin Luther King, is *"the ultimate measure of a man is not where he stands in moments of comfort and convenience, but where he stands at times of challenge and conflict."* You weren't raised to be no one's fucking errand girl. You were raised to be a Queen. Through everything you've been through your still standing. God's grace is shining bright on you. Never forget that. I'll see you soon. I love you so much, please do the right thing," her father said and before he ended the call, he cleared his throat. "And I want to meet him when it's all said and done. If you love him like your sister said you do, then protect him like he better do you. Bye baby," her father said, and he was gone.

Jaylah sat the phone onto her lap with a smile kissing her lips. She looked out the window at the water and sighed. She couldn't understand how the best time of her life could be colliding with the worst time of it. She was on a train headed to destruction fast.

So, fucking fast that she could feel the doom near.

It was coming and there wasn't anything she could do to stop it.

"Good morning love," Oshun said running his big hand up her back.

Her skin shivered as small goosebumps appeared at his touch. Jaylah peered back at him and grinned. With hair wild from her late-night shower. Fair skin dry as fuck from forgetting to moisturize and still she felt like the prettiest woman in the world. It was unreal and she wished her happy bubble was a place she could stay in forever.

"Good morning. Hungry? I can cook," she said excited at the thought of feeding him.

Oshun rubbed his dark honey eyes and shook his head. While Jaylah wore a cranberry silk nightgown that stopped at the bottom of her ass Oshun wore white Armani pajama pants. His erection caught her eye as he stretched in the bed showing off his muscular physique. Jaylah licked her lips and quickly turned hoping Greece would be the place he finally went into her.

"The chef should already have breakfast prepared but thank you, baby. How did you sleep?" he asked rubbing her back tenderly.

Jaylah leaned into his strong hand wanting all of the love and affection that she could receive from him.

"Like a baby," she said softly.

"That's all I want for you is to be at peace."

It was strange because he was the person that was grieving while holding his family together, yet he thought of her.

He always placed her first and that didn't go unnoticed.

"Thank you. Well let's go eat," she said becoming emotional.

Jaylah rose from the bed and headed for the spiral staircase. As she walked down the stairs, she marveled at the beauty of the cave home that sat off the water. It was like nothing she'd seen before. It was angelic, quiet and comfortable.

She didn't want to leave.

Jaylah found delicious smelling breakfast in the dining room. The spread on the large wooden table was enough to feed a family of eight. She inhaled the aroma as strong arms wrapped around her waist. She blushed as he kissed her neck.

"Just wanted to kiss on you before I started eating," he murmured and let her go.

After Oshun blessed the food Oshun made a few calls while eating and Jaylah finished her breakfast. She retreated to the balcony and leaned against the railing. Her eyes closed as the wind kissed her skin.

This was it.

She couldn't stop thinking about it.

She had no choice but to make a move.

"Let's go explore love."

Jaylah nodded. She was sad. So, fucking sad that she had to leave him. She cleared her throat and plastered a smile onto her face.

"Okay!" she said excitedly peering back at him.

Oshun's dark honey eyes stared at her questioningly and he nodded. He walked away and Jaylah exhaled. She had to shake off the pain and make their last moments together count.

Two hours later Jaylah walked hand and hand with
Oshun through the shopping area of Santorini. The island
was nothing short of amazing and so far, everyone they'd
encountered had been extremely nice to them. Jaylah wore
proudly a handmade bracelet from a shop in Oia that Oshun
purchased her. As they entered what was known as the gold
district, the Fira, Oshun took Jaylah into the first shop they
came across.

"Wow look at all of the pieces," Jaylah said smiling.

Gorgeous gold pieces of jewelry lined the glass cases in
the shop. A young man with golden olive toned skin, green
eyes and inky black hair smiled their way.

"Welcome," he said with his heavy Greek accent.

"What's up man, this a nice spot," Oshun said shaking the
man hand.

The man patted his arm while grinning. His friendliness
oozed off his tall lanky frame.

"Thank you, thank you! Very beautiful woman you have,"
he said in a respectful manner.

Oshun looked over at Jaylah and she heated under his
gaze. His dark honey eyes deliberately went over her frame
and she smiled at him. For the day she wore a white tube
maxi dress with pink Chanel espadrilles, a gold heart necklace, her favorite diamond studs and her long hair in a sloppy
bun. Her face was dusted with a light coat of powder as pink
lipstick from Brash Kandy covered her lips.

"Yeah, she's definitely the star of the show. Whatever she wants she can have, spend away love," Oshun said smiling.

Jaylah blushed. Because she had her own money having a man buy her things wasn't the get off. She could get it herself. It was the intent behind the action that made her heart race and her panties moist. He was spoiling her to make her smile and not for his own personal gain. Jaylah winked at him and admired Oshun in is black linen Givenchy shorts that he paired a white linen shirt with. Oshun's jewels shined as they covered his neck and wrist along with a pinky ring. On his face shielding his sexy eyes were a pair of blue tinted vintage Bugatti shades. Jaylah was taken by his masculine beauty that she couldn't get enough of.

Jaylah went from case to case in search of the favorite piece. She was getting ready to leave when a necklace caught her eye. It was yellow gold her favorite with a lobster clasp. From the necklace hung a stunning yellow diamond. Jaylah stared at it in awe as Oshun walked over carrying with him his alluring scent.

"That's beautiful. One of the more expensive pieces we have. Its 25,000 euro's but well worth it!" the man said smiling.

Jaylah's brows hiked upward. She briskly shook her head.

"No that's too much! My bracelet was only 50 euro's. Thank you but no thank you," she said and left out of the shop because the discussion wasn't up for debate. She wasn't comfortable with Oshun spending that type of money on her.

"I talked with Tiffany earlier. She told me that you spoke with her at the cabin," Oshun said walking up.

Jaylah smiled at the mention of Tiffany.

"Yes, she's really sweet. I hate that she's in pain like this, but I do know that once the baby comes, she will be happier," she replied.

Oshun nodded. He moved Jaylah around so that he was closest to the street and placed his hand at the small of her back.

"I feel the same way. She was holding it together but the faster the delivery approaches the sadder she becomes. She wants him here with her and shit we do too. That's why I'm so relieved that they're arresting them pussy ass cops. Sending them to jail will never take away our pain but it will make us sleep a little bit better at night," he replied.

Jaylah smiled.

"I'm sure it will."

Oshun took Jaylah to a nearby gelato ice cream shop and they sat at an available table. After grabbing ice cream Jaylah slurped on her gelato as he stared at her. His gaze was intense, and she wasn't sure why, but she felt like she'd done something wrong.

"Are you okay?" she asked licking her lips.

Oshun nodded while frowning. He grabbed her hand then kissed the back of it lovingly. His eyes stayed planted on her as he pulled a white box from his pocket. Oshun opened the box and inside of it was the beautiful necklace Jaylah liked from the shop but wasn't comfortable with him buying.

She blushed as he removed the necklace from the box and placed it around her neck before sitting back down.

"Sweetheart, I don't need you to speak for me. I don't need for you to wonder about my money and if something is too high. You're special to me and when I want to spoil you, lick on you, rub your back, and even fuck your brains out. Just let me, love. All I need for you to be is Jaylah. I'll handle the rest."

Jaylah nodded with wide eyes. Her cone started to melt and slide down her hand as she looked at Oshun. He leaned over and softened his mild reprimand with a kiss to her lips.

And as the sun set and the night fell onto Santorini Greece Jaylah sat with Oshun on the balcony having a candlelight dinner. The meal was fish and steak and Jaylah was filled with nerves for more reasons than one.

She held the large goblet that contained a healthy amount of cognac while staring at Oshun. Her spirit was telling her that it was time to speak about the rest of the things he saw in her file that he told her Latoya had given him.

"We should talk," she said evenly.

Oshun puffed on his cigar while looking her way. His shades were gone, and she was able to see his beautiful hooded eyes.

"We can do anything you want baby," he replied.

Jaylah inwardly swooned.

Damn he was something like perfection.

"I love you," stumbled from her lips without her knowing. She gasped and Oshun smiled before raising up out of his seat. He went over to her and grabbed the back of her head. His lips crashed into her intensely and they kissed for several minutes before he let her go and retreated to his seat.

"I love you too," he told her.

Jaylah cleared her throat. Things were going to the left when she needed to take them back to the right.

"I was assaulted Oshun. Greedo was gone and I was hurt. I wanted the pain to go away because once again a man that I loved—left me. I gave caution to the wind and let my twin convince me to attend a house party with her," she said and as she spoke about the past like a highlight reel it replayed in her mind.

"You good just relax. Greedo is with Shreeya right now in another state. Don't be a fool twin. Its plenty of other niggas in here to mess with. Look at Kiss," her twin said as they stood in the middle of the floor.

The house party was being thrown five buildings down in their projects and Jaylah wasn't happy about being there. All she could think of was Gavin. His smile, his laugh and his voice. She loved him and all along he'd been cheating on her. He'd called it experimenting before they fell in love, but she was no dummy.

His black ass was cheating.

That stung. She was pissed. Wished she could run to her

*dad and cry on his shoulders so that he could make it all better,
but she couldn't.*

And that angered her as well.

*"What's good with you good twin?" Kiss asked finally
looking their way.*

*Kiss was a higher-ranking street hustler than Greedo. He
along with his best friend Pharaoh were making a lot of money
pushing drugs. Jaylah sometimes saw him in the hood but
because of his financial status they rarely partied in the same
circle.*

*Jaylah looked at the handsome man with the toned
physique, thick lips and smiled. Maybe a little get back wasn't
so bad.*

But could she?

"Hey," she said shyly.

Her twin bumped her hip and rolled her eyes.

*"Hey Kiss! Where's Pharaoh at? Nigga gets with Bebe and
act like he a saint all of a sudden. We both know he still has a
soft spot for me," her twin smiled.*

Kiss nodded while staring at her.

*"That he does. He's always yapping about his bad twin
and how she giving him a hard time and shit. He outside in the
car. Y'all wanna fall off with us?" Kiss asked.*

*Jaylah shook her head. The look in Kiss eyes told her that
he wasn't going anywhere to talk. She felt like get back was
what Greedo deserved but she wasn't ready to have sex with
anyone else.*

No time soon.

"We're good here," she spoke up.

Jael looked at Jaylah and sighed.

"Well at least come with me to see Pharaoh," she said and pulled Jaylah from the party with Kiss following behind them.

"You really are beautiful ma," Kiss told her.

Jaylah smiled but didn't reply. Her thoughts were back onto Greedo and what he was doing.

"Look fuck Greedo! He's with Shreeya out of town, you don't need him!" her twin said as they walked out of the project building.

"Damn, that's good to know," Kiss said and walked past Jaylah and her twin.

Jaylah's twin looked at her and shrugged.

"Maybe I shouldn't have said that," she whispered.

Jaylah smiled. Her twin was extra when she wanted to be.

"Yes, maybe so. Let's go home. Please, please, please," Jaylah begged not wanting to retreat back to the party.

Her twin shook her head. She took off running and Jaylah watched her jump into the arms of one of the finest boys she'd ever seen. He was buffer than the guys she went to school with. He wore nice threads, was easy on the eyes and was leaning against a black S500. Without asking it was clear he was Pharaoh.

"I missed you. I see you all in love now," her twin said still in the man's arms.

Jaylah walked up and the man placed his eyes onto her.

"You the good twin? What's up?" he asked smiling.

Jaylah shrugged and looked the other way. Kiss smirked at her but gave her the space she needed. Jaylah could tell he wasn't the type of man to press anyone for pussy, so she wasn't surprised he didn't try to talk to her again.

"I'm trying to be a good man and you trying to make that hard for me. I still got love for you though. If you need anything Jael, just hit my line. But that you and me shit is dead," Pharaoh told her sister setting her down.

Jaylah watched her twin pout. Pharaoh kissed her twin's forehead before pulling out a ringing phone.

"Aye, that's Bebe. We need to shoot to the Northside. You two stay safe, them niggas upstairs out for self. Watch your drinks and don't smoke they weed," Pharaoh advised walking to the driver's door of the car.

Jaylah nodded listening to him as her sister rolled her eyes. Kiss shot Jaylah one last glance before slipping into the Mercedes. They pulled away and Jael rolled her eyes.

"Fake ass wanna be Malcom X nigga. Bebe not even that cute and she a church girl. Probably lame as hell but let's go back up there," Jael told her.

Jaylah grabbed her twins' hand and frowned at her.

"Let's go home," she suggested.

Jael sighed.

"After this we can. I just need one more drink," she replied and despite Jaylah's protests she went back into the building with her twin.

"When we got back upstairs the vibe was different with Kiss being gone. It was like the boys were unfiltered. Some of them was getting head in the corners. The music was loud as hell and I was scared. I didn't want to stay but my sister kept saying she needed one more drink. She ran into her friend, some guy from the hood and they talked in the kitchen while he made her a drink. He brought me back one as well and immediately after drinking it I felt funny. I went to the bathroom and," Jaylah stopped talking to close her eyes.

"You can stop whenever love," he told her.

Jaylah shook her head. She felt an intense need to tell him about her attack.

"When I was peeing this guy that used to sell for Greedo named Woo came in. He'd tried to talk to me months before hand and I turned him down. He had with him two other guys. They locked the door and I tried to scream but it was like I was planted to the toilet seat. I couldn't move and I was so afraid. They struggled with holding me up because of whatever they gave me, but they didn't let that stop them from raping me. The guys went on the run and was never heard from again and I was bullied for speaking up. It was hell and my only thought was to get far away from that place. I wanted to leave but by the time I graduated high school there was a new rumor in the hood of some other chaotic shit and people had forgotten about me, so I stayed. I just made it a habit to not hangout in that area ever again," she explained.

Oshun sat at the other end of the table with his eyes on

her. The water crashing against the shore filled the silence as Jaylah waited for him to speak.

"I first want to say that you didn't have to tell me that but the fact that you did shows me how brave you are. I destroyed that file love. I wanted for you to tell me about your past, no one else. I'm sorry that you've been through so much pain and I promise you that all of that is behind you. I'm making it my goal in life to keep your pretty ass smiling. Are you sure they weren't taken care of?" he asked.

Jaylah shrugged.

"I don't think they were. I haven't spoken to the police about that case since it happened. I wanted to let it go once I saw they were on the run," she replied.

Oshun nodded as he stared at her.

"Let me show you something," Oshun said standing.

He went over to Jaylah and led her up the stairs and into the master suite. Arranged in the large suite were bright red rose petals covering the floor. On the white marble dresser and nightstand were lit candles. The patio was open giving the room a perfect view of the ocean as 90's R&B music sere-naded the room. Jaylah smiled as she walked to the patio.

"Do you believe that God really forgives us for our sins?" she asked solemnly.

Thoughts of leaving Oshun plagued her mind and battered her heart.

"I believe that if we repent with a clean heart than yes, He will forgive us. Whether that's true or not only God and not the living knows but my spirit tells me it's true. Talk to me sexy, what's up?" he asked.

Jaylah shook her head. She closed her eyes and when she sighed Oshun began to pull her dress down. His lips pressed against her back as she reveled in his touch etching every moment of him into her memory bank.

"Where's the cuffs and whips?" she asked quietly.

Oshun chuckled softly as he leaned down and helped her step out of the dress. His lips pressed against her bottom and she was glad she'd gone panty less for the day.

"Another time. We can fuck whenever. I feel like you need some lovemaking tonight," he replied.

Jaylah turned and stared up into his eyes. She gave him a weak smile as his hands caressed then squeezed her perky breast. Oshun leaned down and flicked his long tongue at both of her nipples while staring into her eyes.

Jaylah moaned and her head fell back. She held onto the top of his shoulders as he kissed his way down her stomach. Oshun eventually made it to her sex and he tasted her nectar sensually, making love to her vagina in a way like it had never been before.

With one of her legs on his shoulder Oshun sucked on her pearl while fingering her tight opening. Jaylah couldn't stop herself from pouring onto his fingers and mouth with her arousal.

"Damn you taste so sweet," Oshun murmured. "I need this pussy slippery so she don't try to stop me from sliding inside of her," he whispered and replaced his fingers with his tongue.

"Oh God," Jaylah moaned. Her thighs shook and her body bucked for him. She released twice more before Oshun was laying her on the bed. She sat up to grab at his member and he shook his head.

"Nah, I just wanna make you feel good baby," he said and grabbed her thighs.

Jaylah swallowed hard as her legs went around his waist. Oshun slowly rubbed his dick at her opening before sliding into her body. Their eyes connected and Jaylah shuddered from the pleasure of him finally being inside of her. For several moments she lay still as Oshun stretched out her pussy. His eyes seared into her as he pulled in and out of her snugness trying to get her used to his girth.

"I love you baby, come here," he whispered and leaned down.

Jaylah sat up and his lips crashed into hers. She closed her eyes and Oshun gripped her hips. His dick pushed into her body faster as they tongue kissed. Jaylah's thighs couldn't stop shaking. She pulled back from the kiss and touched his stomach trying to control his movements. His dick was so big she was scared to take it all.

"—Love," Oshun stopped talking and circled his hips. Jaylah moaned wetting his member up some more. "You gone take this dick. Open up them legs and let me feel all of my pussy, okay?" he asked staring into her eyes.

Oshun pumped faster into Jaylah and pleasurable tears slipped from the corners of her eyes. She nodded as his thick member filled her up.

"Okay baby," she whispered willing to take all that he had to give her.

Jaylah sat on her side of the bed watching him sleep. For two hours she'd listened to his light snoring. Snap photos of his handsome face and even cuddled with him. Between the sex and liquor Oshun was out like a light and she was thankful for that. Jaylah's fair cheeks were drenched with tears. She'd stopped wiping her face an hour ago.

It was useless.

Once again, her heart was broken only thing was this time she'd brought on the pain. She'd went in search of it and now this was the price she had to pay for all that she'd done. Jaylah leaned down and kissed his lips *one* last time.

"I will always love you," she whispered.

Oshun grunted while sleeping on his back.

"Love you too, love," he mumbled before turning onto his side.

Jaylah closed her eyes and bit her bottom lip. Her tears fell again as she gently slipped out of the bed. The note she'd written to Oshun was left under his cellphone securely ensuring that he saw it. She grabbed her purse and glanced back at him. Jaylah stared at him long and hard before walking out of the room and out of his life.

Three days later she nervously sat in front of Brooke her MLN connect. Brooke gave her a big smile as she looked her way.

"Are you sure you want to do this?" she asked for the millionth time.

Jaylah nodded not having to think about it.

"Yes," she said confidently.

"Let's first go on record stating you willingly agreed to this right?" Brooke asked.

Jaylah looked at her and swallowed hard.

"Correct."

"And let's start from the top with your credentials."

Jaylah sighed.

"My name is Jaylah Cole. I work for one of the biggest stations in Baymoor Falls, Michigan HLN20. I graduated college at the top of my class. I have been an anchorwoman for six years now. I was asked a week after the shooting of Malik Lacoste to go undercover by my boss Jerry Hegler."

Brooke smiled at Jaylah.

"Take your time," she said softly.

Jaylah nodded.

"Jerry is like a mentor to me. Strictly platonic before anyone can even ask. He was like a father figure for me. My father is in prison for drugs let's just get that out there right now. Jerry took me under his wing. He showed me the ropes and helped me to become a high-ranking newscaster. So naturally when he asked me to do him a favor I said yes."

"And that favor was?"

Jaylah looked down at her lap. Her eyes lifted to Brooke and were watery.

"I was told to infiltrate the family of Malik and find out if there were in fact drug dealers. From the beginning it didn't feel right. I expressed to Jerry several times that I didn't want to do it. He told me that he needed me to help his fraternity brother who is also the officer that shot and killed Malik Lacoste. Against my better judgement I went along with it...." Jaylah stopped talking and cleared her throat. "Being truthful I myself felt like they could have been shady people. Between losing my father to the prison system and being gang raped I didn't have much faith in black men. Jerry knew that as well and now I'm smart enough to see that he used my flaws against me. I confided in him and he took advantage of that," she replied.

"Did you find anything out?" Brooke asked.

Jaylah nodded. She closed her eyes and took a deep breath before replying.

"I actually did. I discovered how amazing they are. How they have built a community within the inner city that has helped so many people. The things they are doing need to be talked about. They are far from a cartel family," she replied.

"And what exactly did Jerry ask you to do that made you break communication with him?"

Jaylah cleared her throat.

"He wanted me to plant drugs in the family's home or business. I have the messages and emails to prove it along with voicemails."

Brooke nodded while looking at her.

"Do you think Jerry will say that you are switching sides because you fell in love with the older brother of Malik Lacoste?" she inquired.

Jaylah's eyes saddened as she looked at Brooke.

"I'm positive that he will. However, long before I knew I loved Oshun Lacoste, I made up in my head that I would give myself up. This family has done nothing to me. They deserve to grieve in peace. I don't care about my job or reputation. All I care about is finally doing the right thing."

Brooke sat up straight and smiled.

"And to you what would that be?"

Jaylah shrugged.

"To let the world, know that for these cops that did shoot and kill Malik Lacoste, a lot of corrupt people are willing to lie and scheme. I want justice for Malik Lacoste, and I want acknowledgment of the BOC in Detroit Michigan."

Brooke nodded.

"We thank you for being so brave and so honest with us," she said, and the camera man stopped filming.

Jaylah closed her eyes and covered her face with her hands. She counted down from ten as her heart pumped at an unnatural level in her chest. She'd done it! She actually owned up to her truth, but damn was she frightened.

"Jaylah, I have some security that is going to sit outside of your home for a few days. I have a feeling that this interview will cause you some issues, but you gave me the story and like I said before even with the switch up we still want you because you are talented. Would you like to be a part of this network?" Brooke asked.

Jaylah shook her head. Reporting news was now the last thing on her mind. She needed her family.

"No but thank you for the offer. I'm going to head out," she replied looking at Brooke.

Brooke nodded with an empathetic gaze.

"And no money for the interview?" she inquired.

Jaylah shook her head in a daze.

"No, just a receipt showing me you donated to the BOC is all I need," she said drained from the interview.

Brooke smiled.

"I'll be sending you that in an hour. For what it's worth you chose to do good. Never feel ashamed for that. My mom always tells me that the light will always outshine the dark, call me if you need anything," she replied before walking away.

Jaylah nodded and left the building. After grabbing lunch at her favorite sushi place, she headed home. Jaylah spotted Kylie's cherry red Lexus in her driveway and she sucked her teeth. She parked on the side of Kylie's car and grabbed her things before getting out her vehicle.

Jaylah walked to her front door refusing to acknowledge Kylie. Her twin opened the door for her with sympathetic eyes. After revealing to her family that she would come clean her sister and mom decided to drive up north to help her pack. They wanted Jaylah home at least until sometime passed and Malik's trial was over. Jaylah didn't want to leave her place but felt her leaving was for the best.

"Jaylah please. Can we talk? I just saw your interview online and I'm shocked. I had no clue this affected you so much. I want to be there for you. I mean aren't you done with that guy, whatever his name was," Kylie said running up.

"Is this the bitch that was talking all that shit to you?" her twin asked placing her hand on her hip.

Kylie's head reared back, and she frowned. Her hand went to the Tiffany pearls that were on her slender neck and she clutched them.

"Excuse me? Are you Jaylah's sister? This is between she and I? I have always been by her side. Even when you and your family didn't give a shit about her? She might as well be my sister! Don't come around here with your Cardi B attitude trying to scare me—"

Wop!

"Bitch! Shut the fuck up!"

The hit to Kylie's cheek was swift and hard. Her brown

skin reddened in anger as she grabbed her jaw. Jael snickered as Jaylah held her back.

"Why would you do that?" Kylie asked with her eyes watering.

Jael laughed in her face.

"Cause, I thought a bitch that didn't know how to fight said sum. It was nice meeting you and FYI Cardi B might be loud and extra as fuck but she's herself and she loves the skin she's in. Maybe if you started loving yourself a little bit more your husband wouldn't be online jumping in everybody's DM," Jael replied and walked into the home.

Jaylah sighed not in agreement of the slap but amused by her sisters' actions. She looked at someone that she used to call her friend and she shook her head. It was now clear to Jaylah that Kylie brought out the ugly inside of her. They were no good for each other and in truth Kylie felt she wasn't anything compared to her. That wasn't friendship. Real friends uplifted each other and called the other person out on their bullshit. Real friends pushed you to be better, hell motivated you to be better. They didn't encourage you to run into the wall for their own selfish gain. Jaylah was sickened by how ignorant she'd been for so long but as she looked at Kylie hold her reddening face, she felt sadness as well because Kylie was still lost.

"Goodbye Kylie."

Jaylah turned and Kylie grabbed her arm.

"I'm sorry! Damn, is that what all of this is about? Me

hurting your feelings at that bar? Well you hurt mine too! You chose that thug over me? I have always been there for you! I introduced you to all of the right people. I took you to the big parties and made you a who's who in the right circles. This is how you do me? I need you Jaylah! I just found out Jesse is trying to divorce me. It's been on all of the blog sites. He got some groupie ghetto black bitch pregnant," Kylie ranted.

Jaylah pulled away from Kylie and headed for the door. Kylie didn't get it and it wasn't her job to make her understand the error in her ways. She wouldn't be open to change anyway.

"Go home Kylie!"

Jaylah went into her place and closed the door before Kylie could respond. She set her alarm and her eyes landed on her beautiful mom. She dropped her food on the small table by the door and before a tear could fall from her eyes her mom was pulling her into a hug. Her twin joined in on the hug while holding her daughter.

"God's got you and as long as He does there is nothing you have to worry about," her mom whispered.

Later that night Jaylah held her phone while sitting in her family room with her mom and sister. Baby Diamond was resting while they watched "Mahogany" which was their mom's favorite movie. Jaylah rested her head on her twin's lap as she marveled at how stunning Diana Ross was in the movie.

"I would still wear all of her outfits today," Jaylah mumbled.

"Me too," her twin chimed in running her fingers through Jaylah's hair.

"Yes, she was gorgeous, and she still is. So classy, are you hungry Jaylah?" her mom asked.

"I'm okay," she mumbled.

"Yeah me too," her twin co-signed and damn did it feel like old times.

Jaylah snickered as her doorbell was rung.

"This feels good," she noted.

Her mom stood and ran her hand through her medium length black curls.

"It does, now I'm ready for us to get back to Detroit. I don't like us being here alone like this."

Jaylah's brows pulled together.

"I don't either but so far Jerry has left me alone. I deactivated all of my social media pages and blocked a few people. I think Jerry is going to just let it slide seeing as how I have proof that he set all of that up," Jaylah replied.

Her mom gave her a tight-lipped smile.

"Jerry doesn't seem like the kind of man that lets something like that go. He's probably plotting right now on ways he can get you back. I can't wait for you guys father to be released. Let me go check this door, it should be the pizza."

Jaylah relaxed on her sister. She thought of Oshun when her mom's piercing scream made her jump.

"Momma!" her twin yelled pushing Jaylah off her lap.

Jaylah and her sister ran out of the room. Their feet stopped moving as they witnessed two masked men standing in the doorway. The men wore black jogging suits with black ski masks still the ivory colored skin showed along with their neck tattoos that were of swastika's. Both men held small black handguns while standing in the doorway. Jaylah's mom rushed over to she and her sister and pulled them close as the men stared at them.

"Twins, pretty cool. Which one of you are Jaylah?" the taller man asked in a raspy voice that carried a southern drawl to it.

Jael cleared her throat.

"I am," she lied.

"No, I am!" Jaylah yelled refusing to allow for her sister who had a child to take any pain for her.

This was a situation she caused, and she would own up to it.

"Seriously I'm Jaylah," she said pulling away from her mom.

The taller man looked her up and down carefully. He walked up on her and she held her breath. Her twin and mom rushed to her side as the man aimed the gun Jaylah's way. She held her breath maintaining her cool despite the fear she was feeling. He pulled the trigger and her bladder gave out as the gun clicked but no bullet was ejected from the chamber.

"Oh God! Thank you!" her mom cried falling into a crying fit.

Jaylah's urine trickled down her leg as her sister consoled her mom. The man stepped closer to Jaylah and leaned down. His minty breath brushed against her ear as he whispered.

"Next time it'll be loaded. Have a goodnight beautiful."

His lips pressed against her ear and he walked with his quiet friend out of the home making sure to close the door. Jaylah closed her eyes as her body shook with fear. In shock she went to her door and made sure to secure the locks. She set her alarm and looked at her mom and sister. In her mind she replayed running into Jerry maybe even setting off a couple of cops, but never did she see herself being threatened by the KKK. It was frightening because Jaylah knew that if they wanted to, they could like the cop that shot Malik kill her dead and get away with it.

"I'm calling the cops," her mom said standing.

She rushed out of the room as Jaylah retreated to her bedroom. After washing up she climbed into her bed with Oshun on her mind. Wishing he was there to comfort her, maybe even tell her that everything would be okay, but he wasn't. Oshun was gone and what they had was over with. She'd done the right thing and in turn she lost him while putting her life in jeopardy.

Doing good had never felt so bad.

Sadie: I'm worried about you. My spirit is uneasy. Are you okay? When will you be back in the city?

Jaylah looked up from her phone and peered around the restaurant. She was still in Baymoor Falls. The company that was helping move her things pushed her moving date back by a week and for the time being she'd been laying low with her family. After her run in with the white supremacist and no help from the Baymoor Falls law enforcement she was ready to leave her hometown for good. She saw that it wasn't the place for her anymore and she was fine with that.

Her pretty eyes peered down at the phone in worry. Sadie oh Sadie was truly a gift from God. She hadn't shunned her, and Jaylah was very grateful for that.

Soon. I promise I'm okay.

Seconds later Sadie sent her another message.

Sadie: Call me later so I can see that face of yours. Did the police follow up with you on the men pulling the gun out on you?
Jaylah: no, I'll be fine. I swear.
Sadie: Its cool, God is working everything out for your good. Stay safe Jaylah and don't forget to call me when you get home.

Jaylah smiled. She put her phone away as Charise walked

up to her table. In righting her wrongs, she acknowledged the things she said and done to everyone. She owed Charise a huge apology and prayed that she forgave her.

"Look at you, come here miss confessions," Charise smiled.

Jaylah sighed with relief. She stood and gave Charise a tight embrace. Jaylah closed her eyes hating how ugly she was to Charise. Nothing about her behavior had been cute.

"I'm sorry, from the bottom of my heart I am," she whispered to her old co-worker.

Charise rubbed her back.

"Water under the bridge boo. Let's sit and talk."

Jaylah nodded. She pulled herself together and sat at the table. She adjusted her large Dior shades as she looked at Charise. Because of her interview she was trying to be as low key as possible.

"Swear I'm not being Hollywood. I just don't want any more drama. My home was egged a few times. My car won't run, my front window was busted out and well a gun was pulled out on me," she laughed to ease her pain. Jaylah swallowed hard. "I'm not saying any of this to gain your sympathy. I just want you to know why I'm here in all black like this," she explained.

Charise looked at her and shook her head. Like always Charise looked beautiful in her tight jeans that she rocked a "God Is Love" t-shirt with along with black ankle boots. Black girl magic vibrated off her thick frame and Jaylah marveled at that. Charise was truly something special.

"You look beautiful," she felt the need to tell Charise.

A ghost of a smile crossed Charise's face.

"Jaylah I'm worried about you. Online people have mixed emotions about you. They don't understand your plight. I heard about your home being vandalized and everything. I know some people from this organization that can help protect you until everything dies down," Charise said quietly.

Jaylah shook her head.

"That's not needed. I'm leaving soon. I'll be fine and the world doesn't have to get me. I know in my heart that I did the right thing. God is telling me so and I won't try to make people understand that. As long as He's good with me, I know I'll be fine," she replied.

Charise gave her a forced smile. She ordered food when the waitress arrived before speaking again.

"Jaylah, I also accepted this meeting because I wanted to ask you something," she said nervously.

Jaylah grabbed her tea and smiled.

"Go for it."

Charise cleared her throat. Nervousness covered her thick frame as she looked at Jaylah.

"I'm doing this podcast until I can find a new station to work at. It feeds into my need to report the news you know? I cover all things happening in the world but most importantly our people. I want to interview you Jaylah. Show everyone the beauty that I saw in you even when you weren't that pleasant to be around. I know that pain caused you to do a lot of what you did with Jerry and the Lacoste family. Your story deserves to be heard Jaylah. You need to release it and tell the devil to kiss your ass. What do you say? We can go do it tonight?" Charise told her with hopeful eyes.

Jaylah removed her shades and wiped her face. She looked at someone that had once been a close friend of hers and she smiled.

"Let's do it."

CHAPTER 13

TWO MONTHS LATER

Dear Oshun,

I love you. Yes, you're sexy as hell. Like the most handsome man I have ever seen but its beyond that. I love the man you are. The way you provide and protect your family along with hundreds of other people. You are a whole ass man. A gentleman when need be, rough-neck when it's called for and a lover when it's time. I wish that life would have pushed us together under different circumstances. I'm not as good as you think I am but being with you did make me better. I prayed this morning for us. I prayed for you and I prayed for myself. I asked God to place it in your heart for you to one day forgive me. I'm sorry that I was too ignorant to know better. I'm sorry that I allowed for the actions of some bad men to make me hate all black men. Hell, I'm sorry that I didn't love myself enough to see the *beauty that came from being black. I know it doesn't seem like it, but I would do anything for you my king. I see the beauty in you. I love the richness of your black skin and the timber of your deep voice. I'm enthralled by your spirit and I will NOT let them take you down. I will never let that happen. Goodbye.*

Jaylah.

The words that Jaylah placed inside of her letter she'd left to him was implanted into his memory bank. As he sat inside of the newly renovated boys and girls club in the BOC, he couldn't shake thoughts of the beauty. Oshun sucked his teeth in anger. Pain was falling from the sky upon him and for once in his life he wasn't sure how to manage it all.

"I'ma head out and pick up Sophie. Is that check enough?"

Oshun stopped thinking of Jaylah to peer over at his boy. After calming down he saw that Ameer was on his side and while he still didn't like how Ameer had done things, he forgave him. Ameer was his nigga and his intentions were good.

"Nigga that was more than enough," Oshun replied thinking of the $150,000 check Ameer passed him for the organization that Deen started.

Ameer chuckled. He dapped up Brando then Oshun and shook his head.

"Then I'm gone. I'll fuck with y'all later," he said and walked away.

"The trial is going good," Brando said standing beside him.

Oshun turned to his boy that was more like a big brother to him and he nodded. He flicked his nose before peering around the fully furnished building. Everything smelled new and he was certain the kids in the BOC would enjoy it.

"Yeah," he grumbled placing his hands into the pants pocket of his Dior track pants.

Brando patted his shoulder.

"Let's go talk," he said before walking away.

Oshun locked up the building and set the alarm before joining Brando in his red Cullinan. He inspected the inside of the luxury truck liking what he saw. The shit was nice as hell, but he didn't expect anything but that from Brando. His boy was a Yaasmin and in the city of Detroit they were like royalty because of their long money. Not even prison had held Brando down. His boy did that time sitting on his head and was back like he hadn't lost shit.

"Kick it with me before Sterling get to sending me them *where you at baby*, texts and shit that mean its time to take my black ass home," Brando chuckled.

Oshun smirked. He relaxed in the seat and his dark honey eyes peered out of the window. His feelings were so conflicted he didn't know what to say or do.

"My cousin Chevez said his girl still talks to Jaylah," he said lowly.

Brando lit up the blunt as he peered over at him.

"Oh yeah?"

Oshun nodded. He pulled hard on the curly beard covering his chin.

"Yeah. She said that the cops fucking with her and shit."

Brando blew smoke from his mouth.

"And how you feel about that?"

Oshun sighed. He took the blunt from his boy and took long deep pulls wanting to ease the pain filling his body. He eventually gave his boy back the blunt.

"It's crazy because she came into my life trying to fuck me over. Claimed she wasn't on no bullshit when she was. I can't trust her, but I also don't want harm to come her way. I'm mad as fuck because no matter what she did I still love her," he said solemnly.

Brando smirked. He rubbed the waves on his fade and nodded.

"*Let them forgive and overlook.* We can't expect to be forgiven and not show that same compassion Oshun. And on some real shit, she's sorry. No woman or man will give up their bread and butter for no reason. We all fall short my dawg. I know you hold people to high regards because you go so hard and you should. You should get back all that you give but this is your *Queen*. I love the fuck out of Sterling. It isn't much she could do that would ever change that. I mean she'd have to fuck a nigga on our bed and I still would off his ass then just have to do counseling or some shit with her. I mean, I'm in this shit for life with my baby," Brando chuckled.

"Don't let pride and anger guide your steps. When it comes to the woman that's in your heart you move out of love and that's real shit. Fuck what anyone thinks. Fuck how the shit looks. She put her life on the line for you. If they fucking with her, then you need to be protecting her. The same way she protected you when she fessed up to what she was doing and refused to plant drugs in your home. We call you King, my nigga because you exude a kingly mentality. Kings always protect their Queens," Brando replied.

Oshun passed his boy back the blunt while nodding. Brando always hit him with some jewels. He made sure to place something on his mind that was worth thinking about. He fucked with that nigga the long way and was grateful to have someone so real in his corner. He turned to his boy and dapped him up.

"I'ma make sure she's good."

Brando smirked at him.

"My nigga and when the smoke clears bring her over so we can introduce her and Sterling," he said.

Oshun nodded and exited his truck. He went to his penthouse and fell onto the sofa with Jaylah still on his mind. Just needing to see her face he pulled out his cellphone and looked at her photo's. He took his time admiring all of the pictures he took of Jaylah while they were in Greece. They'd been so fucking happy.

"Damn," he grumbled.

He hated that she'd lied to him. He loved her, that he

would never deny but he was also angry with her. She'd turned out to be everything she told him she wasn't.

Oshun stretched out his legs still high from the weed he'd smoked with Brando when a call came through to his phone. He looked at Latoya's name cross the screen and he sucked his teeth. He wasn't fucking with her at all and she knew that shit.

He sent the call to voicemail and she called him right back. Oshun shook his head as he answered.

"Aye, you know it's not that kind of party."

Latoya sniffled and he groaned hating he'd answered her call.

"What's good Latoya?" he asked in irritation.

"It's Gio. We were supposed to meet up and hangout. He'd been complaining about Tamara cutting him off and I felt bad for him. I pulled up on him at the restaurant and he was still in his car. I thought he was on the phone until I saw his eyes were closed," she said sadly.

Oshun couldn't think straight as he listened to her cry softly into the phone.

"So, what you saying?" he asked afraid of her response.

"We're up at the hospital now and he's unresponsive. He wreaked of liquor, Oshun!" she said and broke down into the phone.

Oshun's body moved fast as his heart thundered in his chest. He ended the call and tracked Gio's phone while rushing out of his place.

CHAPTER 14

baymoor falls

Her car sat idle outside of the gate. She was terrified to pull in and was tempted to drive away. "No, you have to do this," her twin whispered.

Jaylah nodded glad she'd brought her family along. Life in Detroit was better for Jaylah. As long as she laid low, she was able to have peace, but she couldn't miss the opportunity to finally see her daughter again. Even if that meant she was forced to be around Greedo.

"There he goes," her twin said with an attitude.

Jaylah looked to her right and she watched Greedo pull past her in a white Lamborghini. Slowly she followed after his car. She chose to park as far away from him as she could.

"I'll be in the car," her twin said smiling. "You can do this and don't forget to take pictures."

Jaylah closed her eyes. She took a deep calming breath and exhaled.

"I can," she agreed.

She hugged her sister before exiting her car. Jaylah grabbed her large gift bag from the backseat of her Mercedes and headed for the front of the mansion.

"*Twin.*"

His voice was sad, and she didn't want to acknowledge him. It wasn't about their past. It was about their daughter and nothing more. She rolled her eyes wishing she could have done the greeting without him.

"What?" she asked looking over at him.

Greedo walked over holding flowers along with two envelopes. He passed her a white envelope and leaned down to kiss her cheek. Jaylah frowned as she peered up at him. Greedo looked handsome like always while sporting a stone washed jean Amiri fit with a black designer fitted cap on his head. His sad eyes bored into Jaylah the way that they used to when they were younger, and she sighed.

"What is it?" she asked again.

Greedo shook his head. He licked his lips and when Jaylah peered over at his Lamborghini, she saw that Shreeya the same woman from years ago that he was caught cheating with occupied the passenger's seat. She looked back to him and smiled.

"Let's go see our daughter," she said and walked away.

"I'm sorry for everything, ma. Know that, and you will always have a piece of my heart," he said following after her.

Jaylah rolled her eyes.

"Give that piece to our daughter," she quipped before ringing the doorbell.

Seconds later the door was pulled open by one of the maids. Jaylah and Greedo were shown into the great room. Jaylah sat on the white tufted sofa and Greedo chose to sit beside her. He whistled as they studied the large room that housed high ceilings, white furniture along with a grand piano.

"I saw your shit online and if you need anything let me know. I can even introduce you to some people in the media world," he said breaking the silence.

Jaylah shook her head. She attempted to pass Greedo back the envelope and he placed his hand on top of hers.

"It's a check, ma. Just take it twin. Damn," he said as three people entered into the great room.

Jaylah frowned at him but when her eyes landed on the prettiest girl, she'd ever seen they watered. She covered her mouth as her daughter walked up with her adopted parents by her side.

"It's nice to meet you all," the adopted dad said and shook Greedo's hand.

Jaylah was too emotional to reply. Her daughter was like a smaller version of she and her twin. She was around 4'9 with long sandy brown hair and bright brown eyes. She possessed Jaylah's nose while having features from Greedo as well. She looked from Jaylah to Greedo as the adoptive mom took the flowers Greedo had for her.

"Aren't you my mom? Because you look just like me. You don't want to hug me?" her daughter Oakley asked smiling.

Her sass reminded Jaylah of her twin Jael. Jaylah nodded as the tears fell down her face.

"*I do*," she whispered.

Her daughter winked at her and every adult in the room laughed but Jaylah.

"It's okay, come show me some love," her daughter grinned before helping her stand.

Jaylah pulled her daughter into the tightest embrace that she could while silently thanking God.

After spending time with her daughter and having lunch with her twin she decided to leave their hotel room to grab gas before heading back to the city. Jaylah was on a natural high from spending time with Oakley. Her daughter was funny, charming and extremely smart. She was also sassy as hell and Jaylah couldn't wait to spend more time with her in the near future.

She quickly pumped her gas and headed back for the hotel to grab her sister. Jaylah turned onto Broad street and before she could make another right cop lights flashed in her rear view. Her happiness wouldn't allow for her to be scared. Instead she was pissed off because she'd done nothing wrong.

Angrily she threw her car in park. Jaylah exited her car before the cop could and walked up on the squad car.

"When will this stop? Huh! I did nothing wrong!" she yelled and hit his window.

The young pale faced officer with skin similar to hers exited his squad car. Hatred sat in his dark brown eyes as his hand lay on his gun.

"Go back to your car now mam," he said carefully.

Jaylah shook her head. What more could they do? They'd threatened her and her family. Ran her name through the mud online. She was sick of it.

"You all couldn't help me when someone put a gun in my face, but you can stop me for no damn reason? This is fucking ridiculous!" she yelled.

Her eyes filled with tears out of anger and the cop pulled out a stun gun. He looked at her with his wide nose flaring.

"Put your hands in the air! You made a right turn without signaling the proper way! All I wanted to do was give you a citation! Calm down! Don't make me use this!" he yelled making sure to say every word loud and clear.

Fury raged through Jaylah as she glared at him. She couldn't imagine being a black man and having to deal with harassment such as that on a daily. That was enough to drive anyone insane.

"Fuck you," she snarled and turned.

Jaylah made two steps back to her car before small prongs connected with her legs from the stun gun. Like she'd stuck her hand on a voltage, blinding white pain scorched through her body. Her eyes squinted in shock and she fell to the ground. Her head hit a nearby brick hard and her vision blurred. She closed her eyes as her body squirmed on the ground. Like a fish out of water she couldn't stop shaking as the stun gun made her nerves go haywire.

"All you had to do was your fucking job. Jerry says hi," the cop said smugly removing the prongs.

He chuckled as Jaylah's body writhed on the ground in pain. She didn't want to cry. She truly didn't want to give Jerry or the corrupt officers the pleasure of seeing her do so, but she couldn't help it.

Blood trickled down the side of her face that was cut open by the brick as she was pulled from the ground. Jaylah dropped her head and her body shook slightly as she was cuffed and shoved into the back of a squad car.

Jaylah closed her eyes and leaned her head against the window. She took deep breaths and was on the verge of calmly asking the officer a question when he pulled up to the news station. Outside of the same place Jaylah built her television career was none other than Jerry. His ivory toned skin was beet red as he leaned against his black Mercedes. He smoked on a cigarette while wearing one of his normal brown two-piece suits. His eyes fell onto the squad car and he smiled wickedly as the cop pulled into the parking lot.

"The least you can do is tell him your sorry and retract

everything you said. If you do that, we can leave you alone," the cop said parking his squad car.

Jaylah sat up as best as she could and watched Jerry like a hawk. He took his time coming to the car and she wasn't surprised. That was him. Smug in such a manner that it didn't make any sense. He finished his cigarette and tossed it onto the ground. His foot grinded on the cigarette and he huffed. The cop exited the squad car and shook hands with Jerry. They spoke animatedly until Jerry turned his attention back to Jaylah. He walked over to the door she'd just been leaning on and pulled it open. The stench of smoke and his Polo cologne filled the car as he leaned in and grinned at her.

"Hey there girl. Thought I'd run into you today. I heard you was back in town, and I had to say my final goodbye. We've been through so much Jaylah. The highs and the lows but this," Jerry shook his head. He placed his murky brown eyes onto her and sighed. "This is the lowest of the low. I am going to give you one last chance to make this right. You will go in that station and recant everything you said. Tell the world that he forced you to say those things. Show pictures that we created for you and all will be well. You can even have your old job back. I don't hold grudges dear," he told her.

Jaylah shook her head. She'd never heard something so damn dumb.

"Jerry let me go. This is against the law," she said sadly.

Jerry clicked his tongue against his teeth.

"It's a shame because I had such high hopes for you, and

you went and acted like the dumb nigger you are. Get your ass over here," he snarled and pulled Jaylah from the vehicle.

"Jerry be cool. Don't take her to the front of the car," the officer hissed running over.

Jerry shrugged him off. Motivated by anger he tossed Jaylah onto the back of his car. Jaylah thought of the cop's insistence for her to be away from the front of the cop car. She crawled to the front of the car and the cop grabbed Jerry's arm.

"Jerry stop!" he hissed.

Jerry snatched away from the cop and rushed over to Jaylah. He kicked her stomach repeatedly making her insides coil with pain. Tears slid down her cheeks as he chose to grab a handful of her hair and slap her twice. Jaylah closed her eyes not wanting to see the pain coming as he used his fat hand to drive his fist into her face.

"Enough!" the officer hissed standing at the back of his squad car.

Jerry smiled. He let Jaylah go and he leaned down into her face. His hot breath kissed her skin as he stared into her eyes.

"Go be with that monkey because I'm done with you and your done in this industry bitch," he snarled and with venom spat in Jaylah's face.

Jerry went to hit her again and was stopped by the cop.

"Jerry Hegler you are under arrest," the cop said loudly while grabbing Jerry's arm.

Jerry's brows pinched together as he peered back at him.

"What the fuck are you doing?" he asked quietly.

The cop finished reading Jerry his Miranda rights. He peered around and Jerry saw that a crowd of people had formed outside of the station.

"You made me do this," the cop whispered and took Jerry to the squad car.

"We have it all on camera! You need to be locked up too!" an older custodian woman yelled holding out her phone. "Do you all see this? That cop just let fat ass Jerry assault Jaylah Cole, he needs to be arrested too!" she yelled.

In pain Jaylah lifted her head and witnessed several police cars pull onto the scene along with her twin that was getting out the back of an Uber.

"Twin!" Jael yelled running over with a hammer in her hand.

Jaylah flashed her a crooked smile as her consciousness left her being.

"The cop that drove you to the station is in our custody as well as Jerry. We were also able to arrest the captain of the police station. I can assure you this won't get swept under the rug. I owe your sister big time and I'll make sure they go down for this," Rashon explained.

Jaylah nodded. She rested on the bed in her mom's home

with the cover pulled up to her neck. Her body was still in pain and she was in shock by all that Jerry had done to her.

Rashon, her sisters' *friend* that also happened to be a special unit's agent for the FBI gave her an empathetic smile.

"Call my personal cell if anybody fucks with you. The cops at the police station can't do shit to me but get the fuck out of the way when I walk through. Don't let the corrupt ones bully you or turn you against us. It's still a lot of good people in law enforcement," he said before walking away.

Jaylah watched the muscular man exit the room and she closed her eyes. A small hand rubbed her back before sliding around to her stomach. She appreciated the love from her twin, but she wanted to be alone.

"Twin please. I want to lay down by myself," she said softly.

Jael hugged her from the back as her eyes watered.

"To see you for a second time sprawled out like that is fucking with me. I'm scared to let you out of my sight. You don't deserve any of this and I wish I could have gotten a few swings on Jerry. He won't get away with this shit with his Peter Griffin looking ass," she snapped.

Jaylah didn't want to laugh but she couldn't help it. Jerry did look like Peter Griffin.

"Shut up, twin. I'm okay," she lied.

Her twin shook her head hugging her so tight that it hurt.

"No, you're not. Our twin shit is back on a thousand and I can feel your pain. I was waiting on you to come back to the room and when you didn't, I called your phone. As soon as the voicemail picked up, I went to the map and tracked you. I found a hammer at the corner store and I called up an Uber. I just wish I would have gotten there in time," she replied.

Jaylah closed her eyes.

"Don't do that to yourself. It isn't your fault he did all of that shit to me. I just want to go to sleep and wake up a year later. My life is so fucked up right now. I don't know what to do," she whispered.

"I do, lets pray," Sadie said walking into the room holding flowers. "And you must be Jael? Pretty like your sister, come here," Sadie said stepping out of her shoes.

Sadie and her twin embraced one another, and Jaylah frowned when Sadie didn't read her sister the same way she read her.

"Wow, you don't have anything to say to her? She's hiding a whole baby from somebody," Jaylah quipped.

Sadie smiled as her twin looked at them curiously.

"I don't. I speak when He tells me to. Right now, your sister isn't ready to hear about the things she knows she has to do. She's not open to change or speaking her truth and I understand that. But eventually everything that's done in the dark has to come to the light. Especially big secrets," Sadie said looking at Jael.

Jaylah watched her twins fair skin turn a shade darker. Jael smoothed out her short hair and smiled at Sadie.

"And on that note, I'm gone but it was nice meeting you Sadie," she said and left out of the room.

Jaylah smiled although it wasn't funny. She told herself that once she was feeling better, she would make her twin tell her about the real identity of the father of her niece.

"I missed you and I'm sad because I saw this coming," Sadie said joining Jaylah on the bed.

Sadie sat at the foot of the bed and rubbed Jaylah's leg. She passed Jaylah the flowers and Jaylah smelled them before placing them onto the nightstand.

"I'm okay. It's just a black eye and bruised rib," she laughed to ease the pain on Sadie's face.

Sadie closed her eyes. She leaned over and grabbed Jaylah's hand.

"I come to you Lord humbly at your mercy. For my friend, no my family I pray for her covering. I pray for her healing; I pray for her strength. I rebuke the devil and all of the demons that he is sending her way. She is a child of God she will be harmed no more. I ask that you cover her with the blood of Jesus. Walk with her, continue to guide her steps as well as mine and show mercy on us. Amen."

"Amen," Jaylah whispered and squeezed Sadie's hand. "You're like the best friend I wish I had," she smiled.

Sadie winked at her.

"The best friend you can have now. I need to talk to you about myself as well. Can you promise to keep this between us?"

Jaylah snorted.

"Well seeing as how I only talk to you from his family, I'm sure I can."

Sadie waved her off.

"No Gods working on that. You two will be back together in no time. I'm doing something that Chevez doesn't know about," Sadie revealed with one eye closed. She took a deep breath and sighed. "It's in my will. Like I have to do this Jaylah. It's on my spirit so tough," she said while frowning.

Jaylah sat up as best as she could.

"And what are you doing?" she pried hoping Sadie wasn't cheating.

Sadie swallowed hard.

"I'm searching for someone. Her sister found me online and said she was pulled into a human trafficking ring. I found one of the girls I was once being held captive with and after searching for months we think we found her. Now we have to figure out a way to get her out. She's only seventeen Jaylah. I see her and I see myself in so many ways. She's been gone for a year and I would hate for her to get lost in the ring or worst. She's gorgeous and girls like her get sold to the highest paying pimp like I did. I have to find her."

The conviction in Sadie's voice told her that it wasn't up for debate. Jaylah however didn't like the idea of Sadie placing herself back into a world that she'd escaped from.

"But what if you're pulled back into that life? You look young as hell and your stunning. Many pimps would love to add you to the stable. This is dangerous and I know Chevez would be against it. What about your girls?"

Sadie shrugged. She looked at Jaylah with her pretty eyes and smiled sadly.

"God showed favor on me. I have to be a blessing to someone that needs it. I'm going to still be a mother to my girls, but I have to also do this. Chevez will have to understand."

"And if he doesn't?" Jaylah asked quietly.

Sadie smiled like her question was amusing.

"Chevez and I have a love that's unbreakable. Even if he doesn't understand why I'm doing this he won't stop me from helping. Or at least I hope he won't," Sadie said and touched her flat stomach.

Jaylah nodded hoping that everything worked out for Sadie.

"Well I'm here for you and any way that I can help please let me know."

Sadie lifted her head and smiled.

"Thank you," she said sweetly.

Two hours later Jaylah awoke to the smell of soul food. The kind of soul food that made your stomach growl and your mouth water. She shifted slowly in the bed and sat up. Her body was sore and in pain while a slight headache was already approaching, however the need to see what her mom cooked was stronger than anything else she felt. She slowly stood from the bed. Her feet moved carefully, and she held her side not able to stand up straight. She exited the bedroom and took her time going downstairs.

Jaylah looked around the kitchen and was stunned at what she saw. All of the women in Oshun's family filled her mom's cooking space. From his three aunts to his cousins' women including Sadie down to his mom. Even his first lady Tegan came out bearing gifts, food and love. Jaylah didn't know what to say as her eyes watered. She expected for his family to hate her.

"I'm sorry. For everything that I did I truly am," she said emotionally.

Angie walked over to Jaylah and pulled her into a hug. They hadn't spoken many words to one another. Even at the cabin it had been high and bye but as she hugged Jaylah, Jaylah could feel her love.

"Thank you for owning up to what you did and *welcome* to my family," Angie whispered, she kissed her cheek and gave her a knowing smile before letting her go.

Jaylah smiled appreciative of the love she was receiving. She carefully went over to the table in her mom's kitchen and sat down. The first lady to Oshun's church Tegan Miles sat down at the table with her and gave Jaylah a big smile. She was stunning with her dark glowing skin and long thick black hair. Jaylah knew from looking her up that she was a lawyer before getting married and now she'd gone on to write books, preach with her husband's ministry and life coach. She was a woman that you could gain motivation from.

"How are you beautiful?" Tegan asked.

Jaylah shrugged.

"Sore, tired and surprised. I would have never guessed in a million years that you all would be here like this. I've done so many things that a part of me feels like I deserve this beating. I was so wrong to Oshun and his family but even black people in general. I let the hate in my heart turn me against my people. It led me to believe that I was different. I brought this on myself," Jaylah replied still holding her side.

Tegan scooted her chair closer to Jaylah and grabbed her hand. She looked into her eyes and smiled.

"If you knew who I was before I was saved you wouldn't believe it. *For all have sinned and fall short of the glory of God.* You aren't the first and you won't be the last person to make a mistake. The blessing is that you learned from it and you were able to stop it midway through. Don't look at what you've done but instead look at how you are now. It was a test Jaylah and you passed it. I hate that you were attacked because of it but you did pass, and you may not see it now, but you will be blessed because of it. I mean already they're shining down onto you," Tegan said and winked at her.

Jaylah nodded praying that what the first lady said was true. She wanted to be forgiven for all that she had done, and God just might show mercy on her but would Oshun was the question.

CHAPTER 15

H is mind was reeling from everything that was transpiring as he sat inside of the small white room with his brother. Gio sipped on a water while frowning. He wore all white sweats with a white skully on his head. He looked at Oshun and sighed.

"I fucked up," he admitted.

Oshun nodded. He passed Gio his phone and watched his brother read over the message he'd received earlier that day. Gio looked up once he was done with wide eyes.

"Is this shit for real?"

Oshun smirked.

"Yeah. Officer Milton took the plea deal and confessed to what he knows," he replied.

Gio's visage relaxed in the plastic chair. He looked at Oshun and shook his head.

"I let this shit fuck me up. I don't have Tamara and now I'm in fucking rehab. I let the family down," he sulked.

Oshun patted his brothers' arm.

"You fucked up brah but you making it right. Nobody's perfect and you know that shit. You focus on getting better and I'll make sure Tamara is good. You know we got her," he assured him.

Gio sighed.

"Man, but what about you? How is Jaylah? I heard about the shit they did to her and I see they locked up her boss and that cop."

Oshun's jaw flexed. He balled his fist as he thought of the people responsible for assaulting Jaylah. No matter what she did it never warranted that type of behavior. He wished that he could have been there to prevent it from happening.

"I should have been there for her. And you saying you fucked up. I fucked up too because even though she lied, she fixed it. She fixed it and went through a lot of shit for us," he replied.

Oshun stared up at the ceiling as he thought of Jaylah. He remembered the best news he'd ever received, and he looked at his brother.

"And this is something to be glad about brah," he said passing him a photo.

After leaving the treatment center to check on Gio, Oshun pulled up to Jaylah's mother's home. He parked in the driveway and cleared his throat.

He was nervous.

He was very fucking nervous.

Jaylah could turn him away and he wouldn't be able to fight her on it. So much had changed but his feelings for her were the same. He loved and he missed her. He was done waiting. It was time for him to reconnect with the love of his life.

Oshun exited his car as his cellphone rung. He saw it was his cousin Deen calling and he answered as he headed for the front door of the two-story suburban house.

"Everything smooth?" he asked.

"I need to ask you a question. Do Jaylah's sister have a kid?" Deen questioned.

Oshun rang the doorbell and before he could respond Jael answered the door while holding a beautiful baby girl. Oshun stared down at Jaylah's sister and the baby while frowning.

"Yeah," he grumbled looking at the baby's grey eyes.

"Good looking," Deen replied and ended the call.

Oshun put his phone away as Jael smiled at him.

"She's asleep and upstairs in the first bedroom to the right," she said stepping to the side.

Oshun stared at Jael briefly and nodded. He wasn't into gossiping. He was certain his cousin would get up with the beauty sooner than later.

"Good seeing you, twin," he said walking by.

"You too," Jael said as he headed for the steps.

Oshun stepped into the bedroom quietly and on the

queen-sized bed slept Jaylah. His heart sank when he spotted her black eye. He stepped out of his shoes and joined her on the bed. Oshun pulled her close as he peered at her battered face. No matter the situation she didn't deserve a beating. He felt fucked up to know that she'd been attacked, and he wasn't there.

"I'm sorry, love," he whispered and kissed her forehead.

Jaylah stirred in his arms. He kissed her nose and her eyes before kissing her face.

"I missed you," he whispered.

Jaylah squirmed. She slowly opened her eyes and swallowed hard when their eyes connected. She tried to pull back, but he wouldn't let her.

"A baby, huh?" he asked and couldn't contain his smile.

Jaylah nodded. Worry sat on her beautiful face as she looked at him.

"I don't need you to be here just because of the baby," she whispered.

Oshun shook his head.

"I'm not. I'm here because I love you and I wanna take care of you. I'm sorry I wasn't there to protect you love," he said sincerely.

Jaylah laid her head onto his chest. She hugged him tight while closing her eyes.

"No, I'm sorry," she countered. "I didn't even know I was pregnant until after the attack. I could have lost our baby," she whispered.

Oshun kissed her forehead trying not to think of the what if's.

"But you didn't. Everything is going to be okay, love," he promised.

Jaylah nodded while holding onto him and for the first time in a while he was able to rest. Oshun had a joy in his heart that he couldn't explain. God was assuring him that their storm was over, and he believed him.

EPILOGUE

His eyes the same ones his father possessed peered down at earth intently. He walked slowly back and forth in front of the gates afraid to go in. Since he'd been gone his family had fallen apart and the sad thing was as much as he loved them, he didn't want to go back. Simply being by the pearly gates gave him a joy that he never felt before.

He licked his lips and peered over at his guardian angel. Malik raised a brow and after a few moments he was able to get an up close and personal view of his family. His daughter was now two months old and man was she a looker. He felt pride as he stared at her gorgeous face. He watched Tiffany laugh and play with her as they sat inside of his bedroom at his mom's house.

Malik's eyes went over to Gio and he chuckled when he

spotted him running towards the bathroom in his home while holding onto his stomach. Tamara was laughing as well with Gio and Malik was happy to see his brother was doing well. He then watched his mom shop and talk with her sisters before his eyes ventured to Oshun. He watched his brother bend down on one knee and propose to the woman he loved. Immediately she said yes as they hugged while standing on the beach in Greece.

Malik smiled happy for them. He looked at the officers involved in his shooting and both men sat in jail cells while wearing prison gear. Malik swallowed hard. He paid close attention to the officer that killed him and saw the cop was reading the bible while a calendar sat on his wall. The officer was counting down his time, to go home. Malik smirked knowing that Officer Polk had at least thirty-five years to go before he would be able to do such a thing. He gave Tiffany one more glance before turning around. He headed for the pearly gates and his earthly body started to fade. His spirit ascended into Heaven as he was welcomed in by the Lord.

The end.

(If you were touched by this story, spread the word about it,
Love Dom!)

Made in the USA
Las Vegas, NV
26 February 2021